Zöe Venditozzi ~ 8 NOV 2017 in a small village graduating with an from the University o AUG 2 a variety of jobs includ nannying and editing tne ... People's Friend. When Zöe and her husband moved to New Zealand she decided to train as a teacher and dreamed of becoming a writer. However, it was only when she returned to Scotland and started having children that Zöe started to write seriously. Zöe gained her Mlitt in Creative Writing from the University of Dundee.

ANYWHERE'S BETTER THAN HERE

Zöe Venditozzi

SANDSTONEPRESS
HIGHLAND | SCOTLAND

FT
Pbk

First published in Great Britain by
Sandstone Press Ltd
PO Box 5725
One High Street
Dingwall
Ross-shire
IV15 9WJ
Scotland.

www.sandstonepress.com

Editor: Moira Forsyth

The publisher acknowledges subsidy from
Creative Scotland towards publication of this volume.

ISBN: 978-1-908737-06-9
ISBN e: 978-1-908737-07-6

Cover design by Mark Blackadder, Edinburgh.
Typeset by Iolaire Typesetting, Newtonmore.
Printed and bound by TOTEM, Poland.

For my late father, David Johnston.
Everywhere and inaudible.

ACKNOWLEDGMENTS AND THANKS

First of all, thanks to Dominic for the constant support and to Luca Tavita, Lola-Ray and Rocco for their distraction techniques. Thanks also to my mum for paying for most of my MLitt which gave me the confidence to call myself a proper writer.

I am also grateful to Professor Kirsty Gunn who was and is an amazing mentor and friend. Anna Day, Eddie Small and Emily Dewhurst kept me going when I was thinking of giving up and Jane Fulton, Jill Skulina and Rachel Waites who read drafts at different stages and made me feel like I was writing something worth reading. Thanks also to Bob McDevitt, agent *extraordinaire*, and to Moira Forsyth at Sandstone who edited the book into shape.

Thursday the 16th of December

Just Before Tea Time
Dark and Damp

Laurie scanned and rescanned the endless rows of soup. This task was clearly beyond her. Each can she picked up was heavier than the last and she had difficulty finding its station on the shelf. The dietary information was baffling; she kept losing her place in the column that showed the calories or saturated fat content or whatever it was she was supposed to give a shit about. She eventually tossed some low-fat, low-salt vegetable stuff into the basket, shrugging the handle further up her arm.

She made her way towards Toiletries veering around an infuriated toddler. There was a temporary stall set up at the end of the aisle. A small woman with a big orangey mouth smeared a yellow substance on what appeared to be tiny squares of lino. She was talking at everyone passing about how great the stuff was. Laurie moved closer and joined the growing crowd of people keen to see this new food stuff. It was some sort of spray-on cheese.

She knew that Ed would love this faux-food. Anything processed was ingenious to him; the more nutritionally deficient the better. She smiled at Orange Mouth and picked up a jar. Easy Cheese – No Cutting Required.

1

She could picture Ed's delight at this new-fangled snack food. She imagined spreading it on Mother's Pride and handing it over to him with a fanfare. The jar clunked against the counter as she dropped it back in place.

The shop was filling up. She uncovered her watch. 5.18.

She turned in to Toiletries. Again the array was bewildering. She grabbed an apple shampoo and a coconut conditioner. Despite how shit she was feeling, she wasn't above smelling sweet.

There was something else she needed but nothing in her memory made itself known. Moving along the crisp and biscuit sections, she willed herself to think of the something else. She mentally walked around her tiny kitchen, peering in cupboards seeing if anything came to her. Nothing – the trick didn't work and she knew that as soon as she put her key in the front door that the mystery item would resurface. She ran through her constant shopping list: milk, bread, toilet paper, cereal, butter . . .

She had wandered into a corral of pensioners. They bumped their trolleys against the edges of shelves. They didn't appear to know each other but were all dressed similarly in pale biscuit-like colours. Did you reach a certain age and then felt the need to dress in comfort food colours? They milled around her, clogging up the aisle, getting in the way of everything. She felt like manhandling them out of her way. As she stood, hemmed in by their chat and indecision, she felt the last drop of patience drip out. Tutting loudly, she put her basket in the nearest dawdler's trolley and headed for the door.

The arcade that led to the bus stops was suffocated by Christmas decorations. They were intricate and fierce, the colours mashing together behind the plate glass. Laurie kept catching sight of the patterns blinking out of the corner of her eye. She'd turn her head towards the movement, convinced someone was motioning towards her. She really ought to get on with decorating the Christmas tree. It was only, what, nine days until the big day? But what was the point? Why bother getting lots of sparkly pointless tat and finding places to put it all? Ed wouldn't notice the tree anyway. He took these things for granted more and more. And there was certainly no excitement in her for the event these days. It was all just a hassle really.

A group of boys was clumped around one of the shelters. She had to pass through their cigarette smoke to see the timetable. Her wrist goose-pimpled when she pulled back her sleeve. 5.27 Almost time for Neighbours. At least the TV would drown out the noise of Ed's computer game.

The journey was slow. The bus negotiated the route to Queen Street in a stop-start, sick-making fashion. When she arrived home she stood outside the block and looked up at the flat. She could see Ed through the lace curtain his mother had insisted on giving them. Laurie could only imagine this was a last-ditch attempt at respectability. They may be living in sin but at least the view of them at it was obscured.

"Chance would be a fine thing," she muttered, reaching into her hand bag for her key. She raked around through all the bus tickets, sweet wrappers and scraps of paper. Her bag was looking more and more like a bin. It was then, of course, she realised.

"Fucking bin bags! Fuck! Fucking fuck!"

She kicked the door closed behind her. Inevitably, it caught on the invisible rise in the concrete floor, requiring her to turn back and push it home. She felt like smashing the glass out. Why did nothing ever work properly around here?

She could hear the shooting before she reached the top landing. As bloody usual, there was a pile of mail by the front door. Not even on the table, just toed out of the way. She moved towards the green glow.

"Hello." She tried to sound cheery.

"Check this. You can actually see his brains splatter." Ed kept his eyes trained on his opposing number's death. "Did you get anything for tea?"

"No, the shop was closed. Power cut."

Her so-called boyfriend accepted this without even turning his head. His hand reached out for the phone and he dialled without looking.

"Yeah. Curry meal for two. Chicken Korma and Passanda. Peshwari naan. MacDonald. Yeah, that's the one. Cool." He hung up.

"You know, Ed, It might be nice to be asked occasionally what I might like."

He finally turned round to her.

"Did you want something else?"

"No. But it might have been nice for you to ask."

A look of confusion passed briefly across his face. Then he swivelled back to the screen.

Laurie walked out of the room and went into the bathroom. She sat down on the toilet and tried to cry. Nothing happened. She stood up and looked into the mirror and gave herself a severe look. Something had to

4

be done. Whatever looks she had were sure to go soon. She was pale and grimy looking. She probably needed to get her hair cut and try some new make up. But what for? Things were definitely going tits up here. There was only so long she could put up with take-aways and being ignored. When she was younger she'd envisioned a different relationship. Even when imagining an unhappy relationship, she'd pictured a Bastard. A thumper or a philanderer. Not this boring nothingness. She'd almost put up with a bit of domestic abuse just to relieve the monotony.

The door bell rang. Laurie dragged herself up and answered the door.

"Awright. Delivery for ya." The guy was about seventeen. He had the ubiquitous fauxhawk and an eyebrow piercing. He wasn't her usual type, but he was good looking. He raised his eyebrows at her. She realised she'd been staring.

"How much?"

"Twelve fifty."

She ducked in for her purse. Twelve fifty, plus tip, of course. It wasn't enough that she'd already be paying the best part of two quid for delivery, she also had to pay the delivery guy. For what? Driving a mile and climbing a flight of stairs.

"Here." She handed over the money, almost everything she had in there. It was mostly pound coins – the least she could do was weigh him down a bit.

"Listen, can I get a lift off you?"

"Yeah, whatever." He shrugged and turned to go back down the stairs. "I've got to go back to the shop anyways."

She put the bag with the curry round the corner into the hall. Ed still hadn't shifted. He'd stay there all night without even looking her way, shovelling his curry in, then some sweets and several cups of tea.

She reached into the bag, took the naan and followed the delivery guy down the tenement stairs.

The delivery car was a dressed up black and yellow Punto. There were lights under the wheel arches and a good deal of chrome. She climbed into the passenger seat and pulled the racing seat belt around herself.

"Where you goin'?" the driver's accent was that strange Pakistani-Scottish hybrid. He was acting less confident now, unsure how to behave in this unfamiliar situation.

Laurie looked out of the window.

"I don't know, Vicky Park? Do you mind if I . . ." She waved the naan at him.

"Please yourself. Roll the window down though. I don't want my car stinkin'"

"Don't you like peshwari?"

"Not all Asians like curry y'know."

"Oh sorry, I didn't mean anything." She felt wrong-footed. Had she been racist? She didn't really know any Asians. There was a Nigerian guy in her office, but that was the extent of her multi-cultural interaction. Had she implied something?

"Nah, I'm only messin'. It just interferes with ma after-shave. Y'know?" He smiled at her.

Still, she didn't unwrap the naan and her stomach was starting to hurt with hunger pangs. The warmth was seeping out through the tin foil and she could smell the almonds.

"Seriously, go ahead." He flicked his head at her. "Go on." He grinned again. She peeled away the foil, careful not to spill the sugary powder. She peeled off a corner and took a bite.

"Here we are." The car pulled up at the wrought iron gates. Now they'd arrived, Laurie didn't want to get out into the cold. Still, she couldn't hang about with the delivery driver all night. She didn't even know his name. He looked at her. She started to wonder why he was being nice to her.

"Well, I suppose I'd better get going." She half-wished he'd ask her to stay but he just kept looking at her expectantly. She opened the door.

"So have you got more deliveries to do?"

"Uh, yeah. It's tea time."

"Yeah I suppose it is." She smiled and waved her naan at him. "Suppose I'd better eat mine!"

She swung her legs out of the car.

"Thanks."

"S'alright."

She still didn't move.

"Are you okay Missus?"

God, Missus? Was she a Missus now? Fuck.

She nodded and climbed out.

"See you around!" He grinned, turned the music up and sped off.

Laurie watched the car disappear down the street, then turned to the park and having no other plan, went through the gates. What now? She supposed she'd have to go home after the naan. She had nowhere else to go. She didn't know anyone in town anymore and she could hardly pop into her dad's unannounced. She made her way up the hill to a bench which was tucked into a little cave of trees. She unwrapped the naan again, realising she'd eaten nothing since breakfast. It often happened like that. She'd just forget to get anything at lunch time because she was staring out of the window of the office. Today she'd stayed in her seat at the call centre when the rest of her team had gone for lunch. She couldn't be bothered to pretend she cared about what she was wearing to the Christmas party. The Christmas party that she had no intention of going to. They rest of them wouldn't under-stand. To them it was the social event of the year.

The naan was still quite warm and she tore into it. Ordinarily, she would have been nervous sitting on her own in the dark like this. Every man would look familiar from Crimewatch. She'd be trying to look nonchalant but would be completely tense and on guard. But tonight she felt as if she was invisible. The rain picked up speed and she could hear it glancing off the leaves of the trees above and around her. The noise was soothing, serving to high-light her chosen solitude. She leaned back into the bench with her eyes shut and tried to clear her mind but became aware of what sounded like murmurs and rustles.

She sat up sharply and held her breath.

A man emerged from the bushes to her left and hurried down the hill towards the gates. No sooner had he reached the gate than another man appeared over the brow of the hill, from the opposite direction, hung about for a bit near the bench then ducked into the bushes the first man had come out of. The noise started again. Laurie recognised the rhythm and let out a silent breath.

Moans and zipping noises seemed to be issuing from all the bushes surrounding the bench. She stood up, crumpled the naan wrapper up and jammed it into her coat pocket. She headed back down the hill towards the high street. She wasn't a prude; she was all for same sex marriage; but to be so near to all that outdoor activity . . . Didn't they have flats? It wasn't like it was illegal anymore. Perhaps the men had partners. Partners who didn't have any suspicions, wives and girlfriends who were just going about their business. Maybe bringing up children, washing their clothes.

Well at least Ed wasn't like that.

He hardly ever left the house.

The rain had slowed now and become a static moistness. She felt like she was walking through the sheerest of cobwebs. If she didn't think of something soon she'd have to go home and face Ed. Would he be phoning around desperately trying to find her?

Unlikely.

She walked down towards town, looking into every shop window to pass the time. As she walked down the High Street she became aware of a knot of young guys approaching her. They took up the pavement entirely, bulging out onto the road. They were shouting and waving beer bottles around. She ducked into a pub on her left. The Weaver's Arms. She'd passed the place by for all the years she'd lived here but had never been inside. Well, tonight was the night it seemed. It would do her good to try something new, have a little adventure.

There were three others in the bar. Two old guys sitting six feet apart against the back wall under a big uncovered strip light and a torn faced barmaid behind the counter, rag in hand. She was so heavily tanned that she looked like one of those bog people that archaeologists seemed to dig up from time to time. Laurie moved over towards a table and realised that she'd need to approach the bar to get a drink. She turned again and walked over to the woman.

"Can I have a pint of lager please?" The woman looked at her again, moved silently to the taps, poured a pint, placed it in front of Laurie and gave her a long look.

"Two pound," the voice was flat, Northern. She held out her hand. Laurie stared at it for a moment, taking in the array of gold rings. Were these remains from the mediaeval times? She could picture the hand, be-ringed and filthy reaching out from the ground to a group of eager young archaeologists. The woman jabbed her hand at Laurie.

"Two pound."

"Okay. I just have to . . ." Laurie had to search her pockets and make up the money in stray change. By the time she looked up again with the money the woman had turned her back and started to rearrange the crisps. Laurie put the two pounds on the counter and made her way back to the booth through the mismatched chairs and tables.

She sat down and took off her coat whilst glancing around. What kind of place was this? It was bereft of any Christmas decorations. The walls were a patchy white and the plaster was crumbling in patches. The floor had two different types of lino that overlapped in some places, causing swells and dips. The barmaid had turned and was now staring at a spot above and to the left of Laurie's head.

The door opened and a heavy set young man in a polo neck walked in and headed straight to the bar.

"Pint, Mags."

The barmaid grinned at the man.

"How are you tonight, Gerry?" One of Bog face's eye teeth was missing.

He shrugged, picked up his pint and sat at the table nearest Laurie's with his back to the bar. The transformation in the barmaid was astonishing. She smiled as she scoured her cloth across the bar and one of her shoulder straps had fallen to reveal even more of her preserved skin.

Laurie looked back down from the bar to surreptitiously check out this Gerry.

He was smiling at her.

"How d'you like it?" He cut through the air with an upturned palm.

"What?" She smiled. "The pub or the atmosphere?"

"Oh both, everything."

She laughed for the first time that day.

"Gerry," he reached across to shake her hand.

Laurie glanced up at the bar in time to see the barmaid's face fold shut. Her pique gave Laurie confidence. At least she was a better prospect than that old hag.

"Laurie." She smiled. "Would you like to join me?"

He moved across to her table.

"So what are you doing here?" He took a big drink of his pint. "Are you on the run?"

She smiled. Was she? She supposed she was. But how pathetic to be on the run from someone like Ed! "Sort of." She sipped her beer. "Yourself? Are you escaping something?"

"Cheap beer, snazzy décor, on the way home from work." He nodded as he spoke.

"Where is it you work?"

"The hospital." He paused then pointed at himself. "I am a hospital DJ."

"Really? I've never met anyone who did that. Is it interesting?"

He thought for a moment. "I'm thinking about leaving actually." He smiled brightly at Laurie. "Anyway, do you want another drink?"

Laurie looked down at her almost full glass.

Gerry smiled. "Well, how about a nip?"

She shrugged. "Why not, eh?"

Gerry turned to the bar. Laurie took the opportunity to check him out a bit more. He was taller than Ed, taller than her Dad. Maybe about six footish? Manly. Looked like he could cut things down and carry stuff around. He was wearing a thick dark green wooly jumper which should have looked daggy, but actually just looked warm and practical. His shoulders had that nice straight line to them that some men had. Ed would never have shoulders like that. He'd never be manly like this guy.

"Mags, my darling, two nips and a pint when you have a moment."

The barmaid narrowed her eyes, no doubt contemplating poisoning either one or both of the drinks.

"So." She needed to keep the chat moving. "Why are you thinking about leaving?"

"It's too heavy." He shrugged. "But I don't trust anyone else to do it."

"Really? I'm not being funny, but isn't it just playing music?"

"It's not actually as simple as that." He looked a bit hurt. "It's all operations, bad news, dark nights of the soul, that kind of thing." He shrugged again.

She thought for a moment. "But there must be good things too. Babies being born."

"No, no. They bring their own CDs. It's all Enya and fucking whale song. Hospital radio's mostly for the old folk, the terminally ill." He picked at a beer mat and flicked it at the scabby table top. "I can't stop thinking about how many people have died listening to one of my shows." He took a deep breath. "Listening to tunes that I've picked." He dropped the beer mat again and gripped his pint with both hands.

"Oh God, I see what you mean." She had never thought about that before and she could feel herself start to get choked up. She hated it when that happened and the feeling of sadness just popped up unbidden.

"It's taking me hours to plan my shows. It's not easy, not easy at all." He drained half his pint. "The thing is: there have been complaints. They want more Abba and less Ennio Morricone." He seemed baffled.

Laurie laughed, the feeling gone again. "I suppose nobody wants to be challenged at that point, do they?"

Gerry laughed too. "I suppose so. You're not really looking to grow your musical repertoire at the end, are you?"

Mags arrived at the table with the fresh drinks. She ignored Gerry and stared again at Laurie.

"Thanks Mags," she smiled up as she spoke. The older woman snorted and turned back to the bar.

"Cheers!" she called out to the retreating back. "She likes you, doesn't she?" Laurie felt a twinge of jealousy. Ridiculous – she didn't even know this man.

They knocked back the whisky. Laurie's eyes watered and she had to stop herself from gagging. She took a big slug of her beer to wash the taste away.

They sat in silence and concentrated on finishing off the beer. Now she was feeling giddy and enthusiastic. She knew she was staring at Gerry's face – at his pale eyes and his nice, straight teeth. She wanted to stroke her hand down his jumper and wind her fingers in his thick, dark hair. She was getting carried away. She drained the last of her drink and stood up abruptly.

"I've got to go, Gerry."

"Really, so soon?" He looked anxious and put out his hand. " Let's go somewhere else." He started to stand up.

She frowned down at him as he tried to untangle his coat from one of the legs of his chair.

"Come on," he said. Whether at her or the difficult coat, she couldn't tell. The coat tugged free. She was starting to feel more than a little foolish. What was she doing? She could see where this might go but she just couldn't be bothered.

"Look, Gerry, I have to go home."

"Will your mum be wondering where you are?" His eyes were kind and clever and he was staring at her. She felt she was being looked at properly for the first time.

She swallowed."Something like that." The problem now, of course, was that she had no idea where she was going. No money, no friends, no transport. She sat down again. If Gerry was surprised by this, he didn't show it.

"Pint?" He pointed to the bar.

"Yes please. But I'm afraid I'll have to owe you. I seem to have run out of money."

"That's absolutely fine. I like it when women owe me."

He waved a tenner around as he said this and pretended to twiddle a moustache but he looked awkward. Possibly he wasn't expecting Laurie to do anything in return, but she knew there had to be some method of exchange. She remembered the guys in the bushes.

She wasn't that naïve.

"So what do you want to do?" He spread his arms out in front of him, palms up. "Dancing? Cocktails?"

She sighed. "Drink, mostly."

"It's not something I'd normally do, but Goddamn it, I'll try anything once." He shook the tenner at the barmaid. "Two pints of your finest ale, M'lady."

Mags wasn't happy but moved to the pumps.

"Now what's going on here?" He made a serious face at her. "Who are you really on the run from?"

"God, it's too boring to go into." She sighed. "Better just to drink, Gerry."

"Really? Do you want to talk about it?"

"No. I definitely do not want to talk about it." She made inverted commas around the word "it". She didn't know why. It made Gerry laugh.

"You're a one-off aren't you?"

"Some might say just as fucking well, eh?" They both laughed again in that silly, helpless way that people do when they're settling in to proper drinking.

"Gerry," Mag's voice made Laurie's temples throb. Gerry got up and went to the bar for the pints. No table service now. Laurie resisted the temptation to lay her head down on the table.

"Enjoy." Gerry smiled at her, placing her pint in front of her.

* * *

They left the bar some time later. Gerry had offered to walk her home. She could feel him holding himself deliberately straighter. Was this the kind of situation where he needed to act sober even though they both knew how much they'd had to drink? Laurie led the way back to the flat. She walked at the edge of the pavement, balancing as she tried not to break into a run. She moved in a little but this brought her too close to Gerry and the other pedestrians. Mostly drunken teenagers, they were oblivious to anyone else. The girls were underdressed and sparkly in strapless tops and short skirts. Their legs were bare and shone under the street lamps. Laurie imagined herself as one of them. Out in a pack focussed on sugary drinks and grabby boys. The thought sickened her. She'd left all that behind her, thank God.

They reached the end of her street having said nothing during the walk.

"Well, here we are: Strathmore Crescent." The once grand tenements peered down at them. She could see the light from the PC in their bedroom. She ducked into the lane opposite her flat. Gerry hesitated for a moment but followed her in. The lane joined the crescent to another street but was rarely used and barely lit.

This seemed to be the correct course of action to take. Laurie felt much clearer headed and focused. She looked back at Gerry but the lack of street lights meant she could make out very little of his facial expression. All she could see was a rather grimly set jaw. Laurie pointed to a stone doorway leading to a drying area and stepped inside it. She leaned against the pillar, looking over Gerry's shoulder as he moved in closer to her. She could just make out the bay window of her bedroom.

What was Ed doing now?

As if she needed to ask.

He would, of course, be in front of a screen making pretend people move about in a pretend place killing each other and stealing cars.

She put her arms around Gerry's neck, but the angle was too steep for her and she dropped her arms to his waist. She rubbed her hand around his mid-back in small circular motions. Gerry seemed willing to follow Laurie's erratic lead. He stood still with his face slightly averted. She tucked her face into his jumper below his collar bone. The wool scratched her and she turned so that her cheek was in contact with the rough surface. They stood like this for a few minutes. Eventually Laurie forced herself to lift her head at an attempt at a kiss. He pulled away briefly and looked closely at her face. Then he wrestled her in and started to kiss her in earnest.

She couldn't get her breath but she felt as if she was in a film and was curiously detached from the action. Gerry had started to move his hands around her rib cage towards her breasts. His touch was too tentative for Laurie. She felt herself becoming impatient. This should be more of a passionate tussle, something exciting: a deal breaker.

She kissed Gerry back fiercely and pushed into him nudging him back against the wall. Perhaps a bite might bring on the feeling she was aiming for. She nipped Gerry on the lip.

"Ow! What are you doing?" He frowned at her. She looked up at her flat again. Gerry turned his head to follow her line of vision.

"That's where I live. But I think I'm going to go away for a bit."

"Oh." They pulled away from each other. "Are you going tonight?"

"I'm not sure." She shrugged. "Probably not."

"You might change your mind in the morning."

"Possibly, but I doubt it."

"Where will you go?"

She shrugged again. "Dunno. But the world's my oyster, isn't it?"

"What if the world's not all it's cracked up to be?"

"It's not like I'd be leaving paradise behind." She looked around herself. "Is it?"

"I've seen worse."

He looked like he meant it.

"Come on," she said. "Sorry, I'm ruining the vibe."

They walked to the mouth of the alley. Laurie looked up at the flat. She turned to Gerry.

"I'd better get going. Thanks for tonight."

"It took my mind off things." He began to raise his hand but dropped it again to his side. He stood and waited as she crossed the road over to her front door.

She pressed the intercom, then looking over her shoulder, she watched Gerry walk back along the street. He disappeared and reappeared under the streetlights until he turned the corner and was gone.

Friday the 17th of December

Just After Midnight
Cloudy

Ed was still up when she walked back into the flat. Any residual feelings of tipsiness disappeared when she saw his thin shoulders in his faded grey t shirt as he stood at the window looking down at the street. He was like a gangly child from behind, right down to the superhero she knew graced the front of the shirt. Ed's hair desperately needed cut. It was sticking up on the crown of his head from the way he'd been sleeping. Whether it was last night's sleep or one of his day time naps, Laurie had no way of knowing. Ed's day was entirely his own, Laurie thought but, unusually, without the usual rancour. There was something endearingly pathetic about him as he stood there looking for her.

He turned back to the room, jumping when he realised she was there, watching him. He pulled his ear phones out of his ears and sat back on the window sill, trapping the stupid lace curtain under his skinny bum. Laurie tsked in annoyance as it came free from where she'd wedged it in behind the ancient curtain pole. The top corner flapped free. It would all fall down during the night. No doubt she'd have to climb up tomorrow and fix it again.

"Where have you been?" Ed was completely oblivious to Laurie's annoyance.

"Out. Did you miss me?"

"Where's the curry?"

"The curry?" Laurie repeated. He hadn't been waiting for her at all. Well, at least, not as anything other than a deliverer of food. "The curry's in the bloody hall. Where I left it." She threw her coat on the bed. "Why are you standing at the window Ed? What are you waiting for?"

"Pizza. When you didn't come back I phoned for some. But I thought I'd order something different in case you came back with the curry." He smiled winningly at her.

When she had nothing to say but kept staring at him, Ed's smile faltered. "What's wrong? Don't you feel like pizza?"

"No Ed, I really don't feel like pizza." As soon as she said it her stomach hurt with hunger. But there was no way she was giving him the satisfaction of asking for a slice. Annoyingly, she knew he'd gladly, unquestioningly, give her half, or more, of anything he had. The problem was that he had nothing of any value to Laurie. His needs were simple. He spent his dole money on take-aways and computer games. All he did was play games, watch TV and sleep. He always appeared to have just woken up, picking at the sleep in his eyes and scratching at himself. Luckily he was unable to grow a beard as shaving would be a real issue for him. She had a mental image of him with a rumplestiltskin beard and felt a giggle coming on.

"Have we got any drink here?" She should capitalise on this surge of good feeling.

21

"What?" Ed had moved back to the computer. "Oh forget it. Just forget it," she muttered.

No response.

"For fuck's sake. Ed! What does it take for you to pay the slightest bit of attention to me?"

The script was so well worn and boring. She was like a cuckoo in a clock coming out at prearranged times always making the same noise. She realised Ed had put the headphones back in again. Would it be possible to strangle him with the cord, or would she have to work on her upper body strength first? God, who was she kidding? Ed would probably help her. He was so amenable as long as you weren't asking him to make something of himself.

She was still standing in the doorway. She looked around their living room. They'd finished university more than five years before but were still living like students. At least then they'd had a student social life. Now they were the only ones of their circle left in town.

The bedroom had piles of stuff everywhere. Clothes were heaped up at the end of the bed, next to the wardrobe, next to the chest of drawers. Magazines and papers were dumped on the bed amongst the unmade bed clothes. The most galling thing about all the crap was that it was Laurie's. She had no one but herself to blame. She knew this couldn't go on. Or rather, it could go on forever and ever, amen.

She took off her clothes and dumped them on the floor with all her other clothes from the week. She yanked the duvet back, flicking the bed-top detritus to the floor. She sighed loudly to no avail.

"If you think you're going to carry on doing that while

I'm trying to sleep, you've got another thing coming."
Nothing. "Ed!"

"U-huh?" He pulled the ear buds out and turned to her.

"You'd better go and wait for the pizza in the kitchen. Some of us have to get up for work in the morning."

"Okay. Good idea."

She wondered sometimes if he was tone deaf. As in not being able to hear the tone in her voice. He patted her leg through the duvet as he walked past. She felt a bit bad about being nasty to him until she realised he was actually fishing around for his Gameboy which was somewhere within the covers. Ed left the room, neglecting to switch off the light. Laurie pulled the cover over her head and fell asleep thinking the same thing she always seemed to think when she fell asleep these days.

What fresh hell would tomorrow bring?

Fairly bright and early
Cold and Cloudy

She woke up before the alarm went off and lay looking out of her side of the bed. From there she had a view of the bedroom doorway which was open on to the hall. She could see both the bathroom and part of the living-room through the door frame. Ed was already up. Anybody would think he had a job to go to. He would be making her a cup of tea and a slice of toast. This was the only thing Ed did for her and even this he managed to cock up. The tea was always much too weak and the toast not toasted enough. She was constantly turning the dial on the toaster up a bit, but to no avail. Ed had seen something on TV about the carbon in burnt toast causing cancer and now he wouldn't let Laurie eat it the way she liked it.

He came into her field of vision, carrying the tray carefully in front of himself. He kept looking down at the tray, his mouth slightly open. Despite the fact she was staring at him, he didn't look up at her until he'd set the tray down securely on the bed in front of her.

"There we go."

She looked down at the tray. One piece of bleached toast slathered in margarine. One cup of piss weak tea. She knew he meant well and she knew that she should appreciate his efforts. She smiled at him, wondering when he'd last seen her genuine smile. In fact, when was the last time she'd smiled genuinely at all? Last night didn't count, of course. It was if she'd veered off her approved script and started being a different character.

He sat and watched her eating as he did every morning. She looked up at him.

"What is it?"

"Nothing Ed. I was just wondering what you were doing today."

"Oh. The usual." He stood up from the bed and started to pick up clothes from the floor. He gathered together a pile's worth and dumped them by the door.

"Not those." She stood up and pulled a couple of things from the pile. "I need those for work." She shook out her trousers and cardigan. Now she'd have to try and find some clean knickers.

"Perhaps you'd like to fit a visit to the laundrette into your busy schedule."

"Maybe," he sighed, sitting down at the computer. "I still have enough clothes left for a while though."

She knew she'd end up wearing her emergency pants to work and that she'd be spending time tonight washing stuff in the sink and then part drying things with the hair dryer.

"Well, as long as you're okay for a while."

He ignored her. She walked into the bathroom and gave herself a cat's lick. She was clean enough. She pulled her clothes on, stuck her hair in a pony-tail and opened her make up bag. What she saw in the mirror depressed her even further. She was getting older; there was no doubt about it. She rubbed foundation into her face and attempted to make herself look healthy with blusher and mascara. The trouble was, she was so pale in the winter that it was hard to look okay without looking like a dolly. She tried to blend her blusher in to make it look natural, but she knew she looked daft. She wet a bit of toilet paper and scrubbed at her cheeks. Slightly better, but now she looked a bit consumptive.

She couldn't be bothered to brush her teeth. She also couldn't be bothered saying good bye to Ed. She picked her handbag up from the hall and left the flat, deliberately slamming the door behind her.

She made it to the bus stop just in time. There were several other people waiting. All of them were listening to headphones and ignoring everyone else. She fished around in her bag for her bus pass as she boarded. There were still a few seats free at the back. She slid across into one and was immediately joined by an angry looking middle-aged woman who glared at her whilst taking up more than her half of the seat. Laurie moved over as far as she could and stared into the hair of the passenger sitting in front of her.

Suddenly it occurred to her. She could get off the bus at any time – anywhere she liked. She need not finish the journey. Or at least not finish her original, planned journey. A surge of excitement rushed through her. She stood up, glancing her hand over the man's hair and pushing past the surly woman. Both people turned and looked at her and she smiled calmly.

"This is my stop," she explained loudly to everyone on the bus. At the exact moment she reached the door, the bus stopped. Feeling like a movie star, she stepped gracefully down from the bus. She turned to the bus as it pulled away from the kerb and performed a pretty little bow to the blank, uninterested passengers.

Friday the 17th of December

All Day
Dull But Brightening Later

It was easier than she would have imagined, wasting the day while pretending to be at work. She'd walked around the streets until lunchtime, sipping from her warm coke bottle and peering in people's windows. Nobody seemed to be at home in the nice Victorian semis that she floated past. Where were the housewives and small children? Did everyone work now or attend an organised day time activity? At first she felt like an apocalypse survivor, searching for another human. She felt empty and calm and knew it wouldn't be too awful if she was on her own. Then her own voice started to annoy her, counting her steps and commenting on things and she started to see the value in other people being around.

She imagined what it would really be like to be friendless and wandering. What on earth would she do all day? She supposed she'd have to keep finding food all the time and safe places to shelter. It was hard to imagine what the day to day reality of being a survivor would entail without knowing what type of disaster she'd survived.

If it was a nuclear holocaust she'd presumably have to keep stopping to be sick and she'd probably collapse a lot.

There was no fun in that scenario. Ditto with an extreme weather situation. Everything would be under water, or upside down. Too messy, too dangerous. It would be better if there'd been some sort of virus that had killed off everybody but her. She'd read a book like that once. Except, in the book, there'd been two survivors who'd become aware of another human's presence and had eventually met and fallen in love and begun the mammoth task of repopulating the planet. There was no mention of the problems of inbreeding. Strangely, the animals of the world had been unaffected by the virus. Stranger still, one chapter had seen the heroine battle against some dinosaurs. Quite where they had come from, the book didn't explain.

Laurie tried to imagine herself battling a dinosaur. She wouldn't know where to begin. She'd have to make some sort of weapon. A spear. But she knew there was no way she was strong enough to pierce the hide of a dinosaur. It wouldn't be sporting to shoot the creature and, besides, there was nowhere to get a gun from anyway. She'd just have to pray she could outrun a dinosaur. If she stayed mostly indoors, she'd be safe from the bigger beasts. But, presumably, there'd be dead bodies everywhere and they would pose a health risk to her. She'd just have to move cautiously. She pictured a dinosaur rounding the corner of the street. It was one of those big ones with the long necks and tiny heads. Its legs weren't very long, so she had a chance at escaping. But what if she was fenced in by dinosaurs? She glanced around, checking exit routes. If only she could climb over the shoulder height garden fence on her left and get inside the house behind it. She could barricade herself in. She tested the fence to see if it would take her weight and was just about to attempt to scramble up, when the postman came through the gate.

"Morning!" he grinned at her.

"Yes it is." She grinned too.

Slinging his bag over his shoulder, he tramped off along the street.

Now what? What did unemployed people do all day? Technically she wasn't actually unemployed but she soon would be. They'd sack her when she just didn't turn up anymore. Whatever she did, she'd have to keep to her normal schedule for the time being. She hadn't the patience to attempt to explain to Ed what she was doing. She'd put that off for as long as she could. Probably until the rent was due. Her heart started to beat harder. She pushed all thoughts of money out of her head. That only lasted until she realised it was lunchtime and she was hungry.

Face facts, she told herself. Find a cash machine. She walked to the Perth Road shops, determined to get a realistic idea of what was going on.

There were two cash points: one outside the Royal Bank and one outside the Spar. She stood between both machines, deciding which to use.

Neither had a queue.

They both seemed to be working.

She kept looking up the street to one and then down the street to the other. She knew that it didn't matter which she used, but she couldn't make up her mind. She couldn't even seem to take a step away from what she judged to be the exact middle point between the cash points. People walked around her as if she was invisible and even when someone jostled her, she still couldn't move. A week ago, even yesterday, she would have been shamed by this public show of lack-of-plan, but now she couldn't even be bothered to pretend to read the adverts in the window or to act as if she was waiting for someone.

It started to drizzle.

She fished around in her pocket for something useful. All she had was her house key and a Kirby grip. She plucked the key out of her coat and held it up.

This key was one of a seemingly endless march of replacement keys – destined for wherever it was all her keys elected to visit after a few months in her company. She had it on a key fob that Ed had given her. It was a little model Barbie doll who was dressed in a bright pink fish-tailed evening gown. She even wore a little tiara in her butter yellow, lustrous hair. Ed had been delighted with the gift, handing it over in its reused wrapping paper which Laurie recognised from the birthday gift she'd given to him a few months previously. He'd even almost managed to get it to hold together using the original sticky tape.

She hated opening presents. They were never right. Usually the gift inside seemed to have been picked for someone other than her. It was worse if it was an item of clothing as the gift-giver always wanted you to try it on. Once she'd been given a hideous blouse that she knew immediately would be too small. Her aunt had insisted she try it on. No sooner had she pulled the top over head, she'd realised it was stuck. Her arms folded sharply within the top, making useless little wings. She'd wriggled sweatily for a minute, knowing she was going to have to ask for help. After a few muffled calls from within the top, within the bathroom, she'd been forced to open the door (no mean feat with your hands trapped inside a blouse) and call out. Eventually her mother had appeared and managed wordlessly to wrench the blouse over her head.

Heartbreakingly, it was too ripped to be worn again.

Thankfully Ed never bought her clothing. In fact she could count the amount of times he'd bought her presents on one hand. Once he'd given her a fiver. The other times it had been useless comedy trinkets like a miniature bong or a tiny minarette that played a scratchy recording of the call to prayer a few times before conking out. She'd actually quite enjoyed the call to prayer. She'd listened to it in bed at night once and imagined she was staying in a ramshackle hotel in Morocco.

There was nothing really she could imagine doing with the Barbie key ring. Well, there was, but she often thought of injuring Ed with objects. It was obvious now that Ed had been imagining her as some sort of Barbie doll. He mock-leered at the pneumatic teats of the dolly bird and nudged Laurie as she held the key ring in front of her face and lifted the dress to see if Barbie was commando. She was, but she had nothing to hide and was as smooth as an egg.

"Uh, thanks Ed." One should always pretend the gift was appreciated.

"It reminded me of you." He smiled at her hopefully.

Laurie struggled to look thankful.

"Did it?" She was more puzzled than annoyed.

Ed's smile faltered. Presumably he'd meant to be complimentary, but had misjudged again.

"Yes. She's, y'know, pretty and her hair's blonde. Her smile's nice." He'd looked down at his lap. He started to reach for the remote control. Laurie had felt sorry for him at that moment. He was a little boy, learning how to be a big boy. She hated to see the kicked dog look about his eyes, but, really, at what point was he going to be able to manage on his own? She knew from magazines that all men required a certain degree of training, but how long did it take? She took a deep breath and snatched the remote from Ed's clammy hand.

She threw the remote across the floor and stood up, pulling Ed to his feet. She gave him a hug and kissed him on the lips. Ed stood motionless, his arms by his sides. Laurie kept kissing him until she could feel him start to get into it. They stood like that for a few minutes, Ed becoming breathless and clutching at her upper arms. It always amazed Laurie how easy it was to switch men on. She doubted many women were as easily manipulated. How easy it would be to navigate through the world if you were prepared to put out. She could always anticipate when Ed would attempt to manoeuvre her to the bed and proceed to have a go.

On that occasion she'd been about to pull away and make an excuse when she'd happened to catch sight of herself in the mirror that was leaning against the wall. From the position she was standing in, she could only see herself from the shoulders down and most of Ed was blocked by her body. It was like watching a film that she was in control of. When Ed tried to pull her towards the bed she resisted and when she felt the tension in him go weak she put her hand up to her breast and squeezed, turning her upper body slightly towards the mirror. Her breath caught in her throat as she watched the woman in the mirror. Ed's eyes were closed. He had no idea what she was doing. He tried again to pull her towards the bed and again she resisted, this time taking Ed's hand and putting it between her legs, over her jeans. He sighed into her mouth as she moved his fingers under her own.

This type of encounter had worked for a few weeks, but then Laurie was bored again. She avoided going to bed at the same time as Ed and feigned sleep when he climbed under the covers. Luckily, he seemed to have taken the hint because he hadn't tried it on for ages.

A drop of rain fell into her eye, waking her from her day dream. She pulled herself together and opted for the Spar's cash machine. She took a deep breath and read the screen. She had a grand total of £139.43. She'd only just been paid as well, so the money was going to have to do her for a few weeks. Longer if she did leave work. She didn't think she'd be entitled to dole because she was leaving her job for no good reason. Well, not one the Job Centre would understand. She doubted she'd get away with saying she was consumed with vague feelings of dread. That when she phoned customers she experienced a sort of sympathy Tourette's where she was compelled to keep asking them how they were and not giving up until she'd heard some sadness in their voice. This impulse to get strangers to tell her their troubles didn't extend to people she actually knew. When her work mates tried to tell her about their love lives she had to make her excuses and leave the canteen. She didn't care about Morag's husband's redundancy or Sue's man's temper. They were like bad actors and she'd heard it all before.

But when Mrs Green in Aberdare told her about not being able to afford to feed her cat anymore, she'd marked the unpaid phone bill as paid. It was the least she could do. She'd started giving every fifth customer a bill credit. So far she hadn't been caught, but she knew the calls were recorded and randomly monitored. Eventually she'd get summoned into the Big Office and punished in some way.

But it wasn't even that that was making her leave work. She just couldn't be bothered with the people she knew any more. She'd rather work on her own. She imagined herself somewhere quiet and isolated and peaceful. Somewhere where she'd have to actively seek someone out to talk to them. Somewhere where even if you passed a person in the corridor, it was completely acceptable just to nod at them and not be seen as ignorant.

Nowhere immediately sprang to mind.

She wasted the rest of the day in the Overgate shopping centre. She had a feeling that she'd be wasting a lot of her time in there so consciously eked out the experience. She didn't want to look at everything on her first visit. She decided to carry out a comprehensive customer relations survey of the centre. It would give her something to do and if anyone questioned her hanging about for days on end she'd be able to imply that she was the mystery shopper. Very ingenious.

At first she'd gone for an expression of mild curiosity as if she'd dropped her child off at playgroup and didn't get into town much. She'd stuck around the slightly mumsy section in Debenhams but she couldn't get over the amount of pastel, cotton items there were. It was as if when you had a baby you had to start dressing in a similarly baby-like manner. She'd cast around at first to see if there were any other mums milling around with time on their hands and no set agenda, but there was only a shop assistant going about turning all the hooks on the hangers to face in the same direction. She completely ignored Laurie, even when Laurie raised her eyebrows at her in acknowledgement. So much for looking after the customer's needs, thought Laurie, making a mental note to jot it down later.

She worked her way through the whole of Debenhams from the children's section to house ware, asking various questions of staff and making up little back stories to explain herself. She flicked through a book of curtain swatches and watched the woman working in the porcelain section. She moved carefully around her little shop section. Definitely not for Laurie. All those breakables needing dusted and arranged. There was far too much chance of disaster in there. The woman smiled at her and put down the crystal elephant she was dusting.

"Good afternoon, can I help you with anything?" The woman was happy in her work.

Laurie wondered if the woman's house was full of this stuff or if perhaps it was completely minimalist and uncluttered.

"Yes, please." Laurie thought for a moment. "I'm looking for a present for someone."

The woman smiled at Laurie. Laurie smiled at the woman.

"Who's the present for?"

"Oh, em . . . It's for . . . Gerry." She thought for a moment. "Yes, I'd like to get Gerry a present."

The woman frowned, but not unkindly. She must get a lot of doddery old folk in here.

"Lovely. So what sort of ornament do you think Gerry might like?"

Laurie was baffled. She didn't have the faintest idea.

The woman led her over to a cabinet that contained dad-type stuff.

"How about football? Does he follow a team?"

There were ugly little football badges made out of porcelain. She couldn't imagine Gerry wearing one, even if she did know if there was a team he followed.

"No. I don't think so."

"Well, we've also got golf and rugby balls made out of crystal."

Laurie shook her head. All she really knew about Gerry was that he liked to drink a pint and a nip and that he was a better kisser than Ed.

"We've got crucifixes."

"Oh no, I don't think he's religious."

"Models of motorbikes?"

"Oh no, he wouldn't be able to drive."

The woman frowned, realising perhaps that Laurie didn't have the first idea what to get this Gerry character.

"Well, what about something like cufflinks?"

Laurie shook her head. He didn't seem like the cufflinks type.

"Sorry. I'm not being much help am I?" said Laurie, looking down at the ground.

"Not at all. Sometimes it's hard to think of a gift for a man. They always seem to have everything they need, don't they?"

Laurie nodded.

"What about music? Does he like music?"

"Yes, he definitely does. He's a DJ."

"Great, now we're getting somewhere." The woman beamed at her. She pointed to a small display case on the cash desk. "Have a look at these." It was all rock and roll paraphernalia. It was a bit naff, but was definitely the best stuff in the section for Gerry.

The woman opened the cabinet and took out an Elvis lighter. It was a Zippo type thing that had a silhouette of Elvis outlined on it in black on one side and "Taking Care of Business" engraved on the other.

"Perfect. I'll take it." Suddenly she felt giddy. She gave the woman a little hug. The woman laughed too, delighted she'd helped.

"Wait 'til he gets a load of this! He'll love it."

And she knew he really would. She paid, left the shopping centre and made for the bar from last night, certain she'd see him there.

* * *

Of course, he wasn't there. It seemed to be the same crew of old blokes from the night before. But then, she realised, looking at the clock over the bar, it was much earlier, barely tea time. She sat down and took off her coat. Then she stood up again and walked over to the bar. As she passed the old guys she winked at them. She was some

38

wise cracking dame in a 50s movie. How different she was to the timid girl from the night before. She smiled, thinking how funny it was that a move towards making a decision could have such a marked effect on a person. The battle axe barmaid stared at her. Laurie wavered slightly, but, pulling her spine straighter, she carried on to the bar.

"Good afternoon," she used her politest voice.

"Aye?"

Clearly, Laurie's formality had no discernible effect on the old boot.

"I would like a whisky and also half a pint of lager. Please."

Without a word, the woman (what was her name again – Mags?) turned from her and got the drinks. Laurie didn't notice that she slammed the glasses down with any less ire this evening. Laurie handed over a fiver.

"Keep the change."

The woman regarded her suspiciously.

"I was wondering if you might know when Gerry would be in."

"Gerry?"

So it was going to be like that. The woman was going to make her work for it.

Laurie smiled. "Yes, Gerry. The guy that was in here last night?"

The woman's blank face was slappable.

"Youngish, beard, tall."

Nothing.

"Nice accent. He bought me drinks."

"That's nice for you."

"Right. I see."

Laurie knocked the whisky back, blinking away tears. She looked steadily at the barmaid as she glugged the lager as quickly as she could. She put the glass down firmly on the bar.

"Enjoy your evening, madam," she pronounced clearly and stalked out of the bar.

As soon as she was outside in the damp twilight she realised that she'd left behind her coat.

"Fuck it!" she shouted and kicked weakly at a lamp-post.

Never mind, she'd get another one. She had her purse and keys in her pocket and it was better to travel light anyhow. She remembered dimly that Gerry worked the midnight shift and as she had no idea where he lived, she decided to go to the hospital. She knew from personal experience that although time in hospitals passed twice as slowly as time outside, they were warm places where people didn't look at you too closely. It was certainly a better location to hang about than the bus station or the park. She did have the option to go home of course, but she had no desire to see Ed. He wouldn't ask her how her day had been, or notice that she was late, or that she was not wearing a coat. His stunning lack of interest would drive her to confess her wanderings in an effort to annoy him and she'd have nowhere to go from there.

She needed to have a clue about what she was doing with herself before she involved anyone else. She pictured telling her father that she'd left work. He'd make a few noises about paying the rent, having a plan for her life – some such nonsense – but as long as she didn't approach him for money, he wouldn't bother himself too much.

He'd have more to say about the situation if it was her brother, Danny, who'd packed everything in on a whim, with no idea of what next. Laurie knew her father was waiting for her to get married to someone with a decent job, prospects, a plan. He didn't have time for Ed. He was polite enough on the rare occasions that they visited her father, but it was plain that he saw Ed as a stop-gap, a practice boyfriend. She'd been vague about her and Ed's living arrangements, letting it seem as if there were other flatmates. At the time she'd told Ed it was to avoid confrontation. She said she was worried about her father's health in light of recent events and that it didn't really matter anyway.

Ed, of course, had mutely accepted her explanation. At the time she'd been irritated by Ed's mute acceptance. His mother knew they lived together and although, not happy about it, she'd made an effort at first to help them. Even arriving one day with a box of kitchen utensils.

"I thought these might come in handy." She'd said, holding the box out to Laurie.

Laurie had looked into it, dismissing the contents immediately as the tat that her sort-of mother-in-law had no need for. So Laurie and Ed had become a kind of living charity shop. She'd smiled at the older woman and thanked her profusely.

"That's great Sandy, really great."

They stood facing each other in the dingy little kitchen for a moment. Laurie could feel Ed's mother resisting the temptation to tidy up, that was the thing about Laurie's sort of mother-in-law. But Laurie ushered Sandy into the living room while she made the tea. She stood in the kitchen and looked at the shittiness that surrounded her. It was pure 70s crap; beige everywhere; tile-effect wallpaper with a field mouse on wheat motif; off white plastic handles on the cupboards; muddy brown carpet tiles on the floor. It would take more than a lick of paint to jazz the place up. The whole flat was like that – clean, serviceable, but dull and tired. She made the tea and put it on a tray. They had no biscuits, but she found two Kit-Kats and a Twix in the fridge.

"Here we go," she said as she came into the living room. Ed and Sandy were sitting on the sofa staring into space. Laurie put the tray down on the tile-topped coffee table.

"Sandy, would you like a cup of tea?"

Of course she would. All she ever did was drink tea.

"Yes, I think I will please." She smiled up weakly at Laurie.

Laurie poured.

She was always amazed at how Sandy could appear to have all the strength of a gnat and still control another human being so effectively. Ed sat beside his mother mutely. He was looking toward the window with an expression of neutrality that enraged Laurie. He didn't like to rock the boat ever. Particularly not with his mother. She could understand why. She was still giving him handouts and he was the only child, after all. His dad hadn't been around for years and Laurie understood that they'd developed one of those us-against-the-world relationships. But still, it grated. At some point Sandy was going to have to make a life for herself. Scuppering Ed's independence wouldn't last forever.

Or would it? Laurie could see Ed and Sandy knocking

about the bungalow together in their old ages. Ed's aging would catch up with his mother's and they'd dress similarly and finish each other's sentences. People would see them around and think them spinster brother and sister.

However, the days of that sort of arrangement were long gone. Nowadays people would probably assume there was some weird sexual element to it and throw stones through their windows and point at them down at the shops.

Laurie poured the milk in first, just as Sandy and Ed liked it. They both liked lots and lots of it; full fat if possible. There was a particular shade of beige Sandy was after and Laurie could never quite get it right.

"That'll do, that's fine," said Sandy, reaching out towards her cup.

"But it's only half full," said Laurie.

"It looks plenty strong enough though." She raised the cup to her mouth and took a sip. "Lovely, just the thing." Her smile was unconvincing.

Laurie held out the plate with chocolate bars on.

Sandy thought for a moment, her hand hovering over the Twix.

"No, no. I'd better not."

"Why? Have you got a special occasion coming up?"

"No!" Sandy pinked up then brought her voice back under control. "No, nothing like that. It just doesn't hurt to look after yourself."

What was that supposed to mean? Although, Laurie seemed to have struck a nerve.

"Lovely day, isn't it?" Ed had come over all cheery.

"Yes," Sandy and Laurie said simultaneously.

"When we've had this, why don't we go for a walk in the park?"

Sandy and Laurie both stared at Ed. The park? Outdoors?

"Oh, I don't think so Ed, not today," said Sandy.

Laurie was thankful. The last thing she felt like doing was taking a promenade amongst the dog shit and sweetie wrappers.

"Cool," said Ed, holding his hands up in front of him, as if stopping traffic.

Laurie tore open a Kit-Kat. Hey ho, she thought, this is the life, as she took the biggest bite she could manage without choking.

Since then, Sandy hadn't been back but she phoned every other day. It was always at annoying times like when the takeaway had arrived or when Ed looked like he might be considering washing the dishes. She never seemed to phone for anything of any pressing urgency yet the calls could often last for thirty or forty minutes. Ed said virtually nothing. She'd once taken the receiver from Ed's limp hand to hear for herself what Sandy was going on about, but there was silence on the other end of the line. At first Laurie assumed that Sandy had realised that Ed was no longer on the line, but the silence carried on until it was broken by the faint clack of snooker balls followed by a polite round of applause.

"That was a lovely shot, Ed," said Sandy.

Laurie handed the phone back to Ed, promising herself that she needed a plan B and sharpish.

This plan B still hadn't shown itself as she stood outside Ninewells hospital. It was a modern-ish building, like a huge, ugly office block. As usual, smokers – some with pyjamas on – clustered around the entrance. She'd been in the hospital on numerous occasions over the last few years but only ever to one department. She'd never wandered the hospital in all her time hanging about there, just in case she'd been needed. She'd followed the same route every time, attaching some superstitious notion to her journey about keeping everything the same to stave off bad news. Of course it hadn't worked and she'd sworn to herself that she wouldn't go back to the hospital ever again. But, as she walked through the door, she felt comfortable in the familiar surroundings and noted that nothing seemed to have changed in the intervening months since she'd last walked out of the automatic doors.

She went over to the notice board but couldn't find a listing for hospital radio. She started to wonder if Gerry had lied about the radio station. She hoped not, she was really looking forward to seeing him. The big digital clock next to the reception area read 9.02. Where had the day gone? She was amazed she wasn't hungry, but then the whisky and lager would have taken the edge off. She had hours to kill before Gerry was due to start work. She didn't even have a book with her. She set off for a wander.

The main concourse was empty, save for a couple of porters standing chatting by a wheelchair and a row of four women sitting on office chairs outside a shut door. All the women sat silently, facing forward with their hand-bags in their laps. A sign stuck to the outside of the door read, "cleaning interviews" in neat blue felt tip. As Laurie stood watching, the door opened revealing two women. One was dressed in a mint green coverall and the other was wearing what appeared to be a suit made of stone washed denim.

"Right thanks Maureen, we'll be in touch," said the one holding a clip board.

Maureen nodded and walked out of the hospital.

"Right. Who's next?" She consulted the clip board. "Janelle Anderson?"

A faded looking woman stood up and followed the interviewer into the office. As the door closed, the remaining three moved along. Laurie walked over to the seats and sat down. The seat was still warm. Now she could pass a bit of time without seeming too conspicuous if security noticed her.

The lady next to her smelled strongly of perfume. It wasn't an unpleasant smell; it was the sort Laurie would expect an older woman to wear. She tried to work out how old this woman was but it was difficult to look at her without making it obvious that she was staring.

"Fuck this for a game of soldiers!" muttered the girl at the head of the queue, standing up. "Ah've been waiting here for an hour now. I've got things to dae!"

"It won't be long now. You're next, aren't you?" said the girl next to her, without taking her eyes off her handbag. Laurie realised that she was actually texting on a tiny mobile phone.

The standing girl pushed her fringe off her forehead and put her hands on her hips.

"Nuh, Siobahn. I'm no havin' it! I dinna even need this joab." She stood over Siobahn who clicked her phone shut and put it into her handbag.

"Alright, Carole, let's go for a drink." She stood up,

linked arms with her friend and they walked out of the building giggling.

The woman next to Laurie looked at her and smiled. "Well that narrows the field a bit, doesn't it?"

"I suppose it does," said Laurie. Maybe this was a sign, thought Laurie.

The door opened. The interviewee looked as if she'd been crying.

"Alright Janelle. We'll be in touch." She looked at Laurie and the other woman. "Weren't there more?"

Laurie and the woman nodded.

"They had to leave," said Laurie.

"Okay," said the interviewer. "That doesn't look good, does it?" She nodded at the woman next to Laurie. "Margaret."

"Pat," smiled the woman.

"This is daft, Margaret. I know you're a good worker, you might as well have the job."

They both laughed for a moment. Then Pat looked at Laurie.

"Have you cleaned before?"

"Yes. Well, in my house."

Pat looked at her watch. "That'll do for me. Do you want the job?"

Laurie frowned. This was all happening a bit fast.

"It's six pounds an hour. You get subsidised food in the staff canteen and we provide the overalls. Interested?"

Laurie nodded.

"Great! See you both tomorrow at 8."

"Okay," said Laurie, "bright and early."

"No, no. It's the night shift, love."

47

"Oh." Laurie thought for a second. "That's perfect."

"Okay then." Pat turned to Margaret. "Do you want a lift?"

"Oh that'd be great. It's perishing out there."

Pat smiled at Laurie. "Are you okay to get home, hen?"

"Oh yes, thanks. Actually I'm meeting a friend here. Do you know where Hospital radio is?"

Pat thought for a minute. "That's up in the old bit, right at the top, above where maternity used to be. You'll need to go up the east stairs." She pointed to the back of the concourse.

"Great. Right then, I'll see you tomorrow night."

"Okay," smiled Pat.

"Cheerio," called Margaret as Laurie headed towards the east stairs.

It was weird but Laurie felt she had walked down every corridor a million times before. The muffled echo of her footsteps gave her progress a dream-like quality that allowed her to wander up and down flights of stairs and amble along identical hallways without any nervousness about what she was doing or where she was going. She passed only a few people on her travels and reasoned that she must be in some sort of geriatric dumping ground. People there were waiting to die, she sensed, and when they did there'd be talk of good innings and fair ages. If anyone had the thought to say anything. There was no sign of relatives pacing or dozing.

The building was full of public art. It was like visiting a gallery. Some of the paintings were quite depressing for a hospital. The people who decided these things should make more of an effort to consider the feelings of the patients and their families in the hospital. It was one thing going to a gallery and looking at pictures of mournful-looking people and dismembered dolls or whatever. But when you weren't choosing to be in a place and were likely feeling pretty crappy, these sorts of images could be quite jarring. There was one picture in particular that Laurie had found difficult to look at and yet, couldn't tear herself away from. It showed a man standing up in a little round boat. He was surrounded by piles of dead fish and he held a newspaper in one hand and what looked like a toasting fork or maybe it was a trident, in the other. She couldn't figure out what it signified.

Eventually it was nearly midnight and she went back to the radio station, such as it was. She'd gone past it once, much earlier, and as there was nothing to look at other than a sign saying Hospital Radio and a red bulb on over the door, she'd kept on moving.

She leaned back against the wall opposite the station door and waited. After some time passed, it might have been five minutes or half an hour, she had no way of knowing, she decided to knock gently on the door. It opened and a middle-aged woman appeared.

"Are you new?" she asked Laurie.

"Em, yes," said Laurie. "I'm here on work experience." Where had that come from?

"Work experience at midnight?" She seemed to examine Laurie. "Aren't you a bit old to be on work experience?" The woman frowned as she ushered Laurie into the room.

"It's through the uni. I'm meant to be shadowing Gerry."

"He's a queer one to pair you with. Doesn't speak much." The woman frowned again. Laurie could almost see her pique at not being given a work experience student.

"Maybe I'm supposed to get him to chat more."

"Yes, maybe so. Maybe you'll teach him a thing or two, eh?" She gave a yelp of amusement and nudged Laurie in the ribs. "Well, he's a bit late, but I've put on the A side of this," she held up a Shadows album cover, "that'll keep things going for a while." She picked up her rain coat and a plastic bag. "Nice meeting you. Have fun!" Then she was gone and Laurie was alone at the controls.

She sat down and put the headphones on. Granny music. She took the headphones off again, deciding to keep checking every few minutes that it was still playing. She prayed that Gerry would show up before she had to take decisive action.

Saturday the 18th of December

Just After Midnight
Chance of Snow

Gerry didn't look surprised at all when he opened the door to the station. Laurie smiled up at him, holding the head-phones clumsily against one ear.

"Watcha," she said in a cockney accent, doffing an imaginary cap.

"Good evening." Gerry made her a formal bow.

Laurie was actually delighted to see Gerry. That was what was really surprising about this turn of events: she was delighted to see him. He looked more attractive than she remembered.

"You don't mind. Do you?" she asked, beginning to rise from his seat – the only seat in the station.

He indicated to her to sit down and walked over to the controls. As he took the headphones from her, his hand glanced against her hand and then her hair, making her feel super-sensitive and clumsy. Then he turned the volume control up on the desk so they could hear the music in the room.

"The bloody Shadows," he said. "What a surprise." He spoke to the ceiling rather than Laurie. "Just once I'd like to take over the reins from someone not playing music

51

from before I was born." Without turning back to Laurie, he reached into the bag that was slung across his chest, and took out a CD. He put it on, faded down the Shadows and turned up the CD. He perched on the desk for a moment listening to the music. The longer they sat, the more Laurie wanted to kiss him. The more she wanted to kiss him, the less able she felt to look at him. Laurie looked down at her hands and started to move her bracelet up and down her arm. Realising what she was doing, she stopped abruptly and clamped her hands shut in her lap.

Gerry slid switches up and down and made green lights flicker on the little windows in the control panel.

"Maybe I should go," murmured Laurie, half standing.

"No, no. I'm just a bit weirded out, that's all." He turned towards her.

His face was still, a closed shell.

She wanted to say to him that she'd already taken a big step coming here, but then he smiled at her and reached a hand out.

"I'm glad you came, I really am."

She smiled back. He dropped his hand by his side and they sat in silence for a minute. Laurie spoke first.

"I just got a job." She laughed. "I wasn't even trying."

"A job?"

"Yeah! Here in the hospital as a cleaner! Weird, eh? The thing is," her face became more serious. "I actually need a job."

"Oh. Did you lose your job?"

"No, not exactly." She sighed. "But if I don't turn up tomorrow, I think I'll be fired."

"Would you be bothered?"

52

"Well, I've no intention of going tomorrow!" She laughed breezily. "Anyway, I have this other job now, don't I?"

Gerry didn't look convinced by Laurie's carefree, plan-free, free-fall.

Laurie gave a little cough. "I'm starving. I forgot to eat today, I just wandered around all day. Oh!" She clapped her hands together. "That reminds me," she fished around in her handbag, "I got you this."

She held out a little tissue paper wrapped package. She chucked it over to him.

He caught it, frowning. "What is it?"

"Open it." She pointed at the parcel.

He held the gift in his hand for a moment, feeling the weight of it.

Laurie could tell he was embarrassed. He didn't even know her. Not yet, anyway.

"Go on. Don't be shy!"

He pulled the tissue paper away, revealing the lighter. He laughed.

"Taking Care of Business! I like it!"

"I thought it was funny and handy. A winning combination in a gift." She laughed and reached out for the Zippo. "A winning combination in life!"

She tossed the lighter from hand to hand.

"We could use it if there was a power cut, or if we went camping, or to light candles. Or cigarettes. Or something . . ." She trailed off, embarrassed.

"It's great, I love it. Thanks."

He stood up, took a step over to her and hugged her awkwardly. But then, after a few seconds, the awkwardness passed and they stood holding on to each other. He stroked the back of her head and she tucked her head into his chest. They made no attempt to kiss and when the song finished, Gerry stepped away to the mixing desk.

"Do you know what? I'm going to put on a compilation so I don't need to keep going back to change the music." He raked around in his bag for a minute, then pulled out something called, "Acoustic Café" and stuck it into the machine.

"There. That's better. Now, for my next trick . . ." he said and left the room.

Laurie glanced around at the station. It didn't fit in with her idea of what a radio station should look like. There were no pictures on the walls of the windowless room, no ornamentation of any kind. There was one bookcase filled with vinyl, stacked neatly in all but one of the shelves. The remaining shelf was filled with cassettes and A4 folders. There were no CDs at all. She got the impression from the shape of things and from Gerry's colleague, that Gerry was probably cutting edge to the other DJs, what with all his new-fangled audio equipment and shiny silver musical discs.

She thought he must be a good DJ though. He had such a nice voice. It was a shame he didn't speak to the patients when he was DJing, she was sure they'd find it very reassuring – those that were able to listen with any thought. She supposed the calm, assured voice came from his doctor dad. Not that all doctors had this kind of voice. But, in Laurie's experience, the best kind of doctors did. It was like calming animals: you had to sound firm and sure. It wasn't only men doctors that had this quality, but she would always prefer to have bad news from a man. Somehow, during her mother's illness, the men had seemed to be better at expressing certain facts as they came to light. When her mother was attended to by women doctors, Laurie had difficulty seeing them as anything other than glorified biological housekeepers. The men better conveyed a sense of understood human tragedy.

The door opened and Gerry walked in holding a wing-back armchair.

"Ta da!" he said setting the chair down next to her and ushering her into it.

"Fancy! Where did you get this?"

"Geriatrics. That's why it's vinyl."

"Ha! I like it. Wipe clean."

"So, what are your plans?" asked Gerry, sitting down in the chair Laurie had just vacated.

"Tonight or generally?"

"Either? Both?"

"Hmm. I don't know really. Well, I know that I'm not going back to my crappy phone job and I am planning to turn up for the cleaning one."

"I suppose that's a start. Is cleaning something you want to do?"

"Not particularly, but working at night when there's hardly anyone around appeals to me. Besides, I'm not qualified for anything really."

"What have you been doing since you left school?"

"Well, Dad," she started to laugh, but the look on Gerry's face silenced her. "Sorry, I was only kidding." Gerry reddened.

"I mean it's not like you're that old. Not old enough to actually be my Dad."

"I know," he looked up at her, "but it's a bit weird, isn't it?"

"Not really. I thought you were just a really hard-living twenty year old." She laughed properly now.

Gerry smiled.

"How old are you then? If it's not too impolite to ask an elderly person that."

"I'm thirty four. How about you? Seventeen? Eighteen? As long as you're legal!"

Now Laurie was embarrassed. Gerry turned back to the controls and twiddled with the mixer. There was a silence for a moment. Laurie swithered about saying she was older, but she had the urge to start being a bit more honest. At times.

"I'm twenty four, twenty five in January. That's not too bad, is it?"

"No. That seems a reasonable age," he smiled.

She noticed he had really nice, straight white teeth. He'd look so much better if he shaved his beard off and cut his hair a bit. Still, he had a certain bearish attraction. He looked capable and warm. He was definitely warm. She looked at the collar of his T shirt. There was a small tuft of brown hair there, but it was impossible to tell with any certainty if he was one of these hair-shirt sorts of men. He probably wasn't, as the back of his hands weren't too hairy and in her limited experience, that was usually a dead giveaway.

Gerry didn't turn away from Laurie's searching eyes, rather, he straightened his back in his chair and sat still.

Laurie stood up. "Well. I think I'd better be hitting the road."

"Really? So soon?"

"Yeah. There's only so long that I won't be missed. Eventually people will realise I'm missing."

"Who's "people"?"

"Oh, you know, flatmates."

So much for being more honest. But she didn't want to talk about Ed yet. She was enjoying being Ed-free and different to her real life.

She stood up and put a hand on his head, moving her hand gently over his hair.

"Can I come and see you tomorrow night after my cleaning shift?"

"Yes. I'd like that." He stood up. He put his arms around her and kissed the top of her head. Where were things going, she wondered. But she didn't really care. For so long she'd known exactly what was happening next and what was expected of her. She'd done okay at school, she'd done fairly okay at university. She had found a job and a flat and a boyfriend. But none of it was satisfactory. None of it was of any real interest to her.

The problem was she had no dream of what she wanted. She didn't aspire to do charity work in Africa or climb Everest or hitch-hike across Europe. All she could think of was a list of niggly complaints. Petty moans about what was, on the face of it, an acceptable sort of life. At least now she had a little secret to keep her going. She was going to have to tell Ed about the cleaning job, but she was keeping Gerry to herself.

Saturday the 18th of December

Early Hours
Chilly

When she got home, Ed was in bed and all the lights were off. She took off her shoes and trousers and jumper, dropped them by the bed as quietly as possible and climbed in, trying not to shake the mattress and risk waking Ed. She lay on her back and listened to Ed's steady breathing, cursing him for his ability to not give a shit that his life was devoid of meaning. It would be so much easier if she didn't care about things. If she could be like everybody else going to their rubbish jobs and getting along with their pointless relationships it would be okay.

She stared up at the ceiling where a strip of light shone through the curtain. What now? What was she going to tell Ed? She'd have to tell him in the morning. She wished he wasn't asleep so she could get it over with. All this secrecy was driving her mad. She was no Mata Hari. Maybe if she rolled over, she'd wake Ed. But she couldn't move. The more she tried to roll over, the less able she was actually to do it. She started to feel as if the side of her body was electrified. Every time Ed breathed out she felt as if the hairs on that side of her body were reaching out to him like when you touched one of those electric experiment things in Junior Science.

Once she'd started paying attention to Ed's breathing, she lost the ability to breathe without thinking. Every breath was an effort. She couldn't get the rhythm right, either exhaling too soon or taking a too long in-breath. She tried to calm herself by looking up at the shadows on the roof, but they started to throb in time to Ed's breathing and the ceiling started to move slowly down towards her, pressing her down. She lay like this, pinned to the bed, silently gasping for breath for what seemed like hours until she managed to inch her hand towards Ed and tap him on the hip.

He turned towards her immediately and gave her a long look. She couldn't make out the detail of his expression in the darkness, but she knew what he was doing with his eyes. It was the thought of that sad puppy dog expression that snapped Laurie out of her fug. She made to turn over. But before she could, he clasped her hand in his.

"Where have you been?"

Immediately she felt scorched. She had no right to this concern. She was nothing but a bitch. A selfish, immature idiot.

She opened her mouth to speak, but Ed spoke again.

"It's okay. You don't have to tell me."

Laurie was perplexed. She was torn between making a full confession and crushing his hand. Was he trying that I'm-giving-you-space emotional blackmail shit? Jesus Christ! She gave him nothing but space. Always had. She was the one with the shitty, steady job. She was the one who made sure there was milk and bread. She was the one who paid the bills and thought about the future and stayed with him despite the fact he never had anything to talk about. What had she ever seen in him? Well, that was all changing now. She'd see how things went with Gerry and she'd give Ed an ultimatum. Before she could say anything, Ed spoke again.

"I was on the phone to Mum today and she's been speaking to my auntie Sheila."

"Yeah?" Laurie had met Sheila a couple of Christmases ago. She was a teacher at the College and was quite funny for someone of her age. At the time Laurie had compared Ed's mum and her sister, marvelling at how different they were. But then, Sheila had never married and that had to mean something.

"And she said to mum that there's a place left on the Community Education course that she teaches on and that . . ."

He broke off and looked up at the ceiling.

"Go on," said Laurie.

"Well, I thought I might do it. The course." He was still looking up at the ceiling.

"Wow. Well, that's great. Are you interested in education?"

"Em, yeah. I am."

Still waters, thought Laurie.

"When do you start?"

"Actually, I went down to the college this afternoon and filled out the forms. I start next week. It's lessons in the college for a day then out on placement in the community."

Laurie knew she should be delighted or relieved or

something, but actually she felt annoyed that he'd done all this without asking her what she thought. And he'd lose his dole money if he did a course.

"Mum said she'll pay my rent while I do the course and I'll get a part time job to pay for, you know, other stuff." He turned and looked at her.

"Well. You've really thought this through, haven't you?"

He nodded, keeping his eyes on her.

"What about . . ." She trailed off, unable to think of anything to question him on. It was a good idea and they'd be no worse off in the short term.

He's getting his life together, she thought, patting him on the shoulder and turning away from him to feign sleep. She kept completely still and let the tears run on to the pillow unchecked. In the morning there'd be a black stain the size of a plum.

Saturday the 18th of December

Evening
Clouds Clearing

Laurie found that the cleaning job was exactly what she had been looking for. The work was easy and monotonous. She didn't have to speak to anyone unless she initiated conversation. She was told where to go and what to mop or scrub. She was equipped with the appropriate soaps and sprays, scrubbers and brushes, all laid out on a trolley that she steered down the quiet corridors at her own speed. The trolley, Pat had informed her, was kept in tip top condition. Maintenance sprayed the wheels with WD40 weekly to prevent squeaks that would disturb patients. Pat was very hot on not disturbing patients.

"We should be invisible. If there's one thing I can't abide, it's a chatty cleaner. We aren't here to talk to people, we're there to keep things clean. This isn't a hotel, this is a hospital. Things must be kept clean. It's bad enough the doctors and nurses not washing their hands properly, we have to make sure that our job is done thoroughly."

She looked at Laurie, obviously expecting a response.

"Of course, Pat, of course."

"Right, good. You just make sure you clean properly where you're assigned and we'll get on great." She handed Laurie some white overalls. "You wear these at all times. If it gets a stain on it – you change it, straight away. There are more of them in there." She pointed to the stock room. "You look like a medium to me. You can change in there."

Laurie put the overall on over her vest and leggings and folded the rest of her clothes up and put them on a chair. She snapped up the buttons on the front. It was a bit big and resembled a lab coat but with short sleeves. Instantly, Laurie felt capable and part of something bigger than herself. She'd often wished she'd had some sort of uniform in her last job. It was tiring having to think of what to wear all the time.

She came out of the cupboard and Pat smiled at her.

"Tomorrow you'll need to wear a pale bra underneath, and I'd suggest you always wear thick, black tights. That way no one can see your knickers." Pat laughed, instantly making her appear ten years younger. "You can be as quiet as a mouse, but there's always some dirty bugger notices your knickers through the skirt and makes a big joke of it. Better to show nothing, eh?"

Pat laughed again at the expression on Laurie's face.

"It's the geriatric ward. When they're awake, some of the men can be a bit of a handful." Her face became sombre. "It's a shame. It's often the men who were lovely and polite who become the worst with the dementia. Gropey, grabby, pass-remarkable." She shook her head. "You'll work out which ones to stay out of reach of.

Anyway, you won't see much of that for the first few weeks. I'll have you on floors and surfaces until you get used to things and then we'll see about ward cleaning. Right. Are you ready to get going?"

"Yes, I am," said Laurie.

Pat stood up and put her hand on Laurie's shoulder. "Welcome to the team Laurie. I think you'll enjoy it here."

"Thanks. I think I will," said Laurie, surprising herself by meaning it.

The first job she was given was to clean the corridors between Wards 22 and 23. Ward 22 was where they housed elderly people who were on the way out, but who didn't require a high level of care. Ward 23 seemed to be populated by elderly people who needed more machinery. She had to pass though this ward to collect the cleaning log in which to write the time she cleaned and jot down her initials. Pat made sure everyone did this for every section of cleaning. Laurie was impressed by her efficiency. Apparently the nurse she asked for the log was less impressed.

"It's there hanging on its designated hook. Just fill it out in future. We don't have time to answer questions about cleaning or forms about cleaning, okay?"

The nurse had been sitting reading a magazine, drinking from a mug that read, "Queen of the Fucking Universe." When Laurie knocked on the open door, the nurse tutted and thumped her mug down. She was about eighteen. She probably wasn't even a nurse. She was probably an auxiliary.

"Sorry to have disturbed you," muttered Laurie, signing the sheet and hooking the clipboard back up again. She had to stop herself from touching her forelock as she backed out of the nurses' station.

As she walked back along the ward to her corridor, she kept her eyes down, not wanting to see and remember the people hooked up and bleeping in their beds.

She made quick work of the lino, enjoying swooping the mop one way and then the other then wringing out the grey water in her special bucket. Her arms tingled from the work and she could feel her heart beating in her chest. She'd sleep well tonight, she thought.

After a couple of hours and just as she was giving her mop a rigorous squeeze, Pat appeared at the doorway.

"That's time for your break. We're all having a cuppa in the staff room."

Laurie pushed her trolley after Pat. She parked up with two other trolleys outside the cleaners' staffroom while Pat held the door open for her.

"Now, Laurie, you know Margaret already," said Pat indicating where Margaret sat, eating a sandwich. Margaret looked up and tried to smile, but a piece of egg mayonnaise started to fall out of her mouth and she scooped it up with one hand whilst doing a little wave with the sandwich. Pat pointed to a plump young woman and smiled. "And this is Marie." Marie was about Laurie's age and she beamed up at Laurie.

"Take a seat Laurie. You must be knackered," said Marie, half rising from her chair. "I know I was when I first started."

"Aye," said Pat, "knackered from talking!"

The three women all roared with laughter. It was strangely reminiscent of coffee time at BT. Why did women do this when they got together? Break time was more tiring for Laurie than working. She found it hard to work herself into hysteria over lame jokes and comments about the other women and their boyfriends and their superiors. It was always taking the piss and making a joke of things. She felt as if women in break rooms took their cue from dramas about women during the war, making the best of a bad situation.

She'd have to find a way to avoid breaks in here.

"Would you like a biscuit Laurie?" asked Marie pointing to a packet of digestives on the table between the seats. Laurie hadn't thought to bring a snack with her and was ravenous.

"Yes please."

"Take a few," said Marie, "please – it's all the less for me." She patted her stomach. She was slightly overweight and had the look of a dinner lady about her; Laurie could imagine her with a ladle.

Laurie finished the biscuit and looked around. It was just a room with six lockers and a little kitchenette with a sink, kettle and microwave.

"This is very civilised," she said. A tray sat on the table with the milk jug, the teapot and a sugar bowl with sugar cubes in it. Marie and Pat were drinking from cups and saucers.

Marie beamed.

"Everyone has their own cup, you can use one of the day shift cups until you bring your own in, if you like." Humming to herself, she rinsed the yellow cup under the tap and gave it a wipe with a tea towel. "Would you like tea or coffee?"

"Tea please," said Laurie smiling up at Marie who stood slightly stooped over her as if she was working in a care home and Laurie was some old dear sitting in a wing chair.

Marie poured slowly and carefully. Pat and Margaret watched her. Laurie did too, feeling soothed by Marie's graceful movements. She lifted the milk jug and looked at Laurie. Laurie nodded and in went a stream of white.

"Sugar?"

"No thanks." Laurie almost wished she did take sugar so she could hear the plink of the cubes into the cup.

Marie handed over the cup to Laurie, a look of anxiety and pride mingled on her shiny face.

Laurie took a sip.

"Perfect."

Marie beamed again. Laurie could tell that this tea tray and the cups and saucers had been Marie's idea. Laurie wondered what Marie's life was like outside work. Did she keep a perfect house full of china and doilies? She seemed too young to care about those sorts of things. But it must be nice to live in a proper, organised house where there was a way of doing things and a routine for times like dinner and breakfast. She'd like to live in a house with a milk jug and a tea tray and a biscuit tin.

Marie was still watching her as she drank down the rest of her tea.

"So Laurie, tell us about yourself." Marie leaned her chin on her hands.

"Oh, there's not much to tell really."

Undeterred, Marie pressed on. "Well, what were you

doing before you came here? You must have been doing something."

"Em . . . I was at University and then I worked at BT sorting out people's bills, that sort of thing."

"Really?" said Marie. "That must have been interesting, eh?" She looked round at the two older women who nodded at Laurie.

"It wasn't really interesting at all," said Laurie. "I hated it actually."

"You hated university?" Marie looked disbelieving. "I always thought it would be dead interesting."

"University was okay. But quite . . ." she couldn't find the word to describe it. It hadn't lived up to her expectations. She thought it was going to be exciting and full of amazing switched-on people who'd travelled and had fascinating stories to tell. But most people just wanted to get wasted and compare drug stories. "Quite . . . anticlimactic really."

"Oh," said Marie. "And now you're here." She waved a hand shyly about her.

Laurie made an effort to smile. She didn't want them to think she thought she was better than them. "Yes. And so far I really like it."

"Good," said Pat. "Nothing like a bit of hard work to take you out of yourself. Is there?"

"And have you got a boyfriend, Laurie?" asked Marie, a slight pinkness in her cheeks.

"I do, yes."

The women nodded, wanting her to go on.

"He's called Ed. We've been together for a couple of years."

The women nodded again.

"He's about to go back to college and do Community Education."

"So is he not working at the moment then?" asked Margaret.

"No, but he said he'll probably look for a part time job now." Laurie certainly hoped so.

"He should see if they need anyone in the kitchen here. They're always looking for kitchen porters. My wee brother used to work there, before he . . ." her voice trailed off and Pat took over.

"Good idea, Marie."

"Oh, I don't know if I'd want him to work here too."

"Why not? You'd never see him. Unless of course you're trying to keep a secret fella from him!" Pat was just joking of course, but Laurie felt herself blushing immediately. Pat laughed. "Oh Laurie, have I hit a nerve? What's the story? Got a fancy man?"

Laurie looked down at her hands.

"Oh God, Laurie, I'm only joking! Don't cry."

And Laurie realised that she was indeed crying. Big fat tears pouring out of her eyes.

Marie came over and crouched next to her and patted her arm. "Let it out Laurie, let it out," she crooned, patting and patting. Laurie had to make a great effort not to get off her chair and lie down on the floor, she was suddenly so tired.

This went on for a few minutes until Laurie got hold of herself and stopped crying. Pat leaned across with a box of tissues.

"What's wrong Laurie?" she asked. She held the box steady while Laurie pulled a handful of tissues out.

Laurie dabbed at her face thinking about whether to tell them. She might as well, it wasn't as if they knew her.

"I don't know what I'm doing." She took a bite of the biscuit she was holding and spoke with her mouth full, pushing the biscuit to one side of her mouth with her tongue. "I've met this guy and I'm still living with Ed."

Marie looked shocked. "What about Ed?" She looked like she might cry now.

Laurie swallowed dryly and glugged back the rest of her tea. "I don't know. Nothing's really happened with Gerry. I don't know if I even really like him like that, y' know?"

Marie looked at her mutely. The older women nodded their heads.

"Oh, I know," said Pat. "I used to go with a lad, Peter, before I got married. My mum liked him and so did my dad. Everybody else liked him more than me. I remember saying to my mum, "you go out with him then," but you can't stay with someone just because he's nice, can you? Anyway, I met my Frank after that and," she opened her hands out in front of her and shrugged, "that was that." She didn't look too pleased with the outcome. Maybe she should have stayed with Peter.

Margaret smiled sympathetically at Laurie. "Just you do what's right for you, Hen. But think carefully before you make any hasty decisions."

It was at times like this that she thought of her mother. Not that her mother would have had anything useful to add and she probably wouldn't even entertain a conversation of this nature, but still, it would be nice to think you could feasibly phone your mother and that she could, feasibly, change.

"Anyway, Ladies," Pat stood up. "Back to the grind."

Laurie stood up too and, after being patted on the arm by Margaret and hastily hugged by Marie, she collected her cart and went back to mopping floors.

Sunday the 19th of December

Three in the morning
Changeable

She stood outside the station door. The red light was on
and she hesitated before she turned the handle. Gerry had
said he was glad she was coming to see him, but she still
felt nervous about this. She knew it was pushing things
along: soon she'd have gone too far to write things off
as a bit of fun and non-cheating. She wouldn't have been
happy if Ed had kissed someone else. But surely as you got
older it took more than a kiss to qualify as an affair? When
the range of actions grew, surely the bar was raised
accordingly? But she knew that this line of thought was
a smokescreen, a rationalisation to make herself feel
better. What she was doing was wrong, but she couldn't
help it, it would take someone coming along to actually
physically move her to prevent her from going in to Gerry.

She smiled. She never would have thought a few days
ago that this would be happening.

Gerry was so different, so much older, than anyone she'd
been with before. His being older had to be a good thing –
he knew more, he'd been around the block. That was what
she needed – a grown up to show her the way in. Gerry had
things on his mind, that much was obvious to Laurie. He

was funny and quite charming, but he looked a bit removed to Laurie. Possibly that was one of the things that appealed to her. With Ed, she could push and push him and he'd take it. Gerry, she knew, would have much less tolerance for that sort of thing. She wondered what would make Gerry lose his cool. She tried to picture him losing his temper, but couldn't force an image into her mind. She thought he was more likely to walk out and keep walking. But that wasn't something to think about now.

Now was the time to think about jumping in, being brave, seeing what happened and to hell with the consequences. She turned the handle and opened the station door. Gerry was sitting side on with his headphones on, staring into space. He turned slowly towards her and his face opened up into a broad smile. He pulled the headphones off and stood up.

"Hi Laurie. Sorry, I was miles away." He pointed at the headphones.

They took a step towards each other, shy again, but only momentarily. Then they grabbed at each other, Gerry crushing her against him and kissed messily, toothily for a few minutes. Then Laurie was blushing, but felt like running around and yelling. Gerry pushed his hand through his hair, picked up the headphones and held them against his ear for a second and then dropped them again. They hung from the lead, almost reaching the floor.

"The music's stopped." He stared down at the headphones and laughed. "And guess what?"

"What?" Laughed Laurie.

"I don't care! Let's go to the pub." He grabbed his coat and bag.

"What about your shift? What about your listeners?" She was quite shocked by his giddiness. She thought all this meant a lot to him.

"Yeah. You're right." Gerry looked chastened. He glanced up at the clock. "I've only got about twenty minutes left. I could put on an album until the next shift." He raised his eyebrows at her, looking for permission.

"Yeah, yeah. Good idea." She stepped over to the pile of CDs he'd left by the machine. "Radiohead?"

He shook his head. She rifled thought the pile. She didn't recognise a lot of the bands.

"Bruce Springsteen?" He shook his head again.

"The Who? The Stranglers? Muse?" Three shakes of the head.

"No, no. Nothing's right. It has to be something . . ." He trailed off and started fishing through his bag. "I know, a classical compilation." He put it in the CD player. "Music from the Movies – perfect."

He put his coat on and picked up his bag.

"Right, you ready?"

"Yes. But I'm choosing the pub this time. Not that skanky old guys' place."

"What's wrong with it?" He looked hurt.

"It's full of old men and that Mags woman gives me the creeps."

"Okay. It'll be closed anyway. Do you know somewhere with a late license? Nowhere trendy. I don't want cocktails. I want a cheap pint."

"Not a problem."

Sunday the 19th of December

Early in the Morning
Becoming Drizzly

Laurie lay motionless as Ed rooted around in the bedroom. God, what time had she come in? It felt like she'd only been asleep for minutes. She couldn't face speaking to Ed. Something had been decided, she felt. She listened to him walking through to the kitchen and picking up the phone. There was only one person he could possibly be calling at this time.

"Hello, it's me, Edward."

He was her only child and yet every time he called her, he still felt the need to identify himself. Laurie shook her head.

"I thought I might come and visit you." His voice caught on *might*. "Today. Now actually." She could hear him throw his rucksack on to his shoulder. "I'm leaving the flat now."

Laurie held her breath until Ed spoke again.

"No, it's just me."

It was obvious that Sandy was asking Ed questions.

"It's okay mum, I know. Listen . . ." he paused. "Is it okay if I stay for a couple of nights?"

He said this more quietly and Laurie wrapped the quilt around her head so that he wouldn't hear her crying and come back.

Early Doors
Bright but Nippy

By mid morning, things looked better. It was one of those sharp sunny days that happen in December. Super cold, but sparkly, making her feel metallic and invincible. After Ed had left and she'd showered, she started to feel better. And now, with her hair still damp, she took a good lung full of air and began to walk into town. The streets were deserted and Laurie felt as if she had the world to herself. Without the camouflage of other people around Laurie looked at everything afresh, as if she'd been away somewhere. It was a revelation to see how shops had opened and closed, bus stops had appeared, graffiti had been graffitied over.

She paused to look at the wall by the bus station. It used to have an image of a busty manga-type girl holding a gun. Now someone had drawn on what was either a mask and cape or a badly drawn burqa. The gun had been painted over with a massive book and the words, "change is coming" was written in capitals on the book's cover. Laurie chose to take it as a good sign and went and sat down on a bench in the stance. The time on the information screen read 8.37.

The only other people around were an old couple sitting on a bench directly underneath an electric bar fire that hung from the roof. They were reading separate copies of the Sunday Post. Laurie moved to the bench across from them.

The couple were both wearing massive fleecy jackets, each decorated with a print of a husky or a wolf or something. Laurie couldn't tell exactly what it was. Some sort of big dog anyway. Hers was shades of beige and his was shades of grey. They had big home knit hats on as well and, although they looked fairly silly, they also looked really warm and Laurie regretted her choice of jacket but no jumper over her shirt. She pushed her hands into her pockets and shuffled down into the neck of her coat.

"Says here that an elderly Scottish woman's holiday turned into a nightmare when she fell down the stairs of a museum in Spain and injured her leg." The man said to the woman.

"Oh dear, that's not so nice, is it?" said the woman, glancing up from her paper.

"Apparently, she was on a coach tour with some other women from her village when she took the tumble requiring 56 stitches and a night in hospital." He held the paper down across his knees. "Here, you don't think that's Irene's tour do you?"

"Ooh well, let's see. She's been away five days." She put her newspaper down on her knee and spread the fingers of her left hand out in front of her. She began to count off the fingers. "Salamanca, Madrid, Barcelona, Seville, oh and not forgetting the night in London before they flew into Spain. Where did it happen Jim?"

The man scanned the article again. "Mmm, let's see . . . Andorra."

"Andorra?"

"Yes, Andorra."

"Is Andorra even in Spain?"

"I'm not sure. Well, it must be, it's in the Sunday Post."

The woman frowned, unconvinced.

"Anyway, I don't think it's Irene's trip. What's the woman called?"

He consulted the paper again.

"Janet McCraig."

"Janet McCraig." The woman repeated and then sat thinking for a minute. "No. I don't know her and I don't remember Irene mentioning any Janet McCraig."

They both looked back at their papers and fell silent again. Laurie couldn't see herself sitting with Ed on a bench in a bus station in fifty years. She couldn't see herself with anyone, anywhere in fifty years.

She thought of Ed's auntie Sheila. Perhaps Laurie's life would turn out like Sheila's. Sheila travelled and sang in a covers band at the weekends. After a couple of glasses of wine at Ed's 21st, Sheila had confided that she couldn't understand her sister's lack of drive. She said that Sandy had been different before she met Ed's dad but that after she married she stayed in her house as much as possible and all but lost contact with her own family. It was Sheila that had kept phoning and visiting and she said that sometimes she felt as if Ed's mum wouldn't be too bothered if she didn't call again.

Maybe Ed would talk to his auntie Sheila while he was staying at his mum's. Maybe she'd encourage him to spread his wings a bit. Laurie knew she should be feeling happier, but she didn't know how she felt. The sight of him playing on the computer when she came home from work never failed to set her teeth on edge and clutch her bag as tightly as she'd like to wring his neck, but the thought of coming home to darkness and silence was not appealing to her. Too much like coming home from school to an empty house and hours to fill before everyone else was back from work or clubs or friend's houses. She couldn't really be bothered to speak to Ed when she was at home, but being on her own was worse. She feared finding herself talking out loud in partial sentences and re-arguing ancient arguments with herself in mirrors.

What did other adults do? According to TV there were loads of girls her age going to work, coming home, cooking, getting dressed in nice gear and going out again to meet lots of similarly happy girls and guys. She just couldn't see herself doing that – organising a social life, caring about it. Besides, how do you organise a social life if you work the night shift? That was assuming she stayed in the cleaning job. It was ridiculous really, she had a degree – why was she even considering staying in a cleaning job? She could do all sorts of other jobs that paid far better and had sociable hours. But these jobs came with responsibilities; meetings; paperwork; suits; lots of other people. Not yet, not for a while. There was no hurry, was there?

She watched the number 22 pull in. She had no need to catch a bus to get to where Gerry lived and she'd almost be there by now if she'd just walked. But she wanted someone else to move her along today.

She stood up and smiled at the old couple. The man immediately snapped his eyes back down to his paper. The woman blinked slowly back at Laurie.

Sunday the 19th of December

Still Early
Sudden Cold Fronts

"He's no in."

Laurie ignored the rough looking woman who had appeared from downstairs as she raised her hand to knock on Gerry's door.

"Ah said, he's no in!"

"I heard you, but I'd rather see for myself." She knocked again.

Gerry opened the door, clearly trying to look as if he'd just woken up.

Laurie stood on his step with her back to the other woman who was leaning against the banister at the top of the flight of stairs. Laurie could feel her scowling.

"Alright?" said Gerry to the women, as he pretended to wipe sleep from his eyes.

Laurie looked over her shoulder. The woman from downstairs swept her eyes from Gerry's face to his groin and back again, the scowl never changing shape, flicked her head up at him by way of greeting and thumped back down the stairs, her house coat trailing behind her.

Laurie raised an eyebrow. Gerry took her by the shoulder and pulled her into the flat and shut the door behind her. They stood facing each other for a second, neither quite sure what to do next, before leaning into each other and kissing. This time it was smoother, more co-ordinated. Laurie was more familiar with the shape of his face, the workings of his tongue. Before Gerry she'd never kissed someone with a beard. Gerry was her first man, really.

She pressed up against him, feeling herself getting carried away. Gerry gripped her tightly and then lifted her up to him like a child and carried her to the bedroom. He lowered her on to the bed and stood looking down on her as she wiggled backwards further up the bed.

"Hi." He smiled at her.

As he stood over her she felt herself start to shiver. "Are you okay with this?" asked Gerry, frowning at her.

"I'm okay. Honestly." Her teeth chattered

Gerry shook his head.

"Not unless you're totally into it, Laurie." He sat down on the bed. "It's too weird otherwise."

"It's just," She sat up properly. "I'm not not into it, I'm just nervous." She felt herself start to get angry. At this point with Ed she'd crank up the insults, see what she could do to rile him, but the sight of Gerry shut her up. Her anger evaporated.

"Come on, let's go and get some food," said Gerry, pulling her to her feet. He gave her a hug then put his arm around her shoulder and steered her towards the doorway.

"Hang on a minute." She stepped over to the chest of

drawers. On top of it was a picture of Gerry, much younger, in an army uniform. She turned to face him, confused by the photo. This didn't fit her image of him.

"Long time ago," said Gerry, pulling on her arm. "Come on, I'm starving."

Ten-ish
Clouding Over

"Tony's Diner" was how Laurie imagined Russia pre-Gorbachev. It had it all: wood panelling, sepia effect Americana posters and the radio playing hits from the sixties. A few cheap looking Christmas decorations were scattered about and a limp Christmas tree stood in a corner with a fall of needles all around it on the floor. Nine or ten ornaments were grouped together around the upper branches and a lop-sided angel drooped over the sorry mess.

The cafe had about twenty tables, most of which were taken by a cavalcade of poor-looking locals. The table next to them held three old women with hardly a full set of teeth between them. They were taking turns feeding an ugly square-headed baby chips from their plates. It gummed the yellow pieces whilst making a groo noise. There was something repellent about the baby and as it rolled its greedy eyes in Laurie's direction she considered telling Gerry she'd rather go elsewhere. But Gerry was smiling at the depressed waitress as she ambled over to their table and before Laurie knew it, he'd ordered them both cooked breakfasts.

Gerry and Laurie sat in silence and looked around. The walls were covered in blackboards displaying menu items.

Laurie scanned fruitlessly for spelling mistakes or unnecessary apostrophes but there weren't any. Mind you, how hard was it to get egg and chips wrong? But she'd seen it done, more times than she'd cared to. The menu held all the usual suspects: pie and chips, bridie and chips, macaroni cheese and chips, sausage and chips. So many chips.

"Do beans count as vegetables?" Laurie asked Gerry.

"No, I don't think so. But there is a healthy choice on the menu if that's what you're worried about."

Laurie laughed. "Oh yeah, what?"

Gerry pointed to the wall above the stage-like serving area. On it was another blackboard advertising a steakwich salad roll.

"Only £2.95. Bargain!" Laurie laughed. "What is a steakwich? And what do you think Tony's interpretation of a salad consists of?"

Gerry considered for a moment.

"Iceberg, one piece of. Two slices of tomato. One slice of cucumber. If it's a really healthy salad."

Laurie looked around herself again. She felt like a fraud.

"What are we doing?"

Gerry reached across and squeezed her hand. "Nothing much – just having a bit of breakfast, hanging about a bit."

Laurie blew air through her nose.

"Look at that guy there." She nodded at a man in his forties or fifties – it was hard to tell – who was dressed in a camouflage jacket and trousers. He appeared to be wearing some sort of green netting around his neck as a scarf. He was reading the paper and sipping occasionally from a mug.

"Why?" asked Gerry.

"I dunno, he's just piqued my interest. He's all dressed for a war or something. Why do people wear things like that? Why wear a uniform if you aren't in the army?"

"Comfort? Preparedness?" Gerry shrugged. "Less to think about in the morning?"

Laurie thought back to the picture in Gerry's bedroom. She waited for a second and cleared her throat. Jesus, why was she so nervous all of a sudden?

"Were you in the army for long?"

He straightened. "A bit, yeah." He frowned down at the formica table top. He didn't want to talk about it.

"Why did you leave? Why did you join?" She laughed but Gerry wasn't amused. He picked at the cuticles on his left thumb with his index finger and shrugged.

"Steady job. I didn't know what else to do." Maybe he'd seen himself as some sort of humble hero – a saver of women and children, who'd remember him forever, Laurie thought. Maybe this guy had the same fantasies.

The hacked-off waitress approached their table carrying two steaming plates. She was wearing a badge that read, "I've been kissing Santa Claus".

"Here ye are," she said, putting the plates down firmly on the formica. Suddenly she smiled moonily at Gerry. "Would you like any sauce?"

"No thanks," said Laurie, but the waitress only had eyes for Gerry. She smiled at him again.

"Tomato please."

"Coming right up," said the waitress and bounded off to the kitchen.

"You've an admirer!" Laurie was inexplicably irritated.

"I seem to bring it out in older ladies."

"So you do!" said Laurie, thinking of Gerry's neighbour and the barmaid in the pub. "Maybe they want to mother you. I can understand that," she smiled at Gerry, then glanced away, embarrassed.

"Come on," Gerry picked up his fork and waved it over her fry up. "Tuck in, before it gets cold."

The food was piled up on the plate shining greasily under the strip lights. She poked the yolk of the egg with her fork and took a deep breath. No, not the egg first. She speared the piece of Lorne sausage which resembled a cross section of brain, ready to be examined. She put it down again, scraping it off her fork with the side of the plate. There were some cold-looking beans, half a dozen pensioner-grey mushrooms, a shrivelled piece of half burnt bacon and two pieces of fried bread which looked to be more oil than bread.

"What's wrong? Not hungry?" asked Gerry, a laden fork half way up to his mouth. His lips had a shimmery layer of grease on them and Laurie imagined herself kissing him and looked away quickly.

She shrugged. She could feel her jaw tightening up and her tongue lying dully against the bottom of her mouth. She couldn't think of a single thing to say, or rather, she could think of several polite, acceptable things to say but knew she wouldn't be able to force the words out. She cast around the room for a distraction. Everywhere she looked she could see food. The old lady sitting behind them was cutting up egg and chips for her Down's Syndrome son. She looked up at Laurie and gave her a big, gappy smile and still Laurie couldn't force herself to get it together. God, if that woman could do it, why couldn't she?

What did she have to complain about? She was perfectly healthy, had a job, somewhere to live, a boyfriend, and another man interested. And what was she doing? Hanging about in a shitty cafe feeling sorry for herself. Pathetic. Her eyes filled up with tears and she felt like punching herself in the face. Plus, here she was with someone who'd really been somewhere . . . and seen something . . .

Gerry started to reach across the table to her but she moved her hand quickly away and looked over his shoulder to the window. It was grey outside and looked like it might rain. Typical. Why didn't they get snow anymore? It was only a week until Christmas, but it felt more like November. Nothing was how it was supposed to be.

It hadn't been for ages.

Tuesday the 21st of December

Lunchtime
Foggy at Times

"What about Christmas?"

Laurie was standing at the window spying on the downstairs neighbours unloading shopping bags from their car. She peeled up a flap of the woodchip by the window frame.

"Dunno." Ed sounded hopeless.

Laurie glanced over at him. He was hunched over on the bed, his rucksack torn open beside him with his neatly ironed clothes teetering over. She wanted to go over and stuff them back in so they didn't come into contact with the manky bedclothes. She could just picture Ed's mum standing sorting and ironing in front of the telly, wishing Ed had a decent girlfriend who'd do the laundry instead. No, actually, she'd be loving that Ed had gone back home and probably begged him to stay for good. Back in his old room, under his old grunge posters, under his old red and black striped duvet, under his mummy's roof.

Looking at Ed now, Laurie couldn't work out why he'd come back. He looked as if he'd been crying. If he had been half as evasive as she'd been, she would have gone straight off, not go home for a few days and then walk back in, tail between the legs. She realised she was staring at him and turned to the street again. Why couldn't she just say something?

Ed cleared his throat. "What do you want to do about Christmas? Are you going home?"

She looked back at him again and considered for a moment. Home? Where was that these days? What did she want to do?

"I don't know. I've been asked to work on Christmas Eve and Christmas night."

"Oh well then," said Ed into his lap.

"But I haven't decided yet. I mean, the money's good. But, I dunno, it would be weird working then."

When they had asked her, she had assumed Ed would be at his mum's and had thought it might be a sensible thing to try and treat Christmas as if it was any other day. She knew at this time of the year she should feel more upset than she did, but really, she didn't much care. It would maybe be different if her dad phoned her, or if she went over there to visit more often. But she didn't see the point these days.

"Maybe before I go to work we could have something to eat, or something . . ."

She trailed off and turned back to the woodchip, gouging at the plaster underneath. A lump of it came away and some stuck underneath her thumb nail. She picked it out, still staring out of the window.

Now was the time to be honest, tell him about Gerry, or at least break off with him.

But she just couldn't do it. For the first time in her life she felt guilty. Properly, head down, eye-fillingly guilty. Ed had never done anything to her. It wasn't his fault. She should just keep things going until after Christmas. He would be into his course by then and things wouldn't seem too hopeless to him. He'd meet people at college and realise that there were other, more appropriate girls available to him. Girls who would like him and not mither him to be someone different.

She looked over at him and he raised his head to give her a brave little smile.

"So. What have you been up to while I've been away?"

He stared into her eyes. She forced a smile.

"Working, mostly. I got a job at the hospital on the night shift cleaning." She looked down, waiting for Ed's reaction. He didn't say anything.

"It's quite a change doing night shift. Messes up your sleep patterns."

He sighed then stood up and began to put his stuff into his drawers.

"What about you? What did you do at your mum's?" She moved closer and hovered behind him.

"Well, I've started my placement."

"Really? So soon? What about police checks and things?"

"Luckily mum had already arranged for the college to send off for a police check."

"That was good of her," said Laurie, trying not to sound sarcastic. "So where's your placement?"

"It's at a youth club place in the City Centre. I'm going to be doing after school sessions. Four to ten. You just chat to them, play on the PSP and that sort of thing. I'm back again today."

Bloody typical. There she was, slogging her guts out in the middle of the night cleaning up body fluids and bloody Ed was going to get a job where he'd get paid to play fucking computer games. Stupid, pointless games where the aim was to kill people. For fuck's sake.

She watched Ed bobbing down to tuck his folded T shirts into his bottom drawer and thought about kicking him, but then remembered Gerry again.

She sat down on the edge of the bed.

"Do you like it then?"

"Oh yeah." He beamed at her. "It's like, for the first time, I feel like I'm doing something pretty important." He coloured and she looked away. Get him. "Anyway, I'd better get a shift on. I start in a couple of hours and I need to go in to college for a meeting." He narrowed his eyes at her. "Is that alright?"

"Obviously." She tried not to sound to eager to get shot of him. She was going to see Gerry before her shift.

"Laurie?" Ed turned to where she was sitting on the bed and raised a hand in her direction as if he might touch her. She stiffened.

He didn't say anything else. Laurie waited for a moment, raising her eyebrows to urge him on.

"What?"

He sniffed and shrugged.

"Nothing."

"Are you sure?" It would be easier if he said something. She smiled encouragingly.

He shook his head.

She looked at her watch. "I'd better get ready too." She hesitated. "I'm meeting a friend before my shift." She could feel her face burning. It was on the tip of her tongue. She just wanted to shout it at him. But it was as if her face had locked up all of a sudden.

"Well," he said, standing up and taking a deep breath. "You'd better prepare yourself then."

He walked out of the room.

Laurie lay back on the bed.

Around One
Clear and Cloudless

This time Laurie had chosen the cafe. She sat with her back to the wall waiting for Gerry to arrive, glancing around at the place. It was trying hard to be European. She watched the customers with their cappuccinos and lattes and wondered when Scotland had bought into the whole cafe culture thing. When she was growing up there were just pubs and normal cafes. If people were ordering a hot non-alcoholic drink it was either tea or coffee. No speciality fruit teas or extra shots or any such nonsense. Now it seemed that everyone had a coffee fetish. She sipped her drink. It was very strong and she'd deliberately asked for it black. She felt she needed to keep her wits about her. The situation with Gerry was developing a momentum of its own.

He appeared at the window and she raised a hand to wave at him, but he didn't see her. She moved her coat from the other seat at the table and swept a couple of crumbs off the table top, all the while keeping her eyes on him. He was standing outside looking up at the sky and he seemed to be taking a few deep breaths. After a minute, he stepped up to the door and opened it. She thought to call out to him but wanted to see the expression on his face when he saw her. Maybe that would tell her what to do.

He stood for a second and scanned the busy cafe then his eyes stopped on Laurie. He looked at her then smiled. She stood up and pushed her chair out from the table as Gerry walked over and took off his coat, dumping it on a chair.

They stood facing each other smiling. Laurie felt her heart speed up as she imagined touching him. Gerry broke his gaze and cleared his throat.

"Latte? Cappuccino? Espresso?" Laurie asked him.

"Tea, I think." He grabbed his coat off the seat and sat down, bundling the coat into a wad on his knee.

Gerry smiled up at the waitress who was walking past. "Excuse me, could I have a tea please?"

The waitress ignored him and carried on walking.

Gerry sighed.

"She'll be back in a minute."

"But that's not the point though is it? People have jobs to do and they should just do them." He frowned at Laurie.

"Look. It's just a cup of tea. We'll get her when she comes back."

Gerry sniffed. "Sorry. I just hate it when people don't do what they're supposed to do."

"I suppose it's that military training," Laurie said. "You're used to people doing what you want them to do, eh?" She laughed. "And if they don't, you can always shoot them!" She considered for a moment. "That would be handy. Having that in reserve." Gerry shook his head. "Not quite," he said.

The waitress appeared again. She was holding a cup of tea which she placed in front of Laurie.

As the girl walked away, Laurie reached across and laid her hand on his forearm.

"She's probably foreign, you know. Maybe she isn't confident speaking English."

"Maybe," said Gerry. He slid the mug towards him.

Laurie took a long drink of her coffee.

"What are you doing for Christmas?" she asked and then looked down immediately into her cup. Her face was bright red.

"Oh, I don't really do anything for Christmas. I'll probably cover someone else's shifts on Christmas night."

"That's nice of you," said Laurie. That was that then. No romantic Christmas day for them. She hadn't even realised that she'd been thinking that might happen.

"What I'd really like to do is stay in bed and sleep all day." He sighed. "But I'd probably get no peace from Theresa downstairs."

Laurie could just imagine her with a Mrs Santa Negligee on, standing guard at his door with a bunch of mistletoe, singing dirty versions of Christmas songs to him through the letter box. She shuddered. What was worse was that she could see Gerry opening the door and letting her in.

"What are you doing?"

Gerry looked closely at Laurie's face. She shrugged.

"Aren't you seeing your family?"

"Not likely."

"Really? Don't you get on with them?"

"No." She paused and licked the side of her coffee cup. "Not now."

Laurie looked at the other people in the cafe. The place was emptying out a little. The waitress walked past their table again and Gerry caught her eye, smiling. She nodded brusquely and walked on.

"How about something to eat?" Gerry asked. "Are you hungry? What about a sandwich or a cake?"

"God! You're like a mother hen!"

She took the menu out of his hands and looked at is for a second, then she covered her eyes with her hands, leaned her elbows on the table and started to cry. She wasn't making any noise, but her shoulders were shaking.

"I'm sorry. I didn't mean to upset you," said Gerry. "I'm such an idiot sometimes."

She sniffed again. "No really, it wasn't you. It's my . . . my general situation at the moment. I don't know what's going on." She picked up her spoon. "It's just . . . I can feel myself just pissing around and I don't know what to do next." She sighed and tapped her spoon gently on the bridge of her nose. "Does it get better Gerry?"

"Does what get better?" he frowned.

"You know, life?"

"Life? Fucked if I know! God, look at me. No offence, but what am I doing here? I should still be in the army, or at least have a proper job!" His voice was a little too loud and Laurie could feel the waitress hovering near. He took a deep breath. "Look Laurie. I'm the last person you should be looking to for some kind of guidance."

Laurie tapped the spoon off her cheek.

"Yeah. I know." She sighed. "I should sort myself out."

"What about your parents? Or a big sister or something?"

She looked at Gerry with something approaching amusement.

"Eh, No. I don't think so." She made a little humph sound and put her spoon down firmly. "They're even more in the dark than I am." She laughed. "They haven't even noticed there's no light on!" She laughed again. "And they don't even know there's a light switch!"

She leaned back and laughed loudly. Gerry watched her thin shoulders going up and down.

Laurie's laughter petered out.

"Okay," she said. "That's a bit better. I'm all over the place."

"It's okay, don't worry about it." He reached out and touched her arm. She grasped his forearm and squeezed it, glancing around the near empty cafe. "Where's everyone gone?"

Gerry shrugged. "Do you want to come back to mine? The flat's not far from here."

"Mm . . . Okay. Why not, eh? Live dangerously." She stood up and pulled her coat on.

"Okay," said Gerry. He fished around in his pocket and took out a fiver. He tucked the fiver under his cup and pulled on his coat, looking around for the waitress. She'd made herself scarce.

"Come on then," said Laurie. She was standing in the doorway, holding the door open with her hip. "It's that way, isn't it?"

"No," Gerry said, smiling. "It's the other way."

"It was fifty/fifty. You can't always make the right guess, can you?"

"No, I don't suppose you can." He put his hand on her shoulder and steered her the right way.

Slightly Later
Sharp

It was bitterly cold and eye-wateringly bright as they made their way along the road to Gerry's flat. Laurie huddled in to Gerry against the wind and peeked over her collar to see the street. Gerry must be well used to much worse conditions in the army. She tried to look a bit less cowed by the cold which was making her ears throb and her nose numb. She must look a right state.

"It's not far now," said Gerry pointing ahead as if they were trudging through snow at the North Pole.

"Roger," said Laurie, but she was so effectively tucked into her coat she had no confidence that Gerry could actually hear her.

They passed a bus which had broken down a few doors from Gerry's doorway. Laurie looked up at all the passengers waiting patiently while two drivers stood in front of the opened bonnet and smoked. The bus was almost full and the people on board were mostly staring into space facing the direction the bus was pointed. It didn't look as if anyone was talking and she was about to comment on this to Gerry when she saw Ed sitting with his earphones on, drumming his fingers on the edge of the window sill, staring dead ahead. She looked at his profile for a moment and considered telling Gerry to look up but then imagined, ridiculously, that Gerry would look up at the same time as Ed looked down and that Ed would know immediately and would run down the stairs and attack Gerry.

She tried to set the scene up in her mind but she just couldn't picture Gerry hitting Ed back. He'd probably allow Ed to pummel him for a bit before he ran out of steam and would then take him for a pint. They'd chat and discover she was really the one to blame in all this and they'd start to hang out together and she'd be on her own and it would serve her right.

Anyway, who was she kidding, there was no way Ed would come downstairs.

Ed must have felt her staring up at him because he turned his head to face her. Laurie pulled her head down as far as it would go into her coat but she couldn't tear her eyes away from his face. He looked morosely at her for a moment before she realised that it wasn't Ed at all. It was just some other young guy.

"Are you coming?" Gerry was calling.

"Oh yeah, yeah," she ran over to the door he was holding open for her.

"Come on, it's perishing. I'll get the heating on." He ushered her ahead of him up the stairs. When they reached the first landing he nudged her quickly past his mental neighbour's door and propelled her up the stairs to his flat. His hand on her back felt nice and she deliberately moved more slowly so he'd have to apply a bit more pressure.

When they reached his flat Gerry had the key ready and the door was open almost immediately.

"Impressive door opening technique. They teach you that in the army?"

"Hardly. We'd use brute force there." He pushed the door shut. "I had to learn the quick door manoeuvre here." He nodded towards the door.

Laurie frowned. "What do you mean?"

"Downstairs." He mouthed the word, "Theresa."

"Oh," said Laurie. "I see." She walked into the flat. "What's the story there? She's old enough to be your gran!"

Gerry smiled and raised an eyebrow.

"It's hardly the same," Laurie said, annoyed. "This," she flicked her index finger between the two of them a few times, "isn't creepy."

Gerry frowned. "It's not?"

"Of course it's bloody not. Stop thinking like that." She shrugged herself out of her coat and held it out to Gerry. "Surely she's seen you with other girls, women, up here. Surely she doesn't think she's in with a chance?"

"I haven't really brought anyone else here." He smiled at Laurie, but he looked a bit uncertain. "Not since I came back."

"Really?" asked Laurie. It was weird. How long had he been back? And back from where exactly? "You mean I'm really your girlfriend?"

"Oh . . . I dunno . . . I just thought we were, y'know . . ." Gerry seemed mortified.

"I'm only kidding about," Laurie said. "I mean, let's not think too much about things like that, let's just see what happens, eh?" She looked up earnestly at Gerry who nodded and turned to hang her coat in the hall cupboard.

"Right. Where's that cup of tea you were talking about?"

"Follow me." Gerry led the way into the living-room/kitchen. He gestured at the sofa and Laurie sat down. As Gerry turned his back to her to fill the kettle, Laurie stood up again and moved over to the dresser where the TV and some of Gerry's CDs were stored. She flicked through the CDs and wiped a finger across the dresser surface. Spotless. She looked up in time to see Gerry grin at her.

"Everything meet with your expectations, ma'am?" He stood to attention as if for inspection.

Laurie was embarrassed to be seen to check such a stupid thing. It wasn't as if she kept a particularly clean or indeed welcoming home.

"It's all ship shape. Oh, hang on, that's the wrong phrase isn't it?"

"Yes, but don't worry. I'm glad I met with your approval." He was smiling, but there was a look of relief on his face too.

"It's actually very clean and . . . well, orderly here."

"But?" Gerry turned away from her to get mugs and spoons out. Laurie could tell he was just playing for time. She knew she should leave it but couldn't help herself. She tried to sound merely curious.

"Well, you've no junk. No stuff. Where are your photos or books or whatever?"

Gerry kept his back to her and dropped a tea bag into one of the cups.

"I suppose I don't have much stuff. Rolling stones and all that."

"What?"

"I've travelled a lot. I haven't gathered much moss." He glanced at her.

This should have been a further cue to just shut it, but Laurie couldn't stop.

"But don't you have any pictures of your family or anyone?"

"No." He paused then seemed to force himself on. "I'm not massively in touch with my family." He opened the fridge and took out the milk. "I see them sometimes but not with any regularity."

Laurie frowned.

"Gerry, do your family know you're here?"

Gerry poured boiling water into the mugs. "No. They don't."

"Oh." She scanned his face but could read nothing in it. "Can I ask why?"

He shrugged. "Oh, various things." He poured milk into the mugs. "We had some difficulties when I first joined up and it's never improved much." He turned round, holding a mug out.

She reached forward and clasped her hands around Gerry's. They stared at each other.

"Anyway," Laurie said.

"Anyway," Gerry repeated, smiling.

Laurie sat down and took a noisy slurp of her tea. "You going to sit down?" She nodded at the sofa next to her.

"I suppose so," said Gerry looking down at her.

"Hey! You'd better not be looking down my top!" said Laurie in an attempt to sound saucy.

Gerry smiled but walked over to the window.

Well, I've managed to ruin that moment, thought Laurie, gulping down her tea even though it was much too hot. Her eyes watered and she wiped at them as she watched Gerry who was looking out into the street.

He was actually much nicer looking than he appeared at first. She admired the breadth of his shoulders and the height of him. He was very manly, but not a man's man. He was quite tender and quiet but there was that distance in him. He was polite and kind, but he wasn't really telling Laurie much. But then, Laurie was very deliberately not telling him much and there was clearly a lot to tell. At what point would they start to tell each other things? Would they have to go through all the horror of the nakedness and the awkwardness before there was more biographical detail?

Gerry turned to Laurie. If this was a film there'd be a rise in the intensity of the soundtrack or the background would blur bringing Gerry's face into sharp focus. There'd be an extreme close up of Gerry looking intense and then one of Laurie looking unsure but interested, possibly biting her lip. Then it all started to go wonky and spaghetti-westernish. She could hear quite distinctly that lonesome whistling that preceded the gun fight. She made an effort to focus. Gerry was still looking at her. The time was now.

He advanced towards her, putting his mug down on the coffee table then taking hers from her hands and doing the same with it. He reached forward guided her to her feet. He stood for a second with his hand on her shoulder, looking into her eyes.

"Something is happening here, isn't it?"

His face was so serious that Laurie felt like laughing, but she knew that would probably be the end of things if she did. Why was he so serious about this? She was the one breaking the rules.

The walls were magnolia painted woodchip. The carpet was a rough cord type, that someone had covered in front of the sofa with a sludgy coloured Indian rug. The furniture was mismatched charity shop stuff; a tiled coffee table, a teak coloured empty bookcase, a formica table by the window with two pine farmhouse style chairs neatly tucked underneath. She wondered if Gerry owned any of it, but knew he wouldn't. She pictured her flat and made a mental pile of all the furniture she owned. She had a red rocking chair that someone had given her when they'd moved away and a coffee table that she'd painted black and white to resemble cow hide. It was a horrible looking table, but because Ed had laughed when she'd seen it, she kept it.

If there was a fire in her flat she knew there was very little she'd have the slightest interest in keeping. She could picture herself calmly walking away from the burning building thinking how glad she was of the opportunity to get rid of everything without having to go through it.

She sighed.

"Are you okay Laurie?" Gerry turned her face towards him.

She smiled half-heartedly. "Do you ever think . . ." She sighed again. She didn't really know how to explain herself. She knew she was a bit of a spoilt brat really. Things could be so much worse.

"What?" asked Gerry.

She shrugged. "I dunno. I can't explain it."

"Try."

"Well," she took a deep breath. "I look around here and at first you think, "God, he's got nothing. Not a thing. That's kind of sad", you know?"

"No. Not really." He was frowning, somewhere between trying to understand and trying not to take offence.

"Oh, I don't mean anything by that." She thought for a second. "I mean that . . ." She paused. "Right. I mean that you've no stuff. You seem a bit like you're like a hobo, sort of."

He laughed but he was annoyed.

"Oh don't take offence. I'm not explaining myself well." She tried again. "At first I thought that was a bit weird or sad or something." She smiled encouragingly at him. "Now I look around and I think, "how sensible. He doesn't have all the crap around him – the meaningless, just collected, nonsense, crap – that I have floating around in my place." She smiled, but she wasn't convincing him. "Don't you see how sensible that is? Of course you do, that's why you're doing it, eh?"

He wasn't frowning now, just looking steadily at her.

"I'm thinking that's what I need to do. Get rid of everything. Travel light."

Gerry's eyes looked wet all of a sudden but Laurie decided to ignore this and make a joke of things. "Travelling light is where it's at – it's the new black. Travelling light is the new 40."

Gerry gripped Laurie's shoulders more firmly. "We're all God's travelling children? We're all the littlest hobo?"

Clearly, he wasn't getting her drift.

"I'm probably not explaining myself very well. Am I?"

Gerry seemed to have managed to avert the tears that had appeared.

"No, you are. I just hadn't really thought about it properly. I hadn't done it on purpose."

"Really?" Laurie was surprised. "I thought it was your army training."

"Well, maybe a bit." He nodded. "But other soldiers that did the same things I've done have stuff and families and so on."

"M-hm," said Laurie. "But maybe they are the ones who've got it wrong."

Gerry gave a queer little laugh. "Do you think?" Laurie forced herself to carry on.

"If you're free of stuff, you're free! Millions of Buddhists can't be wrong."

There was a pause then Gerry laughed properly. "God Laurie, you're something else, aren't you?"

She smiled, not quite sure if that was a good thing.

"We should celebrate," said Gerry.

"What?" said Laurie.

"We should celebrate our new philosophy, our plan for life."

He was grinning from ear to ear. Laurie hadn't seen this look before.

"Ok. What will we do?"

"We'll go out tonight – the cinema then dinner."

"Really?" asked Laurie. This didn't seem a very Gerry sort of plan. "We've got work."

"Come on, we can phone in sick." Gerry said pulling her towards him. "We deserve a night off. It'll be fun!" He pulled back a little. "I'll take you somewhere fancy. My treat. An old fashioned date. "That doesn't break the hobo rule, does it?"

"No. I suppose not. As long as we don't accumulate any stuff," she smiled, "but, actually, I don't have anything nice to wear out to somewhere fancy."

He thought for a second. "Then you should go and buy something." He took his wallet out and handed her a twenty pound note. "Here. My treat."

"Your treat? What is this, the fifties?"

"Oh, don't be like that," he said, hugging her. "I'd really like to buy you something. You don't have to owe me."

Laurie pulled away.

"Really. I mean it. You won't owe me anything. It will be payment enough to be seen with such a beautiful woman on my arm." He bowed.

"Okay then." She took the note and put it in her back pocket. She'd have to be careful, she didn't want to be too beholden to him.

"What time?" Gerry looked at his watch. "It's nearly half past two now. Shall we say half seven?"

Laurie nodded. "Where? Not outside my flat. Obviously."

"No, obviously." He thought for a moment. "How about outside the Art Centre cinema."

"What's on?"

"Who knows, there'll be something though. Something arty that'll fit in with our wandering notions."

"Cool." She turned towards the door. "I'd better get going then and buy something to wear." What she'd actually manage to get for twenty quid was beyond her, but she wasn't about to ask Gerry for more.

"Of course."

He took her coat out of the hall cupboard and helped her into it. He smoothed his hands across her shoulders and leaned down to kiss her. Laurie collapsed into him as he pulled her in and kissed her. Her closed eyes saw nothing but a velvet purple. Pleasant moments passed then she disengaged herself and took a deep breath.

"Nice," she said as she turned the snib on the lock and stepped out into the stairway. She paused for a second and nodded in the direction of downstairs.

"Cheerio Gerry," she said in loud voice. "That was amazing. I'll see you later." She winked at him and he shut the door, grinning.

3pm
Calm but Wind Picking Up Later

It was still teeth shatteringly cold when Laurie walked out into the street but she wasn't bothered much by it. The heat in her body was radiating outwards nicely. She set off for a second hand clothes shop she'd sometimes been into when she was a student. The thought of raking through rack after rack of slightly smelly nylon items didn't fill her with joy, but she felt like wearing a dress tonight and knew she wouldn't be able to afford one from the shopping centre.

The streets were quiet; presumably most people were working or sensibly staying in the warm. She knew she should be grateful to Gerry for the money and for the evening out, but she couldn't work up much enthusiasm for the actual act of shopping.

She passed a shop window covered with handwritten ads for all sorts of services and places to rent. She stopped short and reversed. How much could she realistically afford for a place to live? She couldn't go on living with Ed after Christmas – even in the event of him suggesting she stay on as a flatmate. She could see it happening; the two of them living in exactly the same manner as they did at the moment. Although now, she supposed, Ed had started college and was getting a life of his own. Perhaps

Ed might be glad if she left, there might not be a scene at all. For all she knew he was sitting somewhere right now, with some girl that Laurie had never met, eating pizza silently. He would be much happier without her and she was foolish to think he didn't know that. She started to brighten up. Everything would be fine, he'd be relieved, he wouldn't cry or beg or offer to change in small or huge ways. She wouldn't feel like a heartless murderer.

She looked more closely at the signs. She really would need to get something, somewhere, sorted out pronto. It wasn't like she was going to move in with Gerry. Although maybe something could develop there. At the very least she could stay with Gerry for a few nights, maybe even weeks, until she got a new place organised. But still, better to get the ball rolling.

Studio apartment. No pets, DSS, students, smokers, children. Byrecroft Road.

Call 07973786534 after 6. £500 pcm.

Sounded good, but way too expensive. Maybe she'd have to think about a flat share. She groaned. It would be like living as a student again and it wasn't as if she could bully or harass flatmates to clean the kitchen and there'd be nobody bringing her a cup of tea again. Maybe ever again. Maybe she'd die alone choking on dog food while children pissed on her front door.

Lovely sunny room available in gorgeous West End flat. Potential flat mate must be vegan or at least vegetarian. £300 pcm would be great, but could be negotiated with the right person.

Sounded nice, but possibly very tedious. She leaned forward and looked more closely at the decorated card. It had flowers drawn all around the borders and a squiggly vine woven through the flowers. She scrutinised the vine which actually seemed to be lettering. What did it say? It was hard to read because of being done in a faint green colour and also because it seemed to have been designed that way. Suddenly it came together. It read:

the Great Perfection within me honours the Great Perfection within you.

"Eugh!" Laurie exclaimed, stepping back in shock and startling an old lady walking past. The look on Laurie's face must have piqued the woman's interest as she stepped forward and scanned the window for what had shocked Laurie. Seeing nothing she turned to Laurie puzzled.

"What is it, Hen?"

"Oh," Laurie shook her head. "I saw something I wasn't expecting in the window."

"Oh, whit was it?" The woman looked concerned. "Ah've seen some fair dodgy things in shop windies in ma time, ah'll tell ye."

"It wasn't exactly dodgy." Laurie knew she'd sound ridiculous. "It was sort of . . ." she pointed at the window. "Like, religious."

She expected the woman to shake her head at her in disgust, but the woman wrinkled her nose and said, "Ah've seen adverts in there for," she sniffed and looked around herself, "sexual services." She drew out the the ex in sexual for longer than it really needed. Laurie thought of snakes.

112

Laurie and the woman shook their heads at each other.

"What's the world coming to, eh?" said Laurie.

"Ah ken." The woman kept shaking her head. It was starting to look like she had a tic or something.

"Where is it?"

Laurie pointed at the card in the window. The woman moved up to the glass and peered in.

"Mmmh," she tapped her finger on the glass. "Hippies."

Laurie nodded.

The woman turned to her. "Hippies and Prozzies. Bloody Hell." She smiled brightly. "Anyway. Happy Christmas, love."

The woman waved and sped off along the street. She should stop underestimating the elderly, some of them were faster than you'd expect.

Laurie couldn't be bothered looking at any other signs. She set off again.

* * *

The shop was a dark little place down an alley. It smelled of patchouli, inevitably, and also something earthier: damp and fertile, like compost or school classrooms. Laurie wrinkled her nose. She wasn't into fashion foraging and hated the self-satisfied looks that bin-rakers gave each other when they ferreted out a designer vintage piece. Piece! Ridiculous, describing clothes as if they were art. Piece of nonsense more like. It was over priced when it was new, and certainly over-priced now that it was second hand. Wankers.

What Laurie really needed was a little dress, a cocktail dress. Maybe black. Definitely black. Not too short, but she did want to look more sexy and sophisticated than Gerry had so far seen her. The problem was that Laurie had no idea what her look was. She wasn't trendy or classic or anything. When she went shopping she always tried to get things she'd get use out of but she never managed to get anything that worked with anything else.

Carole, her friend from school, was a great shopper. She always looked immaculate and put together. Once, at the end of a drunken night out, Carole had tried to impart some advice to Laurie. She told her to always buy a complete outfit and then you'd know what went with what. But Laurie had laughed at Carole's serious face and her grown up approach to shopping, even going so far as drawing other people's attention to Carole saying, "Have you met my granny? She thinks she's Coco fucking Chanel."

Carole had laughed, but they hadn't seen much of each other afterwards.

Anyway, that had nothing to do with getting something for her date. Date! How American!

She braced herself taking one last clean breath of air, and entered the shop.

It reminded her of the shop in the kids' programme Mr Benn. All sorts of costumes hung over the sides of the garment rails that were stuffed with the usual mixture of unpleasant plastic blouses and flares and dresses that didn't fit Laurie, or probably anyone else, since the Seventies. Shapes had definitely changed since the olden days.

Laurie didn't make eye contact with any of the other customers, the last thing she needed was someone waxing lyrical about some faux Biba crap or asking her if she'd like her chakras read or some other hippy shit. She could see out of the corner of her eye that there were only two other customers and the woman that was working the till. From what she could make out with furtive glances, the shop assistant was not someone she'd be asking for style guidance from.

She was a big girl wearing a short puffball skirt over what appeared to be a leopard print catsuit. To top it off she was wearing golden gladiator sandals. She must have been frigging freezing. Mind you, most likely the catsuit was polyester and she was sweating up nicely.

Laurie flicked through the rack in front of her. Nothing. There wasn't even anything black. She moved over to the next rack where there was an over abundance of leisure suits but no little black dress. She could feel the assistant coming closer and desperately grabbed three items from the end of the rack.

Before she could ask to use the changing rooms, the assistant pointed her chubby thumb towards the back of the shop.

"They're back there. I'm going out front for a fag." She raised an eyebrow at Laurie. "Don't nick anything."

Laurie tried to smile at the assistant but was unable to speak due to the fact that she was suddenly struck with the notion that the assistant was, in fact, her old piano teacher, Mr Hooper. If not Mr Hooper, then definitely a man, or a very, very manly woman.

Laurie rushed to the back of the shop and pulled the

swing doors shut behind her. She stood for a minute, resting her head against the glass of the changing room. Her forehead suckered on to the mirror and instantly she felt calmer. Not Mr Hooper, but surely not a woman either? What did it matter anyway? God! Who cared? If Mr Hooper wanted to dress up in hideous clothing, what was it to her? He couldn't have had a very happy life teaching piano to spoilt little brats like her who never did their practice and always lied about it. He'd irritated her mother no end by always leaving his empty Ski yoghurt pot on the piano lid.

"I mean really," Laurie's mum used to say to Laurie's dad. "There's a bin right beside the piano. I put it there the second time Mr Hooper came. But no, no he can't be bothered to put the pot into the bin I've provided. No, he's too good, too arty to be thinking about such nonsense as manners and hygiene." Laurie loved it when her mother had a rant about Mr Hooper and would join in and try and persuade her to drop the piano lessons altogether. But always to no avail. For some reason her mother had it fixed in her mind that Laurie must at least reach Grade One. Laurie couldn't see it happening. Between Laurie's complete inability to master the basics contained in "Lovely Tunes for the Pianoforte" and Mr Hooper's utter lack of interest in teaching these supposedly lovely tunes, there was really no chance of Laurie getting her certificate. Luckily for Laurie, after a few months, Mr Hooper announced a new job in Huddersfield and that was the end of that.

Perhaps Huddersfield was where Mr Hooper had discovered his inner Hilary or Harriet or whatever. But no, surely it couldn't be Mr Hooper. It was a ridiculous idea.

"Pull yourself together girl," she told herself in the mirror, pointing a finger at her reflection. "You've got bigger fish to fry, haven't you?" She nodded glumly. "Well get on with it then."

She lifted the first dress off the hook where she'd hung it. It was dark blue and the upper part of it was made out of lace. It had some sort of structure built into it as if an invisible, deflating person was still wearing it.

The second dress was made out of a cotton paisley fabric and was meant to look as if it was a shirt. It had big gold buttons down the front and a little pocket on the left breast with a fake hankie poking out of the top. Hideous.

The third one was black and shiny. It was a decent length but had big shoulder pads and an oversized bow stitched on to the back. It had some potential and she couldn't face going out again so she decided to give it a try at least.

After some struggle and the always horrifying sight of herself in the mirror without clothes on, she managed to get the dress on. She'd need to remove the shoulder pads and the bow for sure, but, other than that, it was okay. She had a pair of shoes that would be alright with it. She took it off again and got her clothes back on. There was no ticket on the dress. She was going to have to ask the assistant. She stuck her head out of the swinging doors but the shop was empty. She decided to have a look around for accessories. A bag would be nice, maybe some jewellery. She found the bags in a box by the counter and flicked through them. There was nothing that immediately stood out, but there was quite a nice oversized clutch bag with a big metal clasp on it in the shape of an owl. £4. Hopefully she'd be able to afford it with the money Gerry had given her. Why did he want her to dress up? Did he see himself as a sugar daddy? No, ridiculous, she didn't think Gerry would be so grubby.

Quite naturally, as if it was an action she took frequently and inconsequentially, she folded the dress over twice into a neat, little package and popped it inside the clutch bag. She tore the price tag away from the bag and tucked it under a pile of fliers on the cash desk. She was just covering the bag with her coat as the shop door opened and picked up one of the fliers and pretended to read it.

The assistant made his/her way back to the other side of the till and smiled at Laurie. She was dressed as a woman, but it was too confusing to think about what to call her, given her massive paws and throbber of an Adam's apple.

"Now. What can I do to help you?"

Laurie felt her heart should be beating quickly at least. But nothing. She wondered what emotions she'd feel if she revealed to the assistant what she'd done. Had she really done anything yet? Or would the crime actually take place once she left the shop, items concealed and unpaid for. She smiled at the assistant, thinking it was hard to focus on anything other than her/his extravagant and really quite pretty eye make up. She'd used a range of shades of blues and purples and Laurie knew from experience that it wasn't easy to use these colours without looking like the victim of some sort of even-handed assault.

"No. Not today. I was looking for something quite specific, but you don't have it."

118

The assistant frowned. "Are you sure? I could have a look in the back for you?"

It was a strangely neither-here-nor-there voice. Quite deep – but not suspiciously so.

"No really. I'm okay." She smiled. "Your eye make up is lovely by the way."

The assistant beamed at Laurie. "Thanks. Thanks very much."

Laurie smiled as she left the shop and stepped back out into the street. It was nice to be nice. She glanced once over her shoulder into the shop.

That was definitely a man.

Fiveish
Storm Threatening

The last thing Laurie was expecting when she walked back into her flat was Ed's mum decorating a puny little Christmas tree. But there she was: a clutch of fairy lights in one hand and tree-top star in the other. She'd obviously put one load of sparklers on and was standing back to wrap a second set around. There was no sign of Ed.

They looked at each other awkwardly for a moment, then both said hello at the same time.

Without Ed there, there was a different kind of tension in the air. Not so much the usual strain of politeness and barely feigned interest. More a frank assessment between equals. The two women looked at each other more boldly.

Laurie spoke first. "Sandy."

The older woman smiled in a way that impressed Laurie. Perhaps there was more to Sandy than she'd previously let on.

"What's going on with you then?" The question wasn't unfriendly, but Laurie couldn't be bothered with the deference she usually showed. She opened the front of her coat out and, without undoing the zip, dropped the stolen bag on to the sofa.

If Sandy had any comment to make, she kept it to herself. She looked between the bag and Laurie and made no move to carry on with the tree. Laurie indicated the tree with a nod of her head.

"Don't let me stop you." She smiled to show she wasn't being sarcastic but Sandy placed the decorations on a chair.

"I can't really be bothered."

Laurie sat down.

"Cup of tea?" asked Sandy.

Laurie moved to get up.

"Oh no, no. I meant I'd make it. I'm parched."

Laurie sank back gratefully against the cushions and shut her eyes.

"Thanks Sandy." She sighed. "Me too." She pointed at the bag without opening her eyes. "Shopping."

"Looks nice," said Sandy. "Is it for an occasion?"

Laurie could feel her standing over her, but was too tired all of a sudden to much care.

"Don't tell me my son's taking you somewhere!"

Laurie opened her eyes as a curious mix of excitement and dread ran through her. Did Sandy know something? Had Ed guessed and said something to her and this whole thing was a ruse to elicit a confession and move things along? Sandy was looking wary.

"No," said Laurie. "It's a work thing." Easy, she told herself, don't reveal anything else. This all had to be done at her pace – not anyone else's. She forced herself to stand up. "Sit down, Sandy. You're the guest. Anyway," she pointed at the tree. "Looks like you've been hard at it."

"Well. I got over here earlier than I expected and I thought, now that you're working night shift," she looked down at her hands in her lap and then up again at Laurie.

121

"You might not manage to decorate yourself." She smiled shyly and Laurie felt like a cow.

Again.

She walked into the kitchen and called through to Sandy as she put the kettle on.

"So what has been happening with you?"

"Well, actually, something quite exciting."

"Really?" She couldn't believe it. "Have you started seeing someone?" As soon as she said it, she regretted it. There was a stony silence from the other room. "Sandy?"

"No Laurie. It isn't that. No."

Laurie opened and closed cupboards needlessly.

"But I have passed my driving test."

"Wow! That's great Sandy!" Laurie popped her head round the kitchen door. "I didn't even know you were having lessons."

"No one did. I was too worried in case I failed." She looked like she'd burst with pride. "But, do you know what? I passed first time." She hopped about a bit. "I couldn't believe the man when he told me. I nearly kissed him." She went bright red and sat down.

"That's wonderful though Sandy. Really it is."

Laurie went back into the kitchen.

"So what made you decide to do it then?" She laid the tea tray. "I mean, I'm not being funny, but you've managed fine all these years, why do it now?"

"Well, Laurie." There was a pause. "Sometimes you reach a point in life where you stop and think, "What's going on? What am I doing with my life?""

Laurie stood dead still and waited. There was another pause.

"And I decided that the time had come to make some changes."

Laurie forced herself to speak. "Oh right. What sort of changes then?"

"Well, Laurie. For one, I didn't want anyone telling me when I could go somewhere or where I was to sit." She took a deep breath. Laurie realised that this was the most Sandy had said to her in one go before. "I wanted to be my own conductor, my own time tabler. Do you see?"

Laurie placed both hands on the counter top and didn't reply. She'd started to cry again. This time it wasn't much – just a few tears. But she knew she wouldn't be able to talk for a minute.

She looked out of the window at the drying green below and waited until the tears had dried up. God, get a grip! What was going on here?

Sandy appeared at the door.

"Are you okay Laurie?"

Without turning round but watching Sandy in the reflection in the darkening window, Laurie shook her head.

Sandy took a step forward. She raised her right hand and Laurie watched it hover a few inches from her back for a moment before Sandy dropped it again. Laurie was thankful. The last thing she needed was Sandy being kind to her – the whole sorry mess would come tumbling out and she'd confess to her would-be mother-in-law before she told her soon-to-be-ex boyfriend. That would be taking it too far, even for Laurie.

Laurie pulled herself together and calmed her face back into some sort of normal look.

"Sorry." She grimaced. "Hormones."

A flicker of distaste crossed Sandy's face. "Oh. Right."

Laurie clapped her hands. "Right! Now wasn't I making some tea?" She busied herself rearranging the items she'd already placed on the tray. "Now, I'm afraid we've no biscuits, Sandy."

"Oh that's fine, fine." She moved towards the tray and put her hands on the edge of the tray. "I'll just take this next door."

"No, no." Said Laurie gripping the edge of the tray. "I'll do that."

The two women stared at each other.

They stood like that for a long second until they were interrupted by the sound of the front door opening and Ed entering the flat. Sandy dropped her hands away but kept her eyes on Laurie.

Ed stood in the doorway and looked between the two of them.

"What's going on?" His eyes flicked between Laurie and his mother.

"Nothing," said Laurie.

"We were just talking about what to get you for your Christmas," said Sandy.

She didn't look the slightest perturbed. She didn't look shifty or nervous. There was no way to tell that she was lying. Laurie was shocked. Shocked and impressed.

"Oh wow. Is it a Scalectrix?"

Laurie was still watching Sandy's face and caught a glimpse of annoyance. There was no telling if Ed was joking. Most likely he wasn't. Laurie started to feel sorry for Sandy. Ed was such a dolt.

"I need to go and get ready," said Laurie, making her escape.

"Ready for what?" Ed's voice sounded so whiny. "I thought we could order in."

"As exciting as that sounds," Laurie called back over her shoulder. "I'm going out."

"Out where?" Ed had followed her into the living room.

"A work thing." She reached down and picked up the clutch bag.

Ed caught up with her and put his hand on her shoulder.

"What work thing?" He squeezed her shoulder. It was almost sore. She shrugged him off.

"A night out. A Christmas night out." She couldn't look at him.

"You didn't say anything."

"Yeah, well." She forced herself to look up. "I don't have to tell you everything."

He narrowed his eyes at her. "Why not?"

The tone in his voice was new. This was most unusual. Laurie narrowed her eyes at him.

"Let's not do this now, Ed." Her tone was weary. Usually that did the trick. It cowed him.

He glared at her. "Do what, Laurie?"

She breathed heavily through her nose and flicked a hand at him.

"This." She pointed at him then at herself. "This," she hissed at him and indicated the kitchen where his mother was surely standing listening.

He shook his head, but she saw his shoulders go down.

She scooted out of the room with the clutch held tightly to her chest.

Sixish
Clouding Over

She shut the door behind her, leaning on it for a moment to make sure Ed wasn't following her. He wouldn't usually come after her looking for trouble, but something was in the air and anyway, some people needed an audience to get their ire going. Maybe Ed was going that way and the presence of his mum might spur him on.

But he wasn't coming. She could hear him and Sandy talking to each other and the clink of the mugs and the teapot. That ought to buy her ten minutes or so. She didn't want to have a proper shower because it would look suspicious and she didn't really have enough time anyhow. She lifted the leg of her jeans and felt the skin there. Not massively hairy, but it looked like she'd be naked with Gerry and she wouldn't be able to stop thinking about how hairy her legs were if she didn't do something about it.

Her makeup stuff was on the chest of drawers. She had a rake about and found some body lotion she'd been given a couple of Christmases before. She took the lid off and sniffed it. Not completely unpleasant but she had a feeling she might get a reaction from it. Rash or stubble? Rash. Hairiness always suggested a lack of cleanliness to Laurie and unclean was the last thing she wanted to be feeling later.

She found a disposable razor in the back of her undies drawer and laid a towel on the bed. Stripping off to her pants, she lathered the lotion on to both legs from the knee down. Immediately her skin began to tingle. She shrugged; there was nothing for it and it would settle down in a couple of hours. She pulled the razor up her left leg from the ankle to the knee and hurriedly repeated until the leg was done. She had a quick look – no nicks. Good. She wiped the hairy razor across the towel, which she'd realised was actually quite damp and smelled rather unpleasant, and swapped legs. This time she was even quicker and unfortunately managed to cut herself twice: once on the calf which hardly bled at all and once on the side of her ankle across the tendon or whatever it was that ran up the side of her leg. It was a bit of a bleeder and stang like buggery. She pressed the towel against it for a minute and then patted the towel firmly against the invisible cut until it had almost stopped. Her legs felt like they were sun burned. She resisted the temptation to claw at them.

Now she had to find clean undies. She looked in the more obvious places first (her underwear drawer, under the chair, under the bed) but found nothing useful. All she had left was a couple of pairs of ugly too-big knickers that she wasn't even sure were really hers, or just some ex-flatmate's that had gotten mixed up with her laundry a million years ago. Next she looked in her other drawers and the bottom of the wardrobe. No knickers, but a fairly clean pair of black tights and her one sexy bra. She could just go knickerless, but the thought of sitting all night in half a set of underwear with her nether regions smothered in a pair of tights like a fleshy bank robber filled her with horror.

She searched through her dirty laundry and found a pair of not bad pants. Wrapping herself in the damp towel, she sneaked through to the bathroom and washed the pants under the hot tap and squeezed out as much water as she could. She'd be able to just about get these dry with the hair drier and surely, next to her body, any residual dampness would burn off pretty quickly.

She did the best she could with the hair dryer and then set about her face. Luckily she wasn't having an outbreak of spots and it didn't take long to get her foundation and concealer sorted out. The problem with doing your make up for a special occasion was always when it came to the eye make-up, usually the eye liner, something went wrong and required an upper face re-do. Laurie liked to do a bit of black liquid eye liner flicking up at the sides in little cat's eyes, but this was a job that required a quick, steady hand and a lightness of attitude that she wasn't sure she could muster. Plus, as soon as you started to fuck up eye liner, it was hard to fix mistakes and get back on track. What she found helpful was to fake a hilarious conversation whilst looking at the process in the mirror.

She leaned her left elbow on the dresser and pulled the skin tautly to the side with her left index finger. She smiled into the mirror and said laughingly, "I know, it was so funny," and quickly flicked the liner on in one smooth tick. Perfect. Now was the hard part: doing the exact same on the other side. It looked quietly awful if one eye had a higher flick than the other or one was thicker or at a wonky, different angle. She swapped eyes and pulled the skin tight again. "I know, totally hilarious!" she tried to giggle, but nothing was forthcoming and it showed in the make up. It was thick enough and long enough, but slightly higher. It gave her a subtly wonky look. She looked at the clock radio. 6.34. There was no time. She'd have to hope Gerry wouldn't notice. She was fairly confident that he wasn't the type to give a shit anyway. She layered on mascara and scrutinised herself in the mirror. Not too bad and, besides they'd both be fairly tipsy fairly quickly and hopefully the restaurant would be quite dark.

Now. The clothes. She pulled the pilfered dress out of the bag and gave it a shake. Mercifully, presumably because of its high nylon content, it wasn't particularly wrinkled. She quickly tore the shoulder pads out and contemplated pulling off the bow too but knew she'd have to get scissors for the job and that would mean going into the kitchen and she couldn't be arsed, so the bow would have to stay.

She stepped into the dress, this time managing to get it on easily. Perhaps the loss of the shoulder pads made it more malleable. She tried to visualise herself later on that night stepping out of the dress in Gerry's bedroom. She wanted to be all careless and smooth, impressing him with her level of sophistication. She'd read somewhere that world class athletes picture themselves running through the finishing line and then the thunderous applause of the spectators and the victory lap, arms raised in magnificent victory. She tried to run through a victorious sex scene with Gerry but got stuck at imagining him with his clothes off. She couldn't seem to imagine him with a realistic amount of body hair. He was either covered in a sort of downy hair suit, or he had one of those waxed, shiny Hollywood type of bodies with plastic-looking stomach muscles. Clearly, neither was at all accurate but she surprised herself by being quite keen to see what he was really like under his flannel shirts and chunky polo necks.

She glanced at the clock again. 6.47. Oh no! She'd obviously spent too long doing her visualisation. She struggled in to the tights, pulled a comb though her hair and put on her black high heels. Quite nice. She looked a bit like a fair haired Audrey Hepburn. Sort of. She went over to the wardrobe and sifted through the drift at the bottom. Miraculously, she found what she was looking for straight away. It was a pair of black elbow length gloves that Sandy had given her last Christmas. At the time she'd smiled and thanked Sandy and thought that they'd never see the light of day, which was probably why they were still balled together. She carefully painted on some dark plum lipstick and assessed herself critically. Not bad, not bad at all. She turned her head upside down and froofed her hair out. Not bad.

She transferred her purse into the owl bag, took her heavy coat out of the wardrobe and went through to the living room to say cheerio.

"Wow!" said Ed smiling up at where she stood in the door way.

Laurie smiled at him kindly. "Is it a fancy dress thing?" he asked innocently.

Laurie scowled and Ed stood up. "I didn't, like, mean anything by it!" he said, a look of panic on his face. "It's just that you look like a movie star," He struggled for words. "Katherine Hepburn, you know?"

Laurie willed herself not to look at Sandy.

"I think you mean Audrey, Ed." She tried to sound as coolly controlled as she could manage.

"Are they the gloves I gave you?" asked Sandy. Laurie was forced to look at her. Surprisingly, Sandy had a look of pride on her face. Laurie nodded.

"Oh Laurie, you remind me of myself when I was your age." She looked as if she might cry.

Laurie shuddered. "I'm off now." She made herself smile. "Don't wait up!"

They both looked at her as if she was their mother going out and leaving them on their own for the first time. She felt guilt settle around her shoulders. She straightened her back.

"Now. If you need me . . ." She laughed artificially. "What am I saying! You won't need me! You've got each other!"

Sandy and Ed glanced at each other. Now Laurie felt like the mad old auntie going back to the care home.

"Have a nice time," said Ed, pulling his head into his hood and picking up the TV remote control.

"Yes." Said Sandy, looking up at Laurie. "You have a good time." Chastened, Laurie left the flat.

7.30 pm
Clouds Clearing

Gerry was standing outside the Art Centre waiting for her. She slowed so she could watch him. There were a few other people standing chatting and smoking and Gerry looked conspicuously non-trendy next to them. They were younger than Gerry – about Laurie's age – and looked too cool for school. The girls had that sneery look on their faces that these art school girls often had. It was as if being brave enough to wear your gran's cast offs and have your hair cut at a daring angle made you some sort of untouchable. Normally Laurie would be intimidated by having to walk through them and in fact, she hardly ever went to the Art Centre for that reason, but tonight she felt toughened and careless. Gerry looked similarly untroubled leaning against the wall looking in the other direction.

The walk over from the flat had started off shaky with a feeling that she'd gone too far but after she'd rearranged herself she was running late and she had to jog the last half mile. As she galloped along, she felt herself acquire a sort of sheen of strength. It was up to her to do what she wanted with her life. It was hardly her fault that Sandy was such a door mat and had raised Ed to be similarly trampled. There had always been a feeling that Sandy thought she wasn't good enough for Ed and although

Laurie understood that many mothers were like that, she half-agreed with her. Laurie knew that she was the wrong person for Ed and that he was the wrong person for her, but she also knew that life was often made up of inappropriate pairings and that people often had to make do with the results of poor choosing and slim pickings.

As she approached Gerry she doubted that he was the Right One either. If the Right One even existed. The idea that there was a soul mate for everyone was ridiculous anyway. What if her soul mate was Peruvian or Nigerian or something and she never visited those places and they never visited the East coast of Scotland? It was a stupid notion that stupid, unrealistic people liked to hang on to to comfort themselves. Often times, she'd noticed, people bandied about the "he just wasn't the one for me" thing as a means of justifying cheating on people or leaving abruptly, or frankly, just being an idiot. At least she wasn't pretending this thing with Gerry had some higher purpose, some admission of love. What she was doing was just sort of selfish. And when she told Ed, he'd be upset of course, but she was confident that he'd be glad of it soon enough.

Gerry turned to her and smiled. He raised a hand and half saluted her. She felt an upsurge of excitement and almost ran towards him. When she got there they were both grinning but stood a foot apart, stuck for what to say.

Gerry reached out and placed a hand on her shoulder. She felt tingly and also a bit sick. She hadn't felt like this with Ed. Or anyone really.

"Hello up there."

"Hello down there." He smiled down at her.

Ordinarily, this level of corniness would horrify her, but

there was something about this situation which let her relax her normally rigid standards. She could feel the art girls staring at her and Gerry and she lunged at him and gave him a big kiss. At first she could feel him resist a little, but then she felt him wind her into him and kiss her back. He tasted of drink, but not unpleasantly so, it was more that his mouth had a hot, sugary taste. She realised she was incredibly thirsty.

"Come on," she said, pulling out of his arms and grabbing his hand. "Let's go in. I don't know about you, but I could do with a drink." She turned back to glare triumphantly at the girls, but there were all facing in the other direction smoking stylishly.

They entered the bar area and were immediately surrounded by noise and other people's body heat. Laurie shucked off her coat revealing her Hepburn outfit. Gerry looked down the length of her and raised an eyebrow. She pulled off the gloves and stuffed them into the owl bag.

"It's a bit over-the-top isn't it?" she asked him quietly.

"No, no," he said. "I like it." He tapped her on the arm. "I really do. You look great, I'm just not used to it, that's all."

"Oh thanks very much," she said.

"You know what I mean." He steered her towards a table that was being vacated.

"Do you mind if we take your table ladies?" he said smiling to the group of older women that were getting up to leave.

She noticed that his accent was slightly posher and his tone was a bit more formal. What was that all about? The women were charmed by it.

134

"Oh no, not at all," said one of them. She was actually blushing. She was as old as Laurie's mother would have been.

"Excuse me," said one of the women, looking into Gerry's face. "Don't I know you?"

"No, no, I don't think so," said Gerry, his smile faltering slightly. "I get that a lot."

"No, I do." The woman thought for a second. "You're Dr Callander's son, aren't you?"

Gerry didn't answer.

The woman persisted. "I'm Iris Corcoran. I used to play bridge with your mother, oh, years ago."

Gerry nodded very slightly. The woman faltered, finally realising Gerry's reluctance to talk to her.

"Well . . ." she said quietly. "Do remember me to them, will you."

Laurie felt a chill.

"Come on Iris," said one of the other women, pulling on her elbow. "Our taxi will be outside."

Laurie watched the women walk up the stairs. The woman who'd spoken to Gerry glanced back over her shoulder and Laurie tried to smile at her, but she looked only at Gerry who was ignoring everybody and taking a long time to hang up his and Laurie's jackets on the back of their chairs. She sat down next to him.

"Did you know her?"

"Oh. Maybe." He stood up again. "What are you drinking?"

Laurie looked at him, but he was gazing over her head. She sighed. "A cocktail."

He laughed. "It's like that, is it?"

She laughed. "Yes, it bloody well is."

"Okay. What cocktail?"

She shrugged. "You choose. Something sweet."

He walked over to the bar and edged his way in. She watched him as he caught the bar man's attention. He was taller than the other men at the bar and he had much nicer, broader shoulders. Tonight he was wearing a dark grey shirt tucked in to black jeans. His hair was still a bit damp at the nape of his neck and he'd trimmed his beard back a bit. He looked really nice and she was glad to be out with him. Whenever she went out with Ed (not that they ever really went anywhere these days) she felt like she was out with her brother.

Ed had never had the allure of a man and although she'd noticed he wasn't looking quite as fresh faced as he usually did, she didn't think that Ed would ever look like a man in the way that Gerry did. He'd probably just end up looking like an old boy. Partly, she supposed, it was down to build. Ed would always be quite wee and slight and Gerry had a breadth to him that would never be diminished by weight loss. But, more than that, Gerry had a manner about him that suggested he'd seen things that Ed would never see.

Maybe that was fanciful thinking on Laurie's part because she knew he'd been in the army and had presumably seen some action there. Whatever "action" meant. She only had the vaguest of ideas of what had happened in recent conflicts in the world. She'd watched very little on the news. It was one thing thinking of war in terms of the distant past. But current conflicts were too real for her. Also the causes of the conflicts were always too confusing and inevitably bogged down with politics and religion.

If you were a career soldier it probably didn't matter what the roots of war were. You just went where you were sent, defended and dispatched as commanded. She looked steadily at Gerry's back. She could picture him in charge of a troop of soldiers. They'd be younger and would look up to him with respect, expecting him to know what was what. He had something commanding about him, as much as he tried to pretend he wasn't that sort of person. People would follow him into battle.

She would, anyway.

He walked back over to the table carrying a pint and a tall glass with something pink in it. He put them down on the table in front of her and backed away, bowing.

"Hope it meets madam's expectations."

Laurie took a sip. It was spicy and sweet and warmed up her mouth and throat as she swallowed.

"Mmmm, nice. What's it called?"

Gerry sat down. "One Exciting Night, apparently."

"Is that so?"

"I thought it was appropriate."

"I'll say." She was determined to make it so and she could see that Gerry was trying hard too. "So, what's in this exciting night, then?"

"Let's see . . . gin, two types of Vermouth and grenadine. I think." He smiled at her. "Is it good?"

She took a bigger drink. "Yes, very." She took another big drink.

"Steady on!" he said. "We've the whole night ahead of us and those things are strong."

Whether it was down to what Gerry had just said or if it really was as strong as all that, she could feel the effects of the drink in her legs already. Her shoulders dropped comfortably. Everything would be okay. They could enjoy themselves, couldn't they?

She sat back and watched Gerry drink his beer. He knocked half of it back and stared at her.

"Everything okay?"

She nodded. "Yes. I was just thinking," she smiled, "you know, still waters . . ."

"What do you mean?" he frowned at her.

"Well . . ." she searched for the right thing to say. "We're sort of seeing each other . . ."

She glanced up at him.

He was looking intently at her.

She faltered.

"Uh huh," he encouraged her.

"Well. I mean. We don't really know anything much about each other. Do we?"

He smiled but not in a way that made Laurie feel like continuing.

"Well, what do you want to know Laurie? Shoe size? Hopes and dreams? Favourite colour?"

"Och, look, nothing." She wanted to walk out of there. Why was she pursuing this?

He made an effort to sound sincere, "No, really Laurie, what do you want to know?"

She considered for a moment.

"Well. I know you were in the army and I think I know now that you're originally from around here – but I don't really know anything else." He was looking over her head with a blank expression on his face. "You don't know anything about me either, do you?" He still didn't look at her. She knocked back the rest of her drink. "Forget it." She stood up. "Do you want another drink?"

He looked at her again and nodded. "But you sit down," he stood up and pressed gently on her shoulder. "I'll get it."

"Okay." She looked up at him, trying to read his expression, but he had that polite look on again.

"What would you like Madam?" he asked in a James Mason voice. Despite herself, she laughed.

"Definitely the same again."

"Coming right up Madam."

Laurie was at a complete loss about what he was thinking about. It could be anything. He could be anyone. For all she knew, he could be a recently released murderer. He could be planning on chopping her up! She started to laugh.

"What?" Gerry asked.

"Nothing, nothing." She shooed him away, "Come on, get the drinks in, I'm parched!"

"Okay. Okay." He backed away.

She watched him walk over to the bar again. Again she admired his broad back and his height. No. There was no way Gerry was a murderer. He was just secretive. But everyone had their secrets, didn't they? She hadn't been wholly honest about Ed with Gerry and, really, what good would it do to tell him everything? Technically she supposed they were having an affair, and it wouldn't do to know too much about the person your sort-of girlfriend was living with. It might make Gerry jealous and difficult.

She tried to picture Gerry being jealous and difficult, but she couldn't make him work up the enthusiasm. He just looked mildly disgruntled.

Gerry arrived back at the table. He handed her the cocktail and sat down with his pint.

"You know we were going to go and see a film?"

Laurie nodded.

"Do you mind if we just sit and drink instead? Have some food here?"

"No. Not at all." The films in the Art Centre were all foreign. She couldn't be bothered to read subtitles. Not that you could admit that to anyone without sounding like a moron. They were always pretty heavy too and she couldn't be bothered with any dead children or wars or grinding poverty either.

"What's on anyway?"

"Either a French film about child abuse or a Dutch one about Bosnia."

"Bosnia?" she studied his face. He was giving nothing away. He just nodded.

"Gerry? Were you in Bosnia?" She tried to look interested, but not intensely so.

"Was that the sort of thing you wanted to know?"

"Yes. I mean, you don't have to go into it or anything. I would just like to know a wee bit about you. You know, some biographical details." She smiled.

Gerry considered for a moment.

"I was in Bosnia and other places: Kuwait, Afghanistan. It was heavy and then I left the army." "Okay." She took a drink. "Can I ask you any questions?"

He thought about it. "I'd rather you didn't."

"Fair enough." She took another drink. "Were you injured?"

"That's a question Laurie." He took a drink. "No I wasn't injured."

Something about the way he said injured stopped her from pressing him further.

"Okay," she said and reached out and put her hand on his.

"Okay," he said and turned his hand over and squeezed her hand.

* * *

The walk home was fun. They played a game where one person sang the first little bit of a song and the other one had to guess what song it was. Despite the fact that Gerry was quite a nice singer Laurie wasn't able to guess any of the songs.

"What do you mean you don't know it?" laughed Gerry as he tried repeatedly to get the key into the lock of his close door.

"Here," she nudged him out of the way. "Let me do that."

She scrabbled the key about for a minute before getting it in the lock.

"I've never heard of it." She turned back to him and he leaned forward and pressed her up against the door.

He whispered into her ear, "You've never heard of "Slave to Love"?" he leaned against her and Laurie caught her breath.

"No," she pushed her pelvis into him. "I haven't."

He pulled her towards him with one hand while he quickly turned the key in the lock and held the door open with his other. Then he half lifted her, half dragged her into the hallway, shut the door behind them and nudged her up against the tiled wall. They stood like that kissing and breathing into each other for what seemed like ages before Gerry stopped and pointed in the direction of the stairs.

"Listen," he whispered.

Laurie could hear nothing but, dimly at first and then becoming clearer until she felt like the other person was right next to her and Gerry, she became aware of someone else breathing. The breathing was jerky and laboured. The other person sounded as if they'd been running or crying.

It must be the lunatic neighbour. Gerry and Laurie stood listening. Laurie expected the woman to go back in, but there was no sign that that would happen. She looked to Gerry for guidance but he seemed at a loss too. They'd have to walk past her, but Laurie's drunkenness, which had been keeping her warm, or at least keeping her from feeling the cold, had worn off and she needed to get indoors.

"Come on," she whispered to Gerry and pulled his arm towards the stairs. Gerry resisted briefly, then followed. As they turned the corner on the stairs, they found Gerry's neighbour sitting on the top step at her landing. She was wearing a Chinese dressing gown and her hair was big on one side and flattened on the other as if she'd just got out of bed.

"Hi Theresa," said Gerry. Laurie was surprised by the tenderness in his voice. She looked up at him gloomily, but made no effort to move out of their way. She half smiled at Gerry and ignored Laurie altogether.

"Are you okay Theresa?"

Laurie groaned. If you asked this sort of person that sort of question, you could be listening to hard luck stories for hours.

Theresa shook her head.

Laurie squeezed Gerry's hand in an effort to get him moving. He squeezed her hand back but leaned towards Theresa.

"Ahm lonely Gerry." She reached a hand up and stroked his cheek. "Lonely."

The woman was very drunk. She'd probably been drinking on her own all day, waiting for Gerry to come back. Pathetic. Laurie felt no sympathy for people like Theresa. As if Gerry would have any interest in her. But then . . . She glanced at Gerry's sympathetic face. Had he, in a moment of kindness, slept with this woman and that was why she was so obsessed with him? She narrowed her eyes at the woman and she knew, immediately, without any doubt, that he had, in fact, shagged this woman. This hideous, older, drunken woman. She shuddered. Gerry turned to look at her, making a pleading face as if to say, just one minute, just one minute to sort this out. But how could he sort it out? He'd led this woman on and given her hope and now there was no way out of it for him unless he moved away.

"Gerry?"

He turned to her pleadingly.

Theresa looked up at her too with hate in her small, pouchy eyes.

143

"It's late," Laurie went up a step. "Come on."

Gerry pulled back from Theresa's hand and rubbed at his forehead.

"Is yer mammy expecting you?" the old bag laughed at her.

"Shut it you," Laurie said, narrowing her eyes at the woman and nudging Gerry to get moving.

Gerry nodded. "See you around Theresa."

"Aye," said the woman, "that you will." She stepped back into her doorway to let them past but remained there watching them turn the corner of the stairs.

Gerry opened the door to his flat and directed Laurie into the hallway.

"Here we are," he said, not looking at her. "Here. Let me take that." He took her coat, shook it out and hung it neatly on a coat hanger in the hall closet.

She followed him into the living room. What now? The atmosphere had gone, Theresa's slovenly appearance had seen to that quick smart.

She hung about by the door of the living room feeling like the last unwanted guest at a party. The guest with nowhere to go, no one to be with.

Gerry stood at the window, his hands in the pockets of his coat. He was making no move to get things started again and Laurie couldn't think of anything to say to get them back on track.

Gerry turned to her. "Laurie," he took a few seconds, "maybe you'd better leave."

"What?" She wasn't exactly surprised but she still felt a kind of shock moving through her.

"I think it would be better if you left." He spoke calmly.

144

His face was patient and grown up. She knew he was trying to move her along gently which in some way made her feel even more upset.

"Why?" She hated the whine in her voice. She was showing him too much. She should be storming out of here.

"I just think it would be better if we slowed things down a bit." He sighed and held his hands out. "Everything's going too fast. We don't know each other at all."

"Is that it?" She stared at him. "Will we see each other again?"

"Do you actually want to?" He frowned.

"Yes." She hated herself. She wished she could just walk out of here and not give it another moment's thought, but it appeared she did have some feelings for him.

"Are you sure?" He looked unconvinced.

"Yes." She felt her shoulders drop and shook her head. "Yes I am." He moved over to her and squeezed her shoulder. "Let's just see what happens, eh?"

It was a parents' "let's see," meaning, "not a hope".

She took a step backwards so his hand fell from her and walked out of the room into the hall way.

"My coat." She scowled back over her shoulder. "I need my coat." She stood in the dark of the hall waiting for Gerry to come out.

She felt like going into his room and lying down on his bed. Whether to fall asleep or at a last ditch, pathetic attempt at seduction she didn't really know. But then Gerry was there, holding her coat out to her, his face kind and still and maddeningly patient.

She took her coat and he helped her into it and laid his

hands on her collar bones. She felt the touch of his fingers, the weight of his hands. The heat from him radiated out across her shoulders.

They stood like that for a moment and then Laurie left the flat.

She didn't look back at him as she made her way down the stairs but she knew, firmly, definitively, that if he'd called after her, she'd have run back up there as fast as she could.

Sometimes she felt like throttling herself.

8pm
Dark and Unsettled

Marie poured Laurie a cup of tea and offered her a Hob Nob, hovering for a second over her. Laurie said thank you and pretended to be looking over Marie's shoulder at the notice board, scrutinising the adverts about hygiene. The other two women were talking about their teenage children in exasperated tones. They were complaining about the mess they made and their complete inability to put empty milk cartons into the bin but it was obvious to Laurie that they loved their kids' uselessness and dreaded the point where they became superfluous.

Had her mother ever had this kind of conversations with her friends? She couldn't see it. She couldn't really see her mother sitting with a group of friends and just chatting. Her mum had been a great one for committees and organisations. Any group chat would have been minuted and worthy; Palestinian aid efforts, woodland trails, community dental visits.

She remembered her mother sitting at the kitchen table stuffing envelope after envelope for some important cause. She must have been eleven or twelve at the time, but she could have been any age – envelope stuffing was an ongoing activity for her mother. She could remember the growl of hunger and the sound of Newsround on the TV behind her as she stood next to the kitchen table waiting for a break in her mother's concentration. She stood for long minutes but her mother didn't notice her, she was so intent on her task. Eventually, probably because Laurie was blocking her light, she'd looked up at her daughter and blinked. Laurie smiled at her and she reached a hand out and put it on Laurie's elbow, squeezed and gently nudged her.

"Go on, Laurie, amuse yourself, you're a big girl now."

She hadn't said it unkindly, but Laurie had left the room. It was such a nothing experience, a non-event, that Laurie couldn't fathom why she kept thinking of it. She could just see her mother's head bent over her work, licking envelopes and firmly running her nails over the flap to seal them. She could feel the pressure on her elbow and the small push as her mother sent her on her way. She was just trying to remember what her mother was wearing when she became aware that someone was asking her a question.

"Earth to Laurie? Come in Laurie?"

It was Margaret, gazing open-mouthed at Laurie while the other two looked on.

"Sorry," Laurie said, shaking her head. "I was miles away."

Pat smiled at her kindly. "Penny for them?"

"Is it man trouble?" asked Marie.

Laurie sighed. "Yes. I suppose it is." Laurie held her hands out in front of her, palms up. "It's my sort of boyfriend." She tried to smile. "We've sort of split up." She shrugged.

"Sort of boyfriend? Sort of split up? What?" asked Pat.

"I haven't split up with my real boyfriend." She shook her head, but she couldn't even work up to feeling angry. "I just don't know what I'm doing." She felt like leaning her head against the coffee table but the angle wouldn't work and they'd all think she was a complete nut job so she resisted the urge.

"Does your real boyfriend know about this other one?" Pat looked confused.

"He hasn't said he does, but I think he might." She stared into her tea cup. "He went to stay at his mum's for a couple of days," she swirled her tea, "but he came back again."

"Oh," said Margaret. "And the sort-of boyfriend, does he know about the real one?"

"Yeah. But I haven't gone into any details." She drank her tea. "I don't think that's the problem. I think he thinks I'm too young."

"Oh God Laurie, how old is he?" Pat was horrified.

"Oh, he isn't a lot older. He's in his thirties, early thirties."

"And how old are you again, Laurie?" Marie's face was puckered with concern.

"Well, I'm in my early twenties."

Pat laughed. "You're a bit young to be being vague. How old *are* you?"

"I'm twenty four." Laurie felt like a hopeless case. She didn't even know these women, but she had no one else to tell.

"Well," Pat sat back, considering. "That's not a massive age difference, is it?" Although she didn't seem convinced. "Do you really think it's that?"

"Has he just come out of a bad relationship?" asked Marie.

"No." She thought for a second. "At least I don't think so. He has just come out of the army quite recently."

"Has he got that Post Stress Trauma thing?" asked Marie, looking knowledgeable.

The other women stared at Marie.

"What?" she said, annoyed. "I saw it on *This Morning*. Dr Chris was saying that it happens more than we think." She nodded sagely at the others. "He said there are a lot of guys coming back from Afghanistan experiencing trauma." She said trauma as if it was in quotations.

Pat and Margaret looked expectantly at Laurie.

"I don't know," she considered then shrugged. "He won't talk about it."

Marie nodded again. "That's one of the signs. They don't like to talk about it because it brings it all back."

"Oh yeah," Margaret nodded. "My granddad was like that. He wouldn't talk about the war and he went very quiet sometimes." She looked off into the distance. "My Gran made us go out and play when that happened. I was only wee when he died, of course."

"But, I mean, that was different, wasn't it? That was, like, a world war. It's not the same now, is it?" Laurie couldn't see how the two things could compare.

"I dunno Laurie," said Pat. "War's war, isn't it? I saw some pretty hellish stuff on the news, and I bet that was only the half of it."

"God," said Laurie, putting her cup down and her head in her hands. "I hadn't thought of that."

"Well Marie," said Margaret, turning to Marie. "What should Laurie do? What did Dr Chris suggest?"

"Oh. I don't know. I went and made a cup of tea and when I came back he'd moved on to Irritable Bowel Syndrome."

The other two women shook their heads in dismay.

"Laurie, is this the hospital radio fella?" asked Pat.

"Yeah," said Laurie without moving her head from her hands.

"And you say he's mid-thirties?"

Laurie nodded.

"Is he quite a big lad, quite nice looking?"

Laurie looked up at Pat and nodded again.

"Do you know him Pat?" Marie was agog.

"If it's who I'm thinking of." Pat considered a moment. "I think he's Douglas Callander's son."

"Dr Callander?" asked Margaret.

Pat nodded.

Laurie racked her brain for Gerry's surname, but he'd never told her. She tried to remember what the sign on his flat door said, but nothing came to her. Was that what the woman had said in the Art Centre?

"How would you know his dad?" asked Laurie.

"I used to work in his dad's surgery on the reception. A long time ago. I remember when he went off to the army." She looked at Margaret.

Margaret nodded. "I remember that too. There was quite a hoo hah."

"What do you mean? Anyway, it can't be Gerry."

"Well," said Pat. "Let's see, Gerry would be about thirty four or five, because he's the same age as our Irene's oldest because they went to the same nursery. And Dr Callander's boy went off to the army the year he left school, didn't he?" She looked meaningfully at Margaret.

Laurie caught her look.

"Hang on a minute! What's going on here? You're not saying something!"

Pat and Margaret looked at each other, considering what, if anything to say.

"What?" asked Marie, sitting on the edge of her seat. "What?"

Pat sighed. "If you were my daughter, I'd want you to know."

Laurie wished she was Pat's daughter. She looked at her pleadingly.

"Well." She took a deep breath. "If it is him, he left for the army in a bit of a hurry."

"What do you mean? In a hurry?"

"He was seeing this girl, Jenny. Nice girl, lived near me. I don't think it was anything serious, they were both supposed to be going off to uni. Both going to be doctors, I think."

Laurie had a quick image of Gerry in a white coat, holding a stethoscope. It seemed daft.

"And?" asked Laurie.

"Well. He went off to the army all of a sudden and then Jenny had a baby a few months later. There was a big fuss. A lot of people stopped talking to the Callanders and then he retired soon after."

"Really?" Laurie didn't believe it. "I doubt that's my Gerry." Her Gerry? Laurie felt herself smiling, despite the story.

"Well. Ask him. When are you seeing him next?"

"I don't know. I don't know if he wants to see me again."

"What happened to the wee baby?" asked Marie with a damp tremor in her voice.

"Jenny had a boy. He must be about fifteen or so now. But they moved somewhere else in town and I haven't seen her since the boy was a toddler."

Gerry with a child? She couldn't picture it. And yet she could completely picture it. He'd be a good dad, she thought,. remembering his warm, comfortable bulk. Cuddly.

"I'm going to go and see him later and I'll find out then."

"D'you reckon?" asked Margaret. "Is that a good idea? What if he has got post traumatic whatever?"

"Well." She thought for a second. "If he does, he'll need a friend won't he?" She felt a warm, saintly glow come over her. Maybe she wasn't so very different to her mother after all.

Wednesday 22nd of December

Just After 3am
Increasing Mist

She had decided during the rest of her shift that she was just going to have to brass neck it. There was no way around it. Fair enough, she didn't know what direction she was going in just at the moment, but she thought she did want to keep seeing Gerry and she was just going to have to be brave and face up to things. Tomorrow she would have to break up with Ed, but first she needed to sort things out with Gerry. She stood in front of the station door and gathered her resolve.

Straightening her spine and taking a deep breath, she raised her hand to knock on the door, but stopped herself just before her hand made contact with the wood. What if he knew it was her and just ignored her? Worse still, what if he locked the door and stood on the other side – unrelenting, silent, glowering through the closed door at her impertinence? Better to just open the door, give him no warning. She straightened herself up, put her hand on the door handle and turned it forcefully.

She jarred her shoulder as she stumbled against the door. He'd locked it! Furious, she pounded on the door.

"For fuck's sake Gerry! Let me in!"

Nothing.

She banged on the door again. There was no sound from the station. She stood looking at the sign on the door, deciding what to do. She leaned her ear against the door straining to hear whether he was standing on the other side, laughing at her stupidity.

But there was absolutely no sound. She realised that there wasn't anybody in the station. Where the hell was he? Oh God, had something happened to him? No, she didn't think he was the type. Was he?

Fleetingly, she considered leaving him a note just in case he had been caught short, but somehow that would be even more humiliating than just talking to him. Besides, what on earth could she write on a scrap of paper?

She turned from the station and started to walk the long way out of the hospital. This route took her through the wards she worked on, past the old people snoring and muttering in their beds. She tried to look as if she was still working, so she wouldn't appear suspicious. To that end, she straightened a few cubicle curtains as she passed along the corridor. One cubicle had several visitors in it, crowded around the bed on plastic stackable chairs. She caught the eye of one of the visitors, an old man who was sitting at the head of the bed, hands folded in his lap, while the other three visitors – his children maybe? – read books. It must be his wife in the bed. She must be about to die, Laurie thought. She smiled at the old man and he nodded back at her. She wanted to do something for him, but had nothing to offer, so she nodded back and walked on through the ward.

It was nice in the hospital at this time of night. Everything was quiet and the dim lights of the wards reminded her of the quality of light in airplanes during night flights. She was full of a sort of maternal magnificence, where she had the impulse to smooth patients' hair and tuck them in and glow kindly as she floated along the corridors. There were no other visitors at any other beds and the nursing staff must have all been chatting in their stations. She felt as if she was the last person in the hospital and the thought was comforting. Some days she wished she didn't have to see another person again and go through all that rigmarole of their feelings and their ideas and their pasts. Why couldn't people just start afresh and see what happened? Why were people always holding on to ancient history and dragging their bloody heels? Her mood turned as she walked past the last few beds. If it was daytime, they'd all be awake, moaning and demanding. She passed the last bed and noticed the occupant – she couldn't tell whether it was male or female – had their eyes open and stared at her balefully. She stopped and started back. The patient stared at her without blinking. The longer Laurie stood there, the more she became convinced that she was staring at a dead person, but she couldn't tear herself away. Finally she heard the sound of nurses pushing the drugs trolley and she left the ward, forcing herself not to look back.

Where on earth would she go now? There was no way she was going home to break the news to Ed, but she knew herself well enough to know that she wouldn't in a million years be able to keep it in once she was with Ed. She had to break things off with him. She was many things, but not really a liar. She hated people who had affairs. If you fell out of love with someone, that was one thing, it happened all the time, but to stay with someone and start romancing someone else – that just wasn't on. She didn't hold that what had happened with Gerry was quite the same thing, because she hadn't slept with Gerry and what was happening (had happened?), wasn't what could be described as a relationship, as such. But she knew that things might go that way and, anyway, she didn't love Ed and that was the point, wasn't it? Being honest.

She was starving. She'd been in such a hurry to get up to Gerry that she hadn't had her second break. She thought she might go to the 24 hour cafe in the concourse. She'd walked past it a few times and it looked okay. She hurried down the stairs to the main level, imagining a cup of tea and a bacon roll.

As she turned the corner into the beige and grey concourse she was able to see the whole sweep of the hospital's arrivals area. There were more people about than she had imagined. Several doctors stood around reception area chatting in their scrubs and hitting each other around the shoulders with what looked like clip boards. A solitary cleaner ran a mop backwards and forwards over a square meter of lino. Laurie shook her head at the man's sloppiness. Pat would have been furious. His line manager must be a great deal more lenient. She was probably smoking out the front of the hospital. Pat had no time for cleaning managers who didn't have her evangelical zeal. Laurie could see her point. How hard was it to just keep things clean? She hadn't yet carried this through to her own flat, but she was hopeful that, by some sort of domestic osmosis, her own home would start to become gradually more organised and nice to be in. But she knew that, soon enough, too soon to encourage her to really get her shit together, she'd be moving out. But she didn't want to think about that now.

There were only three tables occupied at the cafe. Two nurses silently drinking tea at the same table, an old man reading the paper and a guy sitting at the back wall under the enormous 70s tapestry that made everything else look tiny. He had his back to her but she realised immediately that it was Gerry. She decided to watch him for a while, see the lie of the land. She walked around the perimeter of the cafe and stood behind an abandoned health stand so that she could gain a better view of him. She picked out a leaflet on psoriasis and perused the needlessly graphic photos. Shuddering, she looked over at Gerry. He was leaning his head on his hand and was surrounded by the remains of what looked like a cooked breakfast and several cups of tea.

She sighed and put the leaflet back, hiding it behind a leaflet on vitamins. He didn't look at all happy. Laurie walked towards him hesitantly. Would he want to see her? His look of dejection encouraged her; surely he'd want to see a friend? As she came closer, she could see more of his face. His eyes were puffy and he was none too clean. What she'd really like to do with Gerry was get him bathed and shaved – see what he was really like under all that. Without the slightest attempt at hiding it, he took a hip flask out of his jacket pocket and took a drink. This looks like trouble, she thought.

He looked up at her suddenly; he must have felt her staring at him. For a second, it was as if he didn't recognise her, but Laurie watched realisation unfold across his face and stood waiting for a sign to proceed. He attempted a smile so she stepped forward and put a hand on his shoulder. He reached out and pulled her close, pushing his face against her. Laurie held on to his head and felt him breathing heavily, rapidly into her jumper. She waited while his breathing calmed and he gave her one final squeeze. She could feel the flask in his hand pressing into her back. She sat down next to him at the table.

"Hi." She pushed the used crockery to the other side of the table. She nodded at the hip flask which he was still holding. "Is it that bad?"

He put his arm around her shoulders and pulled her to him again. It was an awkward position. Her head was at an uncomfortable angle and she had the distinct impression that Gerry might start to cry. No one was looking at them but Laurie wasn't greatly concerned about that. It was more that she suspected Gerry had been stopping himself from crying for a long time so might keep going and Laurie wouldn't have the slightest idea of what to do with him.

She disentangled herself.

"Can I get you anything?" She fumbled in her pocket for her purse and looked over towards the serving area.

"No." Gerry put his hand on her forearm and when she tried to stand up he held her down. "Stay a minute. I need to talk to you." He put the flask away in his pocket.

She forced herself to face him. He scanned across her face and back again. Irritation rose up in her.

"What?" She tried to sound patient, but it was there, that tone of annoyance. Gerry didn't appear to have noticed. To be so unaware of other people, thought Laurie, it must be so *freeing* not to notice what other people were thinking.

"Laurie." He shook his head slowly.

"Yes?"

He shook his head again.

"What Gerry?"

"I just . . . I feel terrible about what happened."

"Do you?" asked Laurie. She'd so wanted to come and see him after what Pat had told her, but now she didn't know if she had the stamina for all this.

She hated it when men cried. It was heart breaking and irritating at the same time. It used to be that you never saw men crying. When she was growing up she would have thought it more likely for her dad to fly than burst into tears. But now men were crying all the time. Elaborately, shoulder-shakingly. God, the Princess Diana effect.

The TV made it seem as if men had to be sharing their feelings all the time and that inevitably led to much wailing and gnashing of teeth. She wished men would revert to strong silence. Even her dad was at it now. When her mum died she'd seen him, wet faced and seemingly free of shame. She suspected her dad wasn't even particularly heart-broken by her mum's death. It was if he was taking the opportunity to have a cry. Get some sympathy. Maybe that was too harsh, but it wasn't like he gave her any sympathy at the time – and it was her mother who'd died.

She stood for a moment imagining the outside of her family house. She pictured the front cut away like a doll's house revealing the life of her father. He was in the living room watching TV. The same as before. Except now he'd have to make his own tea. She wondered what sort of things he'd make for himself. She liked to think he was trying new things or eating out more, but she knew it would all be heated up items. Maybe she should just move Ed into her dad's house. They could live quite nicely actually. If she moved Ed's mum in as well that would be perfect. Ed's mum would love it. Ed would love it too. Laurie's dad would be delighted to be looked after again. Plus, he wouldn't even have to pay Ed's mum. Then Laurie could just fuck off and they wouldn't need her at all. Perfect.

Gerry handed her a five pound note.

"Here. Get yourself something."

She looked down at the five pound note and thought better of making a "thanks dad" joke. This was becoming too frequent a thing. She wasn't a charity case. The money was old and tattered. Gerry was staring down at his tea again. She looked hard at him, willing him to turn his face to her. She knew he could feel her staring at him, but he picked up his spoon and stirred his tea slowly.

She breathed out.

He turned towards her.

"Honestly. I'm fine." He nodded. "Please, get something to eat."

There was something about his tone that compelled her to go over and pick up a cheese roll and a can of coke. She handed the money over to the man behind the counter. He managed to serve her without looking at her at all. She was glad of it. She felt she might burst into tears if anyone looked at her kindly, or even politely. She knew that if that happened it would be like before, in the break room, but worse, because she wouldn't be able to stop and she wouldn't even be able to pretend to be mad because Gerry would try to help her and make it plain that she hadn't escaped from somewhere.

She opened the can standing at the counter and gulped back a big mouthful. The fizz went up her nose and her eyes filled with tears. She stood, fists clenched, reminding herself it was just her body having a biological reaction and that she wasn't obliged to throw real tears in with the automatic ones. She realised that she was crushing her cheese roll. She took a deep breath, braced herself and walked over to Gerry, forcing a smile as she went.

Gerry appeared to have similarly pulled himself together. They sat in silence for a moment, trying out various smiles until they both began to speak at once.

"Look, about earlier . . ."

"Gerry, I didn't mean to . . ." Laurie reached a hand towards Gerry's arm and withdrew it again.

They both stopped. Laurie nodded her head at Gerry. He took a deep breath.

"Right." He stopped again and stared at the table top.

Laurie's patience ran out.

"Christ," said Laurie. "I've never seen such fascinating formica." She smiled mock-encouragingly at Gerry. "Go on. You can do it."

The thing was, she didn't want to be angry, but she couldn't seem to switch it off. It was like all the times she'd said horrible things to Ed, even when the voice in her head was telling her to leave it alone. But sometimes she just couldn't seem to keep whatever she thought zipped in.

Other people must control that in themselves or there'd be hand-to-hand fighting everywhere you went. She looked at Gerry and tried to listen quietly.

"Right." He paused for a second. "I wasn't very nice to you." He picked at the table top. "The other night."

She nodded, but kept her jaw clamped shut. She wasn't going to help him out.

"I haven't had a girlfriend," he shrugged, "for quite a while." He scanned her face. "I freaked out a bit."

"Okay." She drew the word out. She should ask him what he meant, but she had a fair idea of what he was on about. What really mattered now was whether there was going to be anything happening between them. Otherwise why bother caring about him?

"Did you mean what you said?"

"About slowing things down?"

She nodded.

"Sort of." He picked up her hand. "I know this isn't maybe anything yet really. But I just don't want to get all . . ." he paused and tightened his hold on her, "involved."

"Involved?" She sat back in her chair, pulling her hand from his grip. "We aren't involved Gerry." She acted mildly outraged, put out.

Gerry held his lips in a straight line and stared at her until she looked down into her lap.

"We are though, aren't we?" he said.

The expression on his face infuriated Laurie. She took a deep breath. At this rate she was going to lift off the floor and float away into the night – an anger fuelled balloon. There was something about the sight of someone who was patently trying to be the grown up that provoked all sorts of childish feelings. Laurie resisted the temptation to throw her roll at Gerry's stupid, calm face.

"Look Gerry, it was you that was upset about it." She jabbed a finger at him. "Not me!" Although, of course, she had been upset.

He nodded, looking down at the table again.

That had wiped the smug self-control off his face. Laurie sat back in her chair, relieved that he was on the back foot now.

"Considering this isn't really a relationship," she said quietly, "it certainly feels like one." Gerry kept his head down, saying nothing. Laurie started to feel as if she'd kicked an old dog and was just thinking about patting Gerry on the head when she caught sight of a young man entering the hospital, holding something to the side of his head. She was watching him wondering if he'd suffered some sort of side of head trauma which would lead to him fainting, when she saw it was Ed.

Ed! What the bloody hell was he doing here at this time in the morning? Was he here for her? How could he be? She ducked down in her seat.

She needn't have bothered. He didn't see her. He was too focussed on the mobile phone she realised he was talking into intensely. He nodded as he talked and gestured with his other hand. She hadn't seen him so animated in a long time, perhaps ever. He walked within ten feet of where she sat with Gerry, zeroing in on wherever he was going.

Gerry didn't look up. He'd started to pick at one of his cuticles.

She waited until Ed had turned off down a corridor and then stood up.

"I'll be back in a minute."

Gerry glanced up briefly then down again.

I bet he thinks I won't come back, she thought. Maybe she wouldn't, she'd see what Ed was up to first. She walked smartly over to the corridor Ed had disappeared into and glanced down it to make sure he was far enough away that he wouldn't notice her. She followed him, getting close enough to eavesdrop.

"It's okay, mate. We'll get it sorted out. We will."

The other person talked at length.

"I know, I know. I'll speak to your mum."

The other person again.

"Well," he paused, "alright, I won't if you don't want me to." He nodded.

She felt like whacking him on the head and knocking a bit of sense into him. He was always nodding when he was on the phone. She remembered, just in time, that she was meant to be secretly tailing Ed and that she wasn't meant to be too close behind him. She dropped back just as he stopped.

"Okay. I'll be down there in a few minutes. Just sit tight." He disconnected the call, put the phone into his coat pocket and shook his head a couple of times.

Laurie stepped behind a conveniently dumped filing cabinet and waited until she could hear him walking on. She knew that the chances of her remaining behind him and not getting caught were slim, but she was very curious about who he was talking to and what was going on. Obviously it was a youth-work thing. Probably some maladjusted drama queen teenager who'd identified Ed as a soft touch and was planning on taking him for a ride. She felt an unwelcome pang of sympathy for Ed and his total lack of guile. He probably wouldn't even notice that some kid was taking the piss and, when he did find out, he probably wouldn't care, thinking it was all just part of being a caring person.

Ed stood in front of a wall mounted hospital map. He traced his finger along several areas of the hospital, clearly unable to find where he was. If he'd bothered to come to the hospital as much as Laurie had when her mum was ill, he'd have a better sense of where things were. Laurie contemplated going over and jabbing a finger at their position on the map, but knew then she'd never have this chance to see Ed in the real world as other people saw him. Their relationship was doomed, she knew that. There was no way she was going to carry on the agony, but she had an idea that she'd like to walk away from Ed with some version of respect for him. Perhaps seeing him at work was a way of doing that. Maybe if she saw him being capable and liked, she could treat him like any moderately okay person she'd encounter in life instead of feeling like thumping him every time he breathed.

Eventually he worked out where he was, tapping his finger against the glass twice.

"Right!" he set off decisively towards the swinging doors that led to Casualty. There was no way she could follow him through there without him seeing her and he'd know instantly that she'd been following him. She sighed and turned back to the main concourse where, hopefully, possibly, Gerry would still be waiting for her. She'd find out what was going on with Ed later.

5.30am
Rain

Gerry was still waiting at the table. At least, he was still sitting at the table. When he saw her his expression didn't change much. She almost veered past the table and out of the hospital, but she was nothing if not bloody minded. She pulled her chair out from the table and stood with her hands on the back of the chair, looking down at Gerry who had gone back to picking at the table top. She sat down and they sat in silence for a few minutes until Laurie realised that if they didn't start talking soon, she'd fall asleep.

"So!"

Gerry gave a weak smile.

"So, Laurie."

Laurie looked around to give Gerry some time to get it together. There was only one other table occupied now. It was a nurse drinking slowly from a mug. She held the mug in both hands and blew on it intermittently. The nurse was about the same age as Laurie's mum, but she looked tired and probably seemed older than she really was. Laurie tried to imagine that it was her mum sitting a few tables across from her. She tried to superimpose her mum's features on to the nurse's face, but she couldn't quite recall the shape of her eyes or how her mouth would look

167

when the nurse blew on her drink. She could recall, of course, her mother's face if she remembered particular photos, but it was as if she could no longer make this version of her mum move any more. She couldn't remember how she'd looked when she talked or when she was eating. She could remember very clearly how she looked when she died; the colour of her at least, the ugly yellow tone she had to her skin and her eyes and the sort of waxy quality of her, lying there in the hospice with her arms tucked unnaturally over the top of her sheets.

The nurse looked up at Laurie but she wasn't really seeing her, Laurie could tell. She was at that stage of exhaustion where everything becomes rubbery and useless. Laurie probably looked like a cardboard cut-out to the nurse. But then the nurse scowled at Laurie, forcing her to look at Gerry. Gerry was staring at her.

She smiled patiently, wishing he'd just get on with it. She didn't think she could be bothered much longer.

"Laurie?"

"Mh-hm?" She tried not to look too intently at him and spook him.

He took a deep breath. "There are some things I think I need to tell you about."

"Okay." She waited while he got going.

"When I came out of the army I wasn't . . ." Laurie didn't say a thing. She waited.

"I saw some stuff in Afghanistan and . . ." he paused ". . . other places where I served." He stopped again and picked up his mug.

"Go on," said Laurie, tying not to sound eager.

"I just couldn't keep going through the motions." He

168

swirled what was left in his mug and looked into it. "And I decided that I'd had enough."

"Okay?" She waited for more. Gerry made no move to expand further. She waited, but he'd obviously finished.

"Right. So what does that mean for me?" He didn't look up. "Us?"

He shrugged. "I don't really know." He knocked back what was left of his drink. "I just thought I'd better tell you."

"To be fair, Gerry, you haven't really told me an awful lot."

He shrugged again.

"Well." She watched him as he flicked a packet of sugar around the table. "I mean – are you better now?"

He considered for a moment and put the sugar packet in his pocket. "Better than I was."

"But that still doesn't tell me much about anything else."

He looked at her blankly.

"For instance: you're from round here, aren't you?"

He nodded grudgingly.

"Why not tell me that? Why's it such a big, bloody secret?" Her voice had risen a bit and the nurse was looking at them.

"It's not that it's a secret." He sighed.

"What is it then?"

"It's just . . . I'm not . . ."

"Aw, come on Gerry. Spit it out!"

"Don't be like that Laurie. I'm trying to explain."

He reached forward and took her hand firmly.

"You aren't trying to explain at all." She flexed her

169

fingers inside his hand, trying to wiggle free, but he continued to hold on.

"What you're doing Gerry, is giving me some vague flim-flam to keep me quiet."

"Flim-flam?" He had the cheek to smile.

"You know what I mean." She wrenched her hand free. "You aren't telling me anything that I couldn't have guessed." She jabbed a finger at him.

He was serious again. "Okay. Okay" He let go of her hand. "What do you want to know?"

She couldn't help it. She knew she ought to build up to this, but why make a pretence of it?

"Why didn't you tell me about your child?" She looked over his head at the tapestry. "Your son?" Gerry looked as if he'd been punched in the face. So it was true then.

"I knew I should never have come back here." He put his head in his hands on the table top.

"Look Gerry, I'm sorry, I am." She realised he was crying. "Oh Gerry, Gerry, I'm so sorry." She stood up quickly and moved round to the seat next to him. She put her arm around him and nestled her head close to his. She stroked the back of his head until he stopped crying. He sat up with an effort.

"Sorry. Sorry," he said, shaking his head. "I shouldn't be doing this. It's my own fault."

"What happened?"

"I've never even met him." He shrugged.

"Why not? Don't you want to know him?" She couldn't imagine having a child out there somewhere and not knowing them.

"It's too late."

"Surely he'd want to know who his father was? I would."

"You don't know that though, do you?" he said. "He might not know anything about me. His mum might have met someone else. Even if he did know about me, surely he'd hate me, want nothing to do with me?"

"Have you ever tried to get in contact with his mum?"

"No."

"Never?" She found it hard to believe.

"I decided that it would be kinder if I had nothing at all to do with it," He said. "I just thought that it would be the kinder option."

"Kinder to who? You?" She couldn't believe he'd genuinely thought that.

"To the boy. To her."

"I don't quite get the logic of that."

"If I was hanging around, seeing him when I was on leave, it would only confuse things. And then if anything happened to me . . ." He rubbed his eyes. "Then, you know, no harm done."

"What? No harm done?" Her voice rose in volume. "Are you mental? Of course there's harm done!" She threw her hands up.

"I know. I know that now!" he shouted. "Of course, I fucking know that now! But I was only nineteen – I was a child myself."

"You were not a child!" She shook her head. "You were old enough to get your girlfriend pregnant. And what about her – she must have had to grow up pretty fucking quickly, mustn't she?"

His eyes were full of tears again. "I know, I know . . .

171

I'm a prick, a selfish prick." He kept shaking his head. "I just ran away to the army. And when I was in the army I thought I could make a difference and sort of make up for things."

"You can't just go around making up for things." She sighed, exasperated. "You can't just go around making up your own," she searched around for the right word, "system. Life isn't like that."

"Well, obviously, Laurie," He said. "I know that now. Well, I knew that then, but I tried to just get on with it."

She sighed again.

"I'm paying for it now, aren't I?"

"Are you?"

He frowned at her. "What do you mean?"

"Well, no offence, but it seems like you just do whatever you feel like doing."

"What?"

"Well, now that you're back, you're doing what? Working a job where you don't have to talk to anyone, you don't seem to have any friends, the only people you do see are those wasters in that shitty pub and that mentalist neighbour." When she said "neighbour" she glared at him, remembering the other night.

He stared at her, mouth slightly open, a genuine look of shock on his face.

"And as soon as things might come to something with me you're like, oh no, not real, human interaction, heaven protect me!" She held her hands up to her face like a distressed old lady.

Still he said nothing. She'd gone too far, but she couldn't stop now.

"And, since you've come back, have you contacted the boy?" She couldn't seem to say the word "son".

He shook his head.

"Why not? What's stopping you?" What was she doing? This could only completely over-complicate things.

"I just don't think it's a good idea."

She tried, she really did, but she couldn't keep her mouth shut.

"Well." She gouged at the table top with a teaspoon, "I think that's pathetic." She lost confidence as she said the word pathetic and whispered it, but Gerry heard her well enough.

He was clearly trying to control his temper. She saw the muscle in his jaw clenching.

"Look, Gerry, I'm sorry." He was still shaking his head and wouldn't look at her. "I know it isn't any of my business." She tapped her spoon off his cup, "Gerry, come on, look at me."

He looked at her but that jaw muscle was still going.

"I just think," she began. He looked as if he wanted to hurt her. She took a breath. "I just think that, if you're around and he's around, then you should, like," she paused, "make the effort."

"The effort? Is that what you think it is?" His voice had that edge of anger again. "That I just can't be bothered?"

"No, no!" she protested. "I'm not saying you're being lazy or anything, I know it'll be a nightmare, but you should do it."

He shrugged, the anger defused. "I doubt he'd even want to see me, especially not the way things are at the

173

moment. Anyway, he might not know I'm his," he looked into his cup, "father."

"D'you reckon?" She took his hand. "In a town this size, you wouldn't be able to hide it for long. I mean, I found out, didn't I?" She considered for a second. "Unless they've moved."

"They haven't."

"How do you know?"

"I just do. But it's immaterial – it's too late."

"It's only too late when somebody dies." She felt her eyes tear up. Not now, this wasn't the time.

Gerry took her hand again. "Are you okay?"

She shrugged. "I just know what it's like for it to be too late, you know?"

"What do you mean?"

"Just what I said." She looked at the tapestry, trying to distract herself.

She could feel him scanning her face, but she didn't want to look up at him looking kindly at her.

There was silence for a few minutes.

"I don't even know what he looks like." He took the flask out of his pocket and knocked it back. Surely there couldn't be much left now.

"Do you know how to get in touch with him?"

"I suppose it would be easy enough to get in touch with his mother, Jenny," he said. "If she'd even speak to me."

"She'd probably be glad of the help."

"I doubt it," Gerry tucked the flask away again. "She's probably still cursing me daily."

"Still. You aren't a kid anymore, are you?"

"No," he laughed, "that I am not, Laurie."

"I could help you." She leaned her head on his shoulder.

"What?" he said, "You're a bit muffled down there."

"You heard me. Anyway, I'm nearer his age than you are."

"For fuck's sake Laurie, that's hardly a winning argument."

"Sorry." She nuzzled closer. She could fall asleep like this. They sat for a few minutes.

"I'd make a terrible father anyway."

She pulled herself away and looked at him. "No you wouldn't."

"You were right earlier. I am a coward."

"I didn't say you were a coward."

"I am though. You know I am."

"How can you have been a coward when you were in the army? Isn't that the opposite of being a coward?" She smiled. "That's going out and actively looking for danger, isn't it?"

"I thought I could do it," he shook his head, "but I was shit at it."

"What do you mean?"

"At first, you don't think about it, but then you do and that's all you think about." His eyes were wet. "All."

"But isn't that normal?" She didn't really know what he meant. "Isn't everyone like that?"

"No." He shook his head.

"But they must be. They probably don't show it."

He shook his head. "Everyone else I knew is still there. Still in the army."

"But that doesn't mean anything."

He shook his head again and a tear fell onto the table. He didn't seem to notice it.

"It was awful. Fucking awful. And you start to get used to it. You start to think it's normal." He spoke in a rush. "And then, one day, you remember that it isn't normal and then, that's it, you're fucked." He was properly crying now. Laurie glanced around, but the cafe was empty.

"What happened? Where were you?"

"All over the place. Afghanistan eventually."

"What was it like?"

"What was it *like*?"

She nodded.

"Hellish. At times."

"What do you mean?"

"It was brutal." His shoulders slumped. "Bosnia was the worst."

"And what were you doing there? Come on Gerry, you need to talk about it."

"I was working with the UN."

"Right." She paused. "What did that entail then?"

"That entailed," he said sarcastically, "A lot of spade work."

"What? Digging things up?"

"Mass graves." His sarcastic tone was gone now. She waited for him to go on, but he was looking into space. She nudged him.

"We dug out mass graves so that people could have something like proper burials." His head drooped. "They weren't just soldiers, but old people, women, children," he rubbed his thumb over his eyelids as he spoke, "babies."

She touched his arm. "God, that must have been awful."

"That's one way of putting it." He shook his head again.

"And was that what made you leave the army?"

"No, not really. It was important work. I still think that." He sighed. "But my CO suggested I had a break from it. I didn't want to go, but eventually I had no choice. Things went too far."

"What do you mean, went too far?" What was "going too far" in a war? She hated to think.

"I was having dreams, nightmares. I was drinking too much, starting to cry, talking too much to the locals. Making a tit of myself, the army."

"I don't understand. Don't they expect that?"

He nodded. "Sort of, but it was me. I just wouldn't take a break. It was like I couldn't stop."

"Oh." She nodded, she knew what that was like. "When my mum died I wouldn't let anyone else do anything."

"When was that?"

She couldn't speak. She put her hand up to cover her mouth and pressed hard, hurting herself to stop from crying. But it was no use, she was shaking and shaking, crying really hard, and all she could think of was: *What am I doing? What am I doing?*

Gerry pulled her close and she clung to the front of his jumper with her right hand, still covering her mouth with her left. She wasn't making any sound but her body shuddered as she gulped air in and pushed tears out. They sat like that for what seemed like a long time and Gerry held her close and sometimes stroked her hair until the crying subsided and she sat, squeezed dry, grafted on to

Gerry. She felt him breathing in and out and matched her inhalations to his until she felt like they were taking in the same air together and that their hearts were beating at the same time, circulating the same blood.

She wished that things could just end like this and that time would stop.

Gerry kept stroking her hair and tiredness washed over her. She started to dream about being on a bus with Gerry and two girls she'd been friends with at primary school. The girls had a paper bag with sweets in it that they were passing back and forth, refusing to share with Laurie or Gerry. She reached forward and snatched a sweetie and was about to put it in her mouth when she realised it was a baby kitten. She woke with a start as Gerry gently pushed her up to a sitting position. She opened her eyes to see Ed standing in front of the table.

"Fuck," she whispered.

6am
Freezing Fog

Nobody said anything. Both men looked at Laurie, clearly expecting her to explain the situation.

"Hello Ed." She smiled weakly. "This is Gerry. Gerry – Ed."

She noticed a teenage boy standing a few feet behind Ed staring intently at her and Gerry. She frowned at the boy. Ed stared at her.

She rubbed her eyes. She was so tired; she couldn't really be bothered with all this inevitable confrontation. She imagined Ed shaking Gerry's hand and giving him a few words of advice on how to handle Laurie now that he was the new registered owner. She imagined Gerry walking around her as she stood patiently. He kicked at the sides of her feet, pinched her waist and the fat of her cheek, nodding, but not wanting to seem too eager, so as to keep the price down.

She let out a giggle and both Gerry and Ed looked at her as if she was mad. Who was she kidding? Ed wouldn't have the first word of advice for anyone on anything – least of all on how to handle women, particularly Laurie.

"Sit down Ed, have a cup of tea, please. And then we can . . ." She stood up and made her way to the counter. She couldn't even work up the appropriate level of horror at this situation. Surely she should be panicking, trying to come up with a cover story or something. But she just couldn't be bothered. She turned and watched Gerry and Ed. Ed stood for a second and Gerry half rose and pointed to the seat opposite. Ed sat down and turned and waved the teenager over who sat down next to him. Gerry looked professionally polite as he started to speak to Ed. She was sure she could rely on Gerry not to make a scene. She should feel at the very least nervous in this situation, but she felt like she was beyond that. She actually felt as if she'd become untethered and was watching her life from above, calmly.

Ed half turned in his seat and spoke to the boy who was sitting looking down at his hands on the table. Gerry's face became grave and he stared at the boy. Laurie took a step towards the table to try and redirect things.

"Yes? Can I get you something?"

Laurie turned back to the counter. It was someone different now, the shifts must have changed.

"Em, yes. Three, no four, teas please."

The woman poured four teas from the enormous metal teapot sitting on the stove behind her.

She placed the mugs on a tray.

"There's milk and sugar on the table." She wiped her hands on a tea towel that hung over her shoulder. "Right hen, that'll be four pounds eighty."

Laurie handed five pounds over and waited whilst the woman counted out the change in coppers.

She took the handful of coins from the woman who offered no word of apology for the shrapnel and then dropped the money on to the tray with the tea. She gave the woman a nod and walked back to the table. Gerry was looking pale and shaky again. She knew he must feel desperate to take a slug from his hip flask, but wouldn't feel able to in front of these two strangers. Ed was telling Gerry about his course and his youth work placement. Head down, the boy was drawing circles on the table top with a teaspoon.

Laurie put the tray down and pointed at the cups.

"I got tea for," she nodded at the boy, "everybody." The boy looked at her; his face was pale and his skin was stretched looking. "Are you okay?" she asked him.

He nodded, but didn't say anything.

Ed spoke. "There was an accident, a car accident." He looked at the boy and the boy looked at the table. "That's why I'm here."

"Why? Were you in an accident?" She knew full well that he had not been. But she had an idea that the more Ed was forced to say, the less hellish the fight that was surely coming would be.

"Well." He paused. "I received a phone call."

Something about the way he said it piqued Laurie's interest. "From who?" She asked.

Ed started to fiddle with his mobile phone, no doubt willing it to start ringing. And, unbelievably, it did. The look on Ed's face was not one Laurie had seen recently.

"I need to take this," Ed said, standing up.

"Of course you do," Laurie said.

Ed moved away to the front reception area talking rapidly on his phone.

Gerry was staring down at his tea morosely. She should say something to him, explain about Ed, she hadn't actually told him that she had a boyfriend. But he must have worked it out, mustn't he? He looked like he didn't much care anyway at this point.

Laurie studied the boy. He looked even worse than before. His dark hair curled damply at his forehead. He picked at the cuff of his hooded top. He glanced up at her and then Gerry, who was now gently sloshing his tea around the cup in a circular motion.

She reached out and touched the boy's forearm. "Are you okay?"

The boy breathed deeply and seemed to ready himself.

"You have to help me," he whispered, leaning towards her.

"What?" She leaned towards him, alarmed. "What?"

The boy ducked down into his top as if he were hiding from someone.

Gerry glanced up, not quite following what was going on.

"It's my family – if I go home now . . ." He shook his head, looking down at the table and then back up towards Ed quickly. He spoke in a rush.

"But surely they'll just be glad you're safe," she said.

He kept shaking his head.

"You don't understand." He sounded like he was on the verge of tears.

Gerry was staring at the boy now.

"What happened?" Laurie asked.

He shrugged, still not looking up.

"Come on, you can tell us." But why would he? He didn't know her or Gerry at all. They were nothing to him. But then, he had asked for help.

She touched his forearm again. He looked over at Ed who was still talking on the phone.

"Look. There's . . . stuff, bad stuff, happening at home." The boy gulped.

Gerry and Laurie looked at each other, alarmed.

"Well. Did you tell your, em, teacher or someone about it?"

"Unlikely." The boy frowned at her.

"Well?" Laurie looked at Gerry, "Isn't that what you're supposed to do?" She looked back at the boy who was staring at Gerry. "Tell a teacher? Or there's, you know, that phone thing – Childline?"

The boy actually laughed at her, suddenly looking much older.

He shook his head. "Forget it."

"No, no . . . but what can we do to help?" She didn't want to fail this boy. It might be the most important thing she ever did. "What about Ed? Isn't he helping you?"

The boy stared hard at her. "He doesn't know what to do." He nodded at Ed. "Look at him. He's useless."

All three turned to look at Ed. The boy was right of course.

"What should we do? Gerry?" She nudged Gerry sharply.

Ed was pacing up and down near the entrance to the wards. He was running his free hand through his hair making it stand up at an angle to his head. He must be talking to his boss or the boy's parent. Mind you, she wouldn't put it past Ed to be calling his own mother for a bit of guidance.

She turned to Gerry. "What do you think?"

Gerry had a slightly wild look to his eyes, but his jaw was firm.

"I know what to do," said Gerry, standing quickly, galvanised into action. He startled Laurie and the boy. "Come on, we need to get going before he comes back."

"But Gerry, we can't just . . ." Where was this coming from? He was acting like he was back in the army and they were recruits.

"I don't see that we have an option." His voice was calmly authoritative. Laurie looked at the boy whose eyes were scanning Gerry's determined face. He began to rise from his seat.

"Is this a good idea?" How much had Gerry had to drink? "Wouldn't it be better to . . ." But she didn't really have an alternative plan. If the boy was in danger . . .

Gerry's eyes were nearly bugging out. "Just follow me." Laurie hadn't seem his this intense before. "I know what I'm doing."

"What are you thinking Gerry?" She put her hand up to touch him on the forearm. "You can't just go off with kids, teenagers."

She looked at the boy hoping he would be getting a bit nervous but the boy had a look of satisfaction on his face. She looked at Ed who appeared to be listening to the person on the phone lecturing him. The boy was right – Ed would just do what he was told. He would take him home, deliver him back to whatever nightmare he lived in.

She looked at the boy again. He was acting tough like teenagers did, but underneath it, he must be frightened to even consider going off with complete strangers rather than go home. Maybe sometimes you had to take decisive action to avoid someone getting hurt. Maybe she could just go back to Gerry's with them and talk the boy into phoning Childline – get some sensible advice and then help Gerry to get his shit together.

Gerry gave one commanding nod at Laurie and strode off towards the exit behind the cafe. The boy and Laurie looked at each other. Gerry stopped and turned to them. He nodded his head grimly in the direction of the door.

Wordlessly, they followed him.

The Back of Six
Sleet, Starless

The boy kept pace with her as they followed Gerry across the car park towards the road. It was sleeting slightly and Laurie was very aware of the fact that the boy didn't have a coat on, just a hooded top.

"Pull your hood up at least," she said to him.

He frowned at her and kept his hood down.

She shrugged. "It's up to you I suppose, but it's a bit of a walk to his flat."

"So what are you, like? His girlfriend or what?"

"I dunno. Something like that."

He nodded.

"So have you been to his flat before then?"

She frowned. "Why?"

He shrugged. "No reason. Just asking."

Gerry pushed on ahead. She didn't want to be stuck with this kid, this was Gerry's idea after all.

"Gerry? Gerry! Hang on!" Either he didn't hear her or he was ignoring her because he kept going, his head down into the sleet, leading the way.

They came to a junction where they had to wait for a run of taxis to pass. Gerry ducked between the cabs, but Laurie waited on the pavement, holding the boy back with her. Suddenly, realising she was as close to her flat as she

186

was to Gerry's, she felt very weary and started to think about heading home. Maybe Ed would already be there and she could convince the boy to talk to Ed about whatever was going on. But then the boy very slightly leaned towards her and she felt herself fill up with sympathy about how shit it was being a teenager. She decided to stay a bit longer and see what she could do. The road cleared and she led the boy across. She turned to him.

"I don't even know your name." The boy stared after Gerry who was standing waiting for them across the road. "Paul," he said, without turning.

"Right, Paul."

He turned to her quickly. "No, no, I mean, I get called Jamie."

Laurie frowned. "What?"

He looked away, shrugging and shaking his head. "Okay." She frowned. "Jamie then."

He turned his head to her and his eyes filled with tears. "Paul's dead."

"What?"

What was going on here? Laurie felt panic rise in her. Was this boy unstable? Was that what Ed was doing? Working with mad teenagers? She tried to remember if he'd said anything to that effect.

"My friend, Paul." The boy stopped walking and started to cry. "He died."

"Oh, I'm sorry." She patted his shoulder. "And your name's Paul too?"

"No." He glared at her through his tears. "I told you – it's Jamie. My mate was called Paul."

She decided just to go with it. It was probably just

confusion because he was upset. Maybe he had a head injury from the accident. She scanned his face but there were no visible signs of injury.

"Come on," she nudged him. "Gerry's waiting for us." There was no way Gerry could cope with this on his own. Someone sensible had to be around. She put her arm around the boy's shoulder as they walked but he was slightly taller and completely rigid so it was painful and clearly not actually helping the boy at all, so she withdrew her arm and put her hands in her pockets. At least it had stopped sleeting now and they weren't far from Gerry's place.

The Christmas lights strung from the lampposts in this part of town looked as if they'd been up for years. Some of them had bulbs missing which gave them a deformed appearance. Several of the reindeers had only partially lit antlers and Santa's half illuminated face made him look a bit Phantom-of-the-opera-esque, but Laurie preferred the older, damaged lights over the newer, more minimalist decorations the council had bought in recent years. Christmas should be gaudy and twinkly and imperfect. She had no time for anti-tinselists.

"What are you getting for Christmas, Jamie?" As soon as she asked, she regretted it. What a stupid thing to ask an abused child.

But he didn't seem particularly disturbed. He shrugged. "The usual."

He turned to her. "What about you?" He gestured at Gerry. "What's he getting you?"

"Gerry?" She laughed. "Probably nothing. I don't think it's occurred to Gerry that it's Christmas. Anyway, we're not at a buying presents stage."

The boy considered this. They turned the corner into Gerry's street. Gerry stopped at the tenement door until they caught up with him.

Gerry turned to them and nodded.

"Right." Gerry pointed at the door with his keys. "We just need to get a few things and then we're off."

"Off where?" asked Laurie as Gerry unlocked the door.

"You'll see," he said.

Clearly, she was going to have to have a private chat with Gerry about his game plan. She was more than a bit concerned about his demeanour. What with all the upset in the cafe at the hospital and then this man-of-action stuff, she knew she had reason to be concerned. But it was nice to see him geared up like this. She could see the officer side of Gerry. She liked it: this was her idea of what a grown-up man should be.

She followed Gerry and the boy up the stairs. Inevitably there was movement behind Gerry's slutty neighbour's door. Laurie leaned up to the peep hole in the door and looked into it. She couldn't see anything, but she whispered at the door, "Get over it Theresa," as she walked past. She might have heard an intake of breath on the other side, but that was probably just wishful thinking.

Gerry opened the door to his flat and pointed in the direction of the kitchen.

"Laurie, you make a flask of coffee and get whatever food you can find into a bag." He turned towards the bedroom. "I'll get some things together."

The boy stood ramrod straight, awaiting instruction. Laurie could imagine him in a World War One uniform. She could see Gerry dressed similarly, standing holding a pocket watch in his hand, telling the boys when they'd be going over the top.

Gerry put a hand on the boy's shoulder. "You sit down and have a rest. You'll need your strength."

What on *earth* was he planning? Laurie tried to smile at the boy as Gerry went into the bedroom.

"Go and the stick the kettle on would you? I just want a quick word with Gerry."

The boy hesitated then went into the kitchen. She stood for a moment staring at the wallpaper, trying to decide what the right course of action was. Clearly, Gerry had gone a bit mental. She wasn't sure if he'd had a lot to drink or if it had just been a couple of sips from his hip flask. He didn't seem drunk. But he did seem odd and it was probably best that she didn't leave him on his own with the oddly-behaving boy. Perhaps their oddness would cancel each other out, but it was best not to take the chance. She sighed and then knocked on the door frame of Gerry's room. She didn't want to startle him.

Gerry was packing things into a camouflage duffle bag. There were two sleeping bags rolled up on the bed. Camping? She shuddered.

"Hi Gerry." He looked up at her and smiled. He didn't seem mad now. Just focussed.

"So. What's the plan?"

"We're going up to Perthshire."

"Okay." She scanned his face, but nothing else was forthcoming. "Why Perthshire?"

"My family have a house there. A holiday place – it'll give us a chance to work out what we're going to do."

"Okay." She took a step closer. "But shouldn't we tell someone about Jamie?"

"Laurie, the papers are full of child abuse stories where nobody does anything and the kid ends up dead." He gripped the duffle bag. "We aren't going to just dump him, are we?"

"Well, no, but we don't want to do something hasty and then get into trouble ourselves, do we?"

Gerry laughed. "That's why we're going to Tarnbrae."

"Tarnbrae?"

"The house. We'll have time to regroup there." He went back to packing the bag, then glanced at his watch. "We're leaving in ten minutes. Grab some cards and things. There's no TV."

She frowned. "Okay. But I think we should at least phone Ed." Gerry didn't look up. "He'll be really worried and he might get into a lot of trouble for this."

Gerry looked up, his face very serious.

"No offence Laurie, but I've no time for people who just stand by and do nothing."

"That's not very fair." She was surprised by herself. "We don't know what's happened do we?"

"It's not a risk I'm prepared to take."

She sighed. "Alright." It was obvious that there was no dissuading him. She could also see that the boy would probably rather go off on a hare-brained adventure with Gerry than go home with her to face Ed. "Fair enough. But we need to talk about this properly when we get to the house."

There was no response.

"Okay?"

He nodded, but he didn't look up.

She should tell him about the dead friend, this Paul, but she didn't want to make things even more stressful. She'd wait for the right moment, maybe try and get more info out of the boy first.

She went through to the kitchen.

Jamie was standing in front of the bookcase staring at the picture of Gerry in his uniform. The kettle was boiling and he'd found the flask and some other things which were sitting out on the counter. He glanced over at Laurie then turned back to the photo. She went over to the counter and started to root around for the stuff to make a flask of coffee. She'd need it; she was as tired as she'd ever been. What she should be doing now was having a shower and then going to bed. She poured boiling water into the flask and dumped in a good dose of instant coffee.

She should be in her own flat telling Ed that it was over and that they needed to move on. She screwed on the lid and the cup and gave the flask a good shake. She needed to think about what on earth she'd been up to over the last wee while. She put the flask and a pint of milk and a bag of sugar into a plastic bag.

But sometimes the things you needed had to wait until other things had been sorted out. Surely, she knew that by now. Besides, there had to be a female presence in this situation. Not only to keep Gerry from being accused of something, but also to think about the things he and the boy wouldn't think of.

Gerry walked into the room holding up his kit bag in one hand and a clutch of sleeping bags in the other.

"Right. That's us."

Jamie turned to Gerry and pointed at the photo. "Who's that?"

It was obvious it was a younger version of Gerry.

Gerry grimaced. "Me."

The boy nodded. "So you were a soldier."

Gerry nodded. "I was."

"What do you do now then?" Gerry nodded his head at the door. "Come on, let's get going."

He walked out into the hall.

Laurie picked up the plastic bag. She watched the boy. His hand hovered over the photo. She knew that if she hadn't been there he'd have nicked it. He'd need some watching over. He was probably used to stealing things. She really hoped he wasn't going to cause any trouble for her and Gerry.

"Come on," she said, pointing at the door.

He nodded, wet eyed.

She thought fleetingly about giving him a cuddle but doubted he'd welcome it. "Here. Take this." She handed him the plastic bag. He didn't move but just stood, staring at her. "Go on," she said gently, "follow him."

He left the room. She glanced around, zipped the photo into her coat and followed the other two out of the flat.

* * *

The street was still deserted and Laurie started to get that post-apocalypse feeling. This situation was much more believably post-disaster than when she imagined it usually. There were all the classic ingredients for drama here: the strong, silent man, the woman who might be handy with a knife but was also prone to dramatic crying and a moody teen who will learn the meaning of life while trying to save himself, or something. Actually, Gerry was the perfect hero type. He had a fairly secret past and no real family connections. She had no idea what was going on in his head most of the time. But he had that necessary filmic sadness about him: a sort of wistful rancher cast to his face that women would fall in love with and men would admire.

Jamie was perfect as the teen runaway. He was obviously from a difficult background but he looked bright enough. He was nice looking too – quite tall and dark with sharp eyes that hinted at hidden depths. But what about her? She doubted she was leading lady material. She was too small, too normally proportioned. However, she knew she did have a steely core that could most likely be relied on in a crisis; she'd shown that she could follow the hero's lead, however daft it might seem; and she had a fairly complicated back story of her own.

Gerry walked beside them now, leading the way to a street around the corner. He stopped in front of an old Mercedes estate.

"Here we are." He put the kit bag on top of the car and fished the key out of this pocket.

Jamie stood between Laurie and the car and looked ready to lay claim to the front seat.

"Right Jamie, you're in the back. I'll sit in the front and navigate."

Jamie scowled at her but moved to the back door.

"Go ahead," said Gerry, "the doors are unlocked."

"How come you've got a Merc and you live in *that*?"

Jamie thumbed over his shoulder in the direction of Gerry's flat.

"It was my Gran's. I inherited it." Gerry walked round to the boot and chucked the kit bag in. "Get in."

Gerry and Jamie opened their doors and got into the car. Laurie stood for a second, playing for time. She looked up and down the street at the Christmas lights hanging from the lampposts and at the cars all neatly tucked in at the pavements. She could still easily walk home from here. Gerry was putting the key in the ignition. She felt something pulse through her. She wasn't sure what it was, but she knew she had to go with them, at least to see what happened.

She opened her door. The car smelled of a combination of pine and mint.

"Mmm, old ladies' handbags," she said climbing in. "Your granny kept a good smelling car."

Gerry gave a slight smile. "She never drove it."

Laurie had a picture of an old lady standing at her window staring out at her car from behind a pair of heavy damask curtains.

"Why have a car if you aren't going to drive it?" asked Jamie from the back seat.

"She must have driven it sometimes, I suppose," said Gerry as he fiddled with the controls. Warm air started to fill the car. Laurie settled into the seat.

"It's very comfortable, isn't it?" she said, starting to feel drowsy.

"Where did she drive to?" persisted Jamie.

"I don't know," frowned Gerry.

"Didn't you know her?" asked Jamie.

"Yes, of course. But, I mean, I don't know what she did with herself, do I?"

Laurie looked back at Jamie. He was staring out of the window.

"Anyway," said Laurie, sounding like a cheery mother. "Let's hit the road."

Gerry started the engine and they pulled out into the street. Laurie fell asleep almost immediately.

* * *

She woke up with her stomach lurching as the car spun round a corner. The sky was getting light and the fields they passed were empty of livestock and spotted with scraps of snow. The radio was on quietly. Laurie had no idea about classical music; she only knew the stuff featured in adverts and slow-mo sport montages. She wouldn't be able to name any of these tunes, but she appreciated them nonetheless. Gerry would know what the pieces of music would be called. She suspected he had one of those memories that held on to the names of everything. He was the sort of person you could go to to identify things. Any thing: music, books, animals.

She wondered if he was like one of those survival experts on TV who could make a meal anywhere. Presumably he'd had training in that. They'd have to train them – what if they got cut off from the rest of their troop, or whatever it was called, and they wouldn't get rescued for a while? She couldn't imagine there'd been much to forage in Afghanistan. She'd seen a few news reports over the years that made the place look like it was made of rocks. There couldn't be much sustenance there – other than goats or maybe camels, and you couldn't eat them without drawing unwanted attention to yourself. Now: the jungle, the rainforest, they were fertile places with all sorts of grubs and plants.

Give her heat over cold any day. She craned her neck to see over the upturned collar of her coat. The heating was on full blast in the car, but the hills in the near distance made her feel cold. She closed her eyes again, drowsy. Was this how hypothermia started? The music was very relaxing – she wondered how Gerry could stay awake.

"So is she your girlfriend, or what?"

Laurie kept her eyes closed.

Gerry seemed to be considering this for a moment.

"It's complicated."

The boy tutted.

She heard Gerry tapping his fingers on the steering wheel.

"So . . ." He was struggling for something to say. "Have you got a girlfriend Jamie?"

"What? And get into all that hassle? No chance."

"You're young. Give it time."

"Don't patronise me." The boy's voice was low and calm. "I've seen how getting into it with someone can fuck things up."

"Okay, okay." She'd put money on Gerry holding his hands up placatingly. "I didn't mean anything by that. You're obviously very mature for your age."

"I've had to be."

"Do you want to talk about it?"

197

"Are you interested?"

"I wouldn't be doing this otherwise would I?"

There was a pause then the boy spoke again.

"Why are you doing this?"

There was another pause and then Gerry said quietly, "I just felt like it was the right thing to do."

The boy laughed quietly. "The right thing to do?" He laughed again, more loudly and nastily. She decided to take this opportunity to wake up.

She stretched elaborately. She saw the boy in the rear view mirror. He was watching her. Christ, he was nobody's fool. He was like a cat: eyes narrowed, shoulders hunched a little. In this light his eyes were so dark they seemed all pupil.

Gerry reached across and squeezed her shoulder, relieved.

"Morning."

She smiled at him. It was nice to wake up next to Gerry. She almost told him so but thought better of it.

"Where are we?"

"Not far now." He seemed much calmer. "Does anyone want to stop for a break? There's a place coming up in a couple of miles."

Laurie's stomach cramped with hunger. She turned back to look at Jamie.

"What about you Jamie? Are you hungry?"

The boy's face was red. He shook his head, looking down at his lap.

"You must be hungry. I'm starving." Suddenly she had a thought. "God. You aren't injured are you?" She looked to Gerry quickly. "I didn't think, at the hospital, were you hurt? Are you hurt?" She felt panic rise up in her. What if he had concussion, or internal injuries? Shit! What had they done? A look of panic crossed Gerry's face too. "Gerry!" She turned round to look at Jamie again.

"No, No," the boy said, looking out of the window quite calmly. "It isn't that." He tapped his hand against the window and said almost inaudibly, "I wasn't the one who got hurt."

"Oh, thank goodness," said Laurie, slumping down a little in her seat and choosing to ignore the last thing he'd said. She really was acting like a mother now. "You had me worried there."

The boy looked at her again. "I didn't have you worried. You worried yourself."

"Alright!" she said sharply. "Whatever's happened to you, we're just trying to help. We've really gone out on a limb here." She glared at him. "Now. Do you want something to eat or not?"

He shook his head.

"Well, you're going to *have* something to eat, whether you like it or not."

Out of the corner of her eye she could see a hint of a smile on Gerry's face.

The boy was still stony faced.

She stared at him until he looked back at her. Now his face wasn't quite so set.

"I don't have any money," he said very quietly.

She felt herself soften. This must be what it was like having a child: lurching from one emotion to another and all the time susceptible to injury.

"Don't worry," She tried to reach back to touch the

boy, but he shrank away from her. She withdrew her hand hastily. "We'll sort it out."

He wouldn't look at her.

"It'll be okay Jamie. We'll sort it out."

He shook his head at his reflection in the window.

Gerry squeezed her shoulder . His face was serious but as calm as she'd ever seen it.

"Here we are," he said, nodding at a single storey building coming up on their left. It was like a big scout hut with a curved, glassed bit that came out of the side. There was what looked like a fibre glass life-sized model of a black and white cow on the roof. It looked down balefully on the car park. Gerry pulled into a space that faced the cow.

They all looked at the cow. Laurie started to laugh. "What's that all about?"

"It's a milk bar," said Gerry looking slightly hurt. "It's been here for years."

"We used to stop here for a milkshake when I was little."

They both turned to look at the boy.

He coloured. "Ages ago."

"I've never been up here before," said Laurie. "Wherever here might actually be."

"Haven't you?" asked Gerry. "We never used to go on holiday really. My dad was too busy." Inexplicably, she felt her throat thicken. She had a picture of her mum standing looking out of the kitchen window on to the back garden.

"Must have been awful," muttered Jamie.

She looked down at her hands. She felt like telling them

about her mum, but there was no point in competing for who had the most miserable parental situation. Besides, clearly he would win – otherwise they wouldn't be here, would they?

At least she was an adult; she had some control over the shape of her life.

"Come on," said Gerry. "Let's get some breakfast, eh?"

Laurie clambered out of the car and stretched. She must have slept in a weird position, because her neck felt as if it had a kink in it. The boy walked over to the side of the car park and spat over the fence into the field next door. Gerry watched him with his hands in his pockets. He pushed his shoulders back and stretched his back.

"Gerry?"

He turned to her and smiled. He looked happy. He walked round the car, still smiling, and hugged her, kissing the top of her head. She let herself relax into his woolly jumper and breathed in his smell.

"Do you think we're going to get into trouble?"

"Don't think about that just now." He squeezed her closer. "Let's just take it a day at a time, eh?"

It was easy to follow Gerry's lead.

"What we all need is some hot food."

"I agree. What's that saying about armies and empty stomachs?"

"Never a truer word." He let go of her and took a step towards the boy who was still looking out over the fields.

"Come on Jamie, let's get out of the cold."

Gerry ushered them up the steps into the timber built café. Laurie went in first.

The place was straight out of the Sixties. The walls were

panelled with wood laminate and there was a curved serving area with glass cases heated with lamps where various food items were laid out for the taking. The formica-topped tables had plastic squirty tomato sauce bottles and glass vinegar bottles on them. There were no other customers. A big clock in the shape of a tractor showed the time as nine am. She took Gerry's wrist and turned it to see the time. It was half past seven.

She pointed out the clock and Gerry glanced at his watch and smiled. "I'd imagine time's fairly irrelevant here. You two go and get a seat, I'll order."

Neither Laurie nor Jamie moved.

"Go on," he nudged the boy's shoulder. "I'll be over in a minute."

"Where would you like to sit Jamie?" Laurie asked.

He pointed, so she led the way.

"Here?" she asked standing over the centremost table.

He nodded and pointed to the ceiling. "We're right under the cow. My mum didn't like sitting here. She said it made her feel 'udderly uncomfortable'." He smiled at her. He had a lovely smile, he was really a very attractive looking boy, when he wasn't scowling.

"Parental jokes, eh?" She laughed, although her parents weren't ones for jokes generally. She wondered where it had gone wrong for Jamie. Maybe drugs or drink were involved. She wondered if there was a dad on the scene. Probably not, there rarely was these days. She felt some sympathy for the mum. Clearly it would be hard being a single parent. Lonely, too.

Laurie sat down facing the window and Jamie surprised her by taking the seat next to her. He glanced at her then pointed out of the window. The road was empty.

"It's like we're the only ones alive."

"I know. I always think that. I'm always planning what I'd do in that situation, you know, if there had been a disaster or something, if everyone else was dead and I was the sole survivor." She had spoken hurriedly, excitedly and now she looked at Jamie, embarrassed. But he was nodding.

"I make escape plans," he said to her.

"Escape plans?"

"I know, it's daft, but sometimes when I'm lying in bed I think about what I'd do if there was a tsunami and the water was rising." He was staring at her. "You know, which window I'd go out of, what I had in my room that would be useful. You know, that sort of thing . . ." He trailed off and looked down at the table top.

She reached out and touched his arm. "No, no, I totally do know. I think about that sort of thing too. Except I think mostly about . . ." She paused; she hadn't ever told anyone about this. "I think mostly about everybody else dying of something like a virus and me being the only one left."

He was nodding again. "Yeah, I sort of like that one too. I think about going into supermarkets and getting provisions and building camps and things."

Gerry approached the table. He was carrying a tray loaded down with mugs and what looked like bacon rolls.

"What are you two talking about?" He put the tray down on the table. "I was watching you from the till – looked very interesting."

"Nothing," they said in unison and then laughed.

Gerry raised an eyebrow at Laurie then started to dole out the breakfast. "This should be enough to keep you going." He handed Laurie her tea and roll. "It'll have to be – it cost a bloody bomb."

"Oh, sorry, do you want some money?" She reached into her pocket, knowing there wasn't anything in there. Not again! When this was all sorted out she was going to give Gerry back what she owed.

"No, no." He held his hands up. "Not at all, it's my treat."

They sat for a few minutes in silence. Laurie felt that the longer they sat, the less she could think of to say. It seemed as if the other two were thinking the same.

Slowly the place started to fill up with other travellers.

She looked at Jamie. "Looks like we're not the only ones left after all."

He smiled at her.

"What's that?" said Gerry. "The only ones left?"

"On nothing," said Laurie, elbowing Jamie in the ribs. It was good to build bonds, wasn't it? She could always explain to Gerry later. But Gerry looked slightly hurt so she put her hand on his forearm. He didn't look up but smiled slightly.

"So," she asked, scanning the other customers. No one seemed to be looking at them. "What's the plan here?"

"Plan?" asked Gerry.

"Yeah, you know, with Jamie."

Jamie stared out of the window.

"Well, I hadn't really thought too much about it."

"Well, Gerry," she said pointedly. "I think we need to have a wee think about what the fuck," she grimaced and

204

looked at Jamie, "Sorry Jamie, we're planning on doing here."

Gerry shrugged.

"Gerry, this isn't a see-what-happens, take-it-one-day-at-a-time, cross-each-bridge-as-it-comes type of scenario."

Neither of them seemed interested. She sighed. "Well, I tried. When we get arrested, don't say I didn't try."

"Arrested?" said Jamie. "Why would you get arrested?"

"Jamie, I'm not being funny," she said. "You can't just go around whisking kids you don't know off to the country – no matter how bad their situation is." She sounded like a teacher, but, really, somebody had to be the grown up.

"Somebody would have to give a shit for the police to be interested." Jamie looked at her glumly. "And I'm not a kid, I'm fifteen."

"I'm sure somebody is missing you." She patted his arm.

"That," he eyeballed her, "is un-fucking likely."

"Well, still . . ." She glanced around, resisting the urge to tell him to watch his language. She didn't want anyone thinking she was a bad parent. "We need to be careful, don't we?"

She tried to look around the cafe subtly to see if there was a CCTV camera.

"What are you doing?" asked Gerry.

Jamie started to laugh. "You're looking for a camera, aren't you?"

"I don't see that it's funny," said Laurie. Gerry was smiling. "Gerry. It isn't funny."

"No, you're right Laurie, it isn't funny." He smiled. "But, really? This place with a camera?"

She glanced around again at the wood panelling and the lino on the floor and at the ancient manual till. She looked at the old lady working the till. The old lady was staring into space. Probably thinking about the good old days, thought Laurie.

"Okay, fair point. But surely somebody will report you missing." The boy looked unconvinced. "What about Ed? He'll need to tell someone, won't he?"

"Hah! Wee Eddy will do fuck all." His tone was casually dismissive. "He'll be shitting himself."

Laurie glared at Jamie, "Wee Eddy? Wee Eddy? What the fuck's that supposed to mean?" She felt herself half rise up from her seat.

"Calm down Laurie. He doesn't mean anything." Gerry clamped his hand around her wrist.

"Nothing, nothing," said Jamie, scarlet. "That's what we call him, "Wee Eddy". We just think he's a bit of a . . . a bit of a tit . . ." he trailed off.

"Who's we? You and all the other kids hanging about in the street? He's just trying to *help* you." Who did this kid think he was?

He looked down at the table.

"You know, if you go around being a dick to people that are just trying to help you then you aren't going to get on very well, are you?" The boy tore his roll up in to pieces. "It's just he's only been around a few nights and he acts like he's one of us." He glanced up at Laurie then back at his shredded roll.

"Isn't that what he's meant to do? Get to know you?"

"Yeah, but . . ."

"Yeah, but what?"

"He's just a bit, you know . . ." He looked up at her and shrugged. "He goes on about gaming a lot and music and he's just trying way too hard."

"What wrong with trying?" asked Laurie.

"Nothing, I suppose, but," he looked around in the air trying to find the right words. "He's like one of those, "just call me Frank," teachers."

Laurie knew what he meant. She'd had teachers like that, trying too hard to ingratiate themselves and be cool. It was always embarrassing. She was probably so angry with him because she knew he was right about Ed.

Poor Ed. He'd be worried about what to do now: who he should phone; what her involvement was.

"That's how come I had his phone number. The youth workers don't normally give you their numbers, but he did." He looked out the window. "I don't even know why I kept it in my phone."

"It's a good job you did or we wouldn't be here," said Gerry.

The boy nodded. He didn't look convinced.

"Look. We could turn around and go back now." She looked at the boy then at Gerry. "It wouldn't be a problem, would it Gerry?"

Gerry was scowling. There seemed to be no reasoning with him.

She looked to the boy, but he shook his head.

"No."

"Are you sure? It isn't too late." She knew she sounded pathetic. She was talking too fast, too like a girl. "We'd be back in time for lunch. You could just say that you stayed at a friend's house." They should go home. They should finish their food and just get back in the car and go home and then everything would be fine.

"No," the boy said again. "I can't." He looked at Gerry. "I've come too far now."

Laurie narrowed her eyes at Gerry.

"No offence Jamie, but would you be able to give Gerry and me a minute to just have a wee chat?"

The boy looked at Gerry. "It's okay. Just go and look at the gift shop." He pointed to the far corner of the cafe where there was a display of tartan tat. He smiled and gave Jamie a fiver. "Get yourself a souvenir."

The boy took the money from Gerry slowly and nodded. As he headed over to the corner Laurie stood up and moved round next to Gerry.

"Gerry, I don't think this is a great idea. We don't know anything about this boy, do we?"

"We know he's in trouble." His face was closed.

"Gerry, to be fair, we don't actually know that."

Gerry frowned at her. "Of course he is. Teenagers don't go off with people they've just met for no reason, do they?"

"No, I suppose not. But what if he's in trouble with the police? He's not very forthcoming with the facts, is he?"

"Well, neither am I, but that doesn't seem to bother you too much." He smiled. The sudden change was breath-taking.

"Don't, Gerry."

Now he looked serious again.

"Laurie. Look, you might find this hard to understand, but there have been times in my life where I haven't done the right thing." He picked up a sugar container and tapped it on the edge of his cup. "Quite a few times."

"But Gerry, that was different. That was in a war."

"I'm not just talking about that. There have been other times where I haven't been the man I should have been." She nodded, not wanting to lose him.

"And then, here comes this," he scanned the ceiling above Laurie's head, "opportunity. Right when I'm thinking about all these things." He gripped Laurie's hand. "It's like a sign, isn't it?"

A sign? Oh God, what was he on? She would just have to humour him and hope he was just tired and a bit, what would her mother have called it? Overwrought? Overwhelmed? She tried to think of what her mother would have done in this situation. The churchy side of her would say to help someone in need – whether Gerry or Jamie needed more help she wasn't sure – but her mother would never have got into this situation in the first place. It was one thing fundraising for black babies, quite another to do unplanned social welfare stuff after the night shift.

"A sign of *what* though, Gerry?" She would just have to play it calm.

"Well . . ." He ran his hand through his hair. "It's like a chance to be a proper . . . you know . . ."

"A proper what?" Then it dawned on her. Why had it taken her this long to twig? "Gerry, you cannot just go around collecting troubled teens to make up for your own fuck ups." She felt her voice rising and struggled to bring it under control. She didn't want anyone to get suspicious.

She glanced around. There were four or five tables taken. No one seemed to be paying the slightest bit of attention to them. Most of them were staring into space not talking. One couple were quietly murmuring and passing what looked like photos back and forth. The woman at the counter was watching Laurie but, by the look of her, she'd been around long enough to have seen her fair share of domestics in here. She smiled at the woman and the woman smiled back and started to wipe a cloth over the counter.

Gerry was crying. He wasn't making a sound, his shoulders weren't moving and his face was completely still, but tears rolled down his cheeks on to the table.

She leaned into him. "Oh Gerry, Gerry, it'll be okay. We'll work out what to do when we get to the cottage, okay? Okay?" She kissed the side of his face then glanced over at Jamie. He was standing staring at Gerry. She waved him over: it was time to get going again. She had to see this thing through. She couldn't abandon Gerry now. She licked the salt water off her lips.

The Back of Nine
Sharp and Cloudless

They drove in silence. Laurie looked out of the window and watched Scotland unfold from the road to the sky. She wasn't normally one for admiring scenery, but there was something about the cold morning and brittle sky that made the landscape seem clean and untouched. You could imagine that no one had ever set foot on the hills in the distance and that no one ever would stand on them. She wondered if Jamie was thinking the same thing, but when she glanced at him he appeared to be sleeping. She stroked Gerry's arm. He didn't look at her; he just kept his eyes on the road. She stroked his arm harder, trying to get him to look at her. She moved her hand down to his thigh and stroked his thigh. She moved her hand up closer to his groin and he looked at her briefly and shook his head.

She sighed and leaned against her window.

"Is it far now?"

"No."

There were very few buildings out here and they didn't pass another car at all. What would happen if they were to break down? What if that happened and it started to snow?

"Gerry? If we were stranded, would you know what to do to save us?"

He smiled. "For a bit, yeah."

"What would you do? Tell me." She snuggled down into her seat.

"Well. Where would we be stranded?"

She waved her hand out of the window. "Here. Somewhere about here."

"We're not far from the house. I'd make my way for the house."

She shook her head, "No, no, where's the fun in that? Just imagine there is no house and there's no one else around. Just imagine it's us and you need to save us."

He took a breath. "Okay. Well, first we'd need a shelter. I take it I can't use the car in this scenario?"

"Now you're getting it."

"Okay, let's see . . . Right: shelter first. We'd need to dig in somewhere. Make an ice house if we had to. Then we'd need to secure some provisions. Catch something like a rabbit or . . ."

"A deer," said Jamie from the back. He was leaning forward. She knew he'd like this.

"Yes. Or a deer. But they're pretty hard to catch. I'd need a gun or – "

"No guns," said Laurie.

"No guns? Hmmm . . ."

"It's not a gun-type situation. You need to improvise. You may have one knife. But it's a small one."

Gerry laughed. "Okay. Small knife: one of. Well, I'd make a bow and arrow."

"Good, good. That's more like it." Laurie cosied down into her coat again and shut her eyes. "Then what?"

"I'd make a hole in the ground with a sharp stone that I'd find."

"Like it," said Laurie. "Cavemanish."

Gerry laughed again. It was nice to hear his laugh.

"What's the hole for?" asked Jamie.

"To evade capture."

"What? Are we on the run in this too?" asked Jamie.

"It's his training Jamie, he can't help himself," said Laurie from inside her coat.

"Did you have to do a lot of survival training in the army?"

"A fair bit."

"For the snow?" The boy must be leaning forward again, his voice sounded close to Laurie's head.

"For all sorts of terrains and weather situations."

"What's it like having all those people depending on you in like, life or death, situations?"

Gerry sighed. "You get used to it."

"Did you like it in the army?"

Jamie was doing a better job at getting information out of Gerry than she'd managed.

"I didn't really know anything else. I was only a few years older than you when I joined up."

"Why did you leave?"

"I'd had enough."

"What do you mean?"

"What I said Jamie," Gerry's tone was sharp. "I'd had enough."

"Alright, alright," said Jamie. "I'm only asking."

"I don't much like talking about it. That's all."

"Have you got shell shock?"

Laurie held her breath.

"Shell shock!" said Gerry. He shook his head and there was a pause before he answered. "It's not called that anymore."

"Whatever it's called now, have you got it?"

She could feel Gerry looking to her for help, but she kept her eyes closed. She wanted to know what his answer was but he was saying nothing, it seemed.

"It's called Post Traumatic Stress Disorder now," said Laurie eventually, still not opening her eyes.

"Whatever," said Jamie. "Well?"

Gerry sighed. "I don't want to talk about it," he said quietly.

"Obviously you do," pressed Jamie. "Otherwise you'd just say you didn't have it."

"Everyone who's seen action has a bit of PTSD," Gerry said quietly.

Jamie finally had enough sense to shut it. They went on in silence for a bit longer and Laurie must have dropped off because she woke to Gerry stroking her hair off her face.

"Come on Laurie."

She opened her eyes.

"We're here."

About Ten
Icy

It was a white-washed farmhouse with green painted trim around the windows and front door. A set of antlers was fixed above the front door and what looked to Laurie like a wagon wheel was leaning against the side of the house. Jamie and Laurie stood looking around while Gerry searched for a key.

"It's been a while since I was last up here. The key isn't where I expected it to be." He pushed his fringe off his face. "Give me a minute."

He disappeared round the side of the house.

"What do you think?" Laurie asked Jamie. "I bet it's bloody freezing in there."

"Not when there's a fire."

"I suppose." She shoved her hands deeper into her pockets. "At least Gerry will know how to get a fire going."

"I do as well." He toed the ground. "Gerry's not the only one around here that can do things."

"Sorry."

They waited for a few minutes. There was no sign of Gerry. The boy tutted and walked over to a window. He reached up and ran his hand along the frame.

"Nothing," he sniffed.

He walked over to the other ground floor window and repeated his action.

"A ha." He turned and held a big key out.

"How did you know that would be there?"

"I didn't. I just thought I'd try."

He turned the key in the lock and opened the door. "Are you coming?"

"Shouldn't we wait for Gerry? It's his house."

"It isn't his house. It's his mum and dad's."

"I know, but still."

"Come on, let's get the fire on."

She looked around. There was still no sign of Gerry.

"He's probably whittling a key out of a twig," she said.

"Come on," Jamie said stepping into the house.

"Okay. It is freezing."

He closed the door behind her. They stood in the hallway in front of the staircase with two closed doors: one on their left, one on their right.

"Come on – in here." Jamie opened the door on the left.

She followed him into the living room. There were a few mismatched armchairs, a display cabinet with lots of china and a big, over-laden book case. Jamie walked over to the fireplace and opened a knee high wooden box that sat next to it.

"Good." He pushed his sleeves up to his elbows. "There's stuff in here."

Laurie sat in one of the armchairs and watched the boy twisting newspapers and arranging them in the fireplace. He was humming as he worked and Laurie relaxed into the wing chair and forgot to go and tell Gerry that they'd made it into the house. The boy sat back on his heels and surveyed the little pyramid of newspaper twists. He seemed content with his work and without looking into the box by the fire, he fished around inside it until he found a box of matches. He stood up.

"Right. I'll be back in a minute."

Laurie nodded at him. She ought to ask where he was off to, but she was feeling sleepy again. He left the room. She tucked her arms into her armpits and stared at the fireplace. There was a framed picture of a dog sitting in pride of place in the middle of the mantel piece. No human pictures. Gerry's family must be one of those who cared disproportionately about their pets but were quite careless about actual humans. She picked it up and examined it under the light, angling it to make the detail clearer. It actually seemed to be a photo of an oil painting. Who paid to have an oil painting done of their dog? Somebody quite rich, obviously. She looked around the room. It was shabby, as if Gerry's parents had just used any old, left over furniture to decorate the place. The sofa and chair matched but were uncomfortable and worn. The carpet was patchy in places and an unpleasant shade of green. But the fireplace was nice and big and a roaring fire would make the place much more attractive.

"What do you think then?" It was Gerry, standing in the doorway.

"Very nice. Quite the country pile."

"Not quite." He put down the bag he was holding. "How did you get in?" He frowned. "Where's Jamie?"

"Jamie found a key and now I think he's finding some firewood." She nodded towards the fireplace.

"Oh." He looked at Jamie's work. "He's done a good job."

"You look surprised," said Laurie, feeling defensive of Jamie.

Gerry shook his head. "No. Well, I suppose I am a bit surprised."

"He probably has lots of hidden talents." She sat down but the sofa was so cold her bum was freezing. "Maybe he was a cub or a scout or something."

"Yes, probably." He leaned down and readjusted one of the newspaper twists. "The key must have been in a very obvious place."

"It was on one of the window frames."

"I should have thought of that."

"It was lucky that Jamie did."

Something flickered across his face but she wasn't sure what. He turned back to the fire.

She got up and stood as close to him as she could without touching. They stood together like that for a second and she felt the air between them contract and tingle with energy. She came up in goose bumps as if her skin strained to touch him. She could hear his breathing quicken but he made no move. They stood like that for a long minute until she became aware of Jamie waiting in the doorway. She took a step away from Gerry. "Jamie. You're back," Gerry said. He nodded at the wood the boy was carrying. "Oh good, let's get this show on the road then."

Laurie sank down into the puffy sofa and watched Jamie and Gerry get on with making the fire. They didn't speak to each other but worked together quickly and efficiently. They soon had the fire going.

218

"I suppose we'd better unpack," she said, getting reluctantly to her feet. "Is it okay if I?" She indicated the rest of the house.

"Sure," said Gerry, sinking down into the sofa.

Interesting, she thought to herself. Men gather fire, women unpack grub. She'd rather deal with food over wood any day. The other door in the hallway led to the dining room. She flicked the light on and stood for a second trying to imagine Gerry and his family here over the years. She had a shadowy image of his parents, but try as she might, nothing more than Gerry's face superimposed over where their faces should be would come into her mind. So it was on to a scene of differently sized and dressed Gerrys that she looked.

Mother sat at the seat nearest the kitchen pretending to be self deprecating about the feast before them. Father naturally sat at the head praising Mother's cleverness and a little bearded Gerry sat with his back to her, quietly minding his manners and saying all the right things. She didn't think to add siblings or other family members because she got the impression that they were a fairly self-sufficient bunch. They seemed happy enough, if a bit too mannered.

She sat down in the remaining seat and looked around the room. There were a couple of framed maps of the local area and a really quite striking oil painting of a mountain above the fire place. She didn't know much about art, but she admired the way the artist had made the mountain look ominous rather than pretty. She wondered if it was a real mountain, or if the painter had made it up completely or put together a few different places. She supposed one mountain was very similar to another really – as much as mountaineers or geography teachers might dispute it. They all went up to the sky; they were all dangerous; they all made good subjects for painting. She hoped that it was imaginary, that way it wouldn't be wrong.

"How are you getting on?" Gerry put his hand on her shoulder and she leaned her head against it.

"I'm so tired. I could go to bed right now." He stroked her head and she felt herself become unmoored, fading away to sleep.

"Not yet," said Gerry, pulling her to her feet. "A good soldier always makes a decent camp before retiring for the night." He cuddled her and she really felt as if he might have to carry her up to bed. She made no attempt to resist the sleep. Gerry must have felt her slackness because he squeezed her arms firmly and pushed her gently away, forcing her to stand.

"Come on," he said. "It won't take long. Then I'll tuck you in myself."

She followed him into the kitchen.

"Okay. The pantry's through that door, there's a little fridge in there." He pointed to a small door set into the wall. "You can see the sink, all the cupboard space etc." He swept his hand around the small kitchen. "And through there," he pointed to another door off to the left, "Is the bathroom." He opened the door. "Such as it is." She looked into the room. Very basic. An old bath with no shower. A toilet. Wooden floorboards. Walls painted white and with a scattering of mould along the wall above the skirting.

"I know," he said. "But it's better than nothing. When I was little we washed in the stream and went to the toilet in a bucket."

"Nice," she said. "So much for posh."

"Posh?" He turned to her. "Where did you get that idea from?"

"Oh I dunno, dad's a doctor, house in the country, nice accent . . ." She petered out.

He smiled. "You're right – very compelling evidence."

"You are posh though, aren't you?"

He considered for a moment. "Maybe posher than some."

"Posher than me?" She was smiling but she felt a little flare of anger.

He looked steadily at her and she felt very much younger than him all of a sudden.

"You started this. Not me."

She sighed. "Okay, you're not posh."

He laughed. "But I made that up about the bucket. We actually did it in the hats of the servants and they disposed of it."

She punched him in the arm.

"Not bad for a girl."

She punched him again, slightly harder. She had this residual feeling of anger. She wasn't sure why.

He rubbed his arm. And then hugged her. "You do in here and I'll get the bedrooms ready."

Bedrooms. She hadn't thought much about what that would mean. They hadn't properly slept together. How would this all work? She decided not to ask him and just see what happened.

Mid Morning
Becoming Milder

They all sat in the dining room drinking the last of the coffee from the thermos. Nobody had much to say and it was obvious they all needed to sleep, but nobody seemed prepared to make the first move.

"We ought to put some Christmas decorations up."

Jamie looked at Laurie as if she was stupid. "What for?"

"For Christmas." She stopped herself from adding "idiot". But it was clear she was thinking it.

"Is that a good idea?" asked Gerry.

"Why not, eh? It's good to be festive. My mum always said you should celebrate everything."

"Isn't she going to be pissed off you aren't around for Christmas?" asked Jamie.

Laurie shook her head. "She died last year, so no, not really."

She felt fleetingly guilty for forcing the boy's head down with embarrassment.

"Oh, Laurie." Gerry put his cup down. "I'm sorry, I didn't realise."

She shrugged. "Why would you?" She smiled brightly. "Anyway. What do you think?" She looked at the two of them. "Mind you, I don't know where we'd get any decorations from anyway."

"Actually. There should be some stuff in the attic." He stood up. "We used to come up here a lot for Christmas."

Laurie smiled at Gerry. He was completely relaxed now and he looked very comfortable here. All that tearful angst from back at the hospital was gone. He wasn't frightening at all.

He pulled Laurie to her feet. "I think we should all have a nap first and think about that later."

She followed him out of the room.

"I'm staying here," Jamie called after them.

"Suit yourself," Laurie muttered. She didn't care whether the boy heard her or not.

Gerry led the way up the curved staircase and she stopped behind him when he paused at the half landing and looked out of the window there.

She sat on the edge of the window sill and looked out with him. You could see a run-down outhouse building, the garden, the little slopes that bordered the yard area and the track that cut between the fields and led to the main road down the hill. A tour bus passed but it was impossible to make out if there were any tourists on board. Surely not at this time of year. It was too cold for fair-weather trippers and not cold enough for winter sport people. Plus, who'd want to have a holiday over Christmas? Wouldn't most people want to stay at home with their families or friends? But then, what was she doing here? For God's sake – going on the run with a troubled teenager and an ex-soldier with some sort of post-trauma thing. Hardly Christmas card material. But what did she have to stay for at home? A clearly soon-to-be (if not already) ex-boyfriend, and, at best, uninterested family and a crummy flat.

She realised that Gerry was staring at her and she turned to him. He was looking at her very intently, but not in a creepy way. She tried to pay attention to what he looked like rather than vaguing out completely.

She looked at his dark eyes and tried to not blink. He had really nice eyes and was, in fact, much more handsome that you might think on first seeing him. His eyebrows were very good – not too bushy and a nice arched, but not feminine, shape. His nose was manly but not *old*-manly. And although he would look far better with a proper shave, he was attractive. She was attracted to him. She hadn't really thought properly about that until now. Everything was so casual and almost accidental before that she hadn't really thought too hard about things. Well, she'd thought about other things. But now, here she was standing a few steps away from a bedroom that surely they were en route to and they'd run off together to help the boy downstairs and it was quite romantic really.

She wasn't one for romance normally. Not the kind of romance that she was supposed to be into anyway. It would have been nice to get flowers or something from Ed, but at the same time, she would have known he was just doing what characters on TV did for each other. It wouldn't have been a gesture that he'd thought up himself. For what must have been the hundredth time in the last week she thought, poor Ed. He was trying his best, but he just didn't have a clue. And there were lots of other girls who'd really appreciate him – or at least wouldn't feel like killing him daily, hourly. She thought of Marie at the hospital. She'd be perfect for Ed. She made a mental note to get them together after Christmas.

Gerry stroked her face and she realised that once again she'd been thinking of something else.

She shut her eyes as Gerry leaned forward and kissed her. She tried to imagine that her mind was a big blackboard and that she was giving it a nice clean wipe. She leaned into the kiss but her mind started getting all scribbly again so she wiped it and wiped it, but it wouldn't stay clean. She opened her eyes and Gerry was staring at her as he kissed her. She pulled back.

"Right. So what's going on here?" she asked.

"Well . . ." He flicked his head over his shoulder towards two shut doors. Presumably bedrooms. Then he dropped his hand from her shoulder and his face went smooth and unreadable.

She felt her breath get jerky and she clenched her fists. Tears threatened and she thought how unfair it all was. She just wanted to go through life unthinkingly. She just wanted to say to herself, yeah, good idea, just do it! But she never could. She could never just jump in. There were always thoughts that stopped her in her tracks and made her freeze.

Well. Not today – today she was going to get on with things. She forced herself to smile at Gerry.

"I'm sorry," she said. She took a breath. "I just feel a bit weird." He didn't say anything, just looked at her steadily, kindly enough, but not too kindly. He wasn't going to do any of this for her.

"It's probably lack of sleep."

"Probably." He half turned. "You take the room on the left. Jamie and I will sort something out later."

"No!" She steadied her voice. "No. There's no need for that. I just need a nap, I'll be fine later."

"I'm not bothered, Laurie."

But he was. He was bound to be. And she was bothered too, she realised.

"No, really, Gerry." She grabbed at his arm. "I'll be fine later."

"We'll see." He smoothed her hair briefly. "Just have a rest. It's been a big day."

He gave her a little nudge towards the bedroom and then went downstairs. She opened the door to the room. It was low ceilinged but large and held an elaborately carved double bed which was covered with pillows. She sighed and bent to unzip her boots. She would have liked to brush her teeth and have a wash before she slept, but there was no way she was going downstairs now; not with Jamie sitting there, watching her; no way with Gerry being nice and polite but thwarted all the same. She just couldn't face it.

She sank down into the bed and kept sinking. The bed was virtually springless, it was so soft. If there was one thing she hated, it was a soft bed. There was no way she'd be able to sleep in it. She got up again and went to try the other bedroom. Much smaller, this bedroom was instantly cosier. It had two single beds, but she didn't care. They could always push the beds together if need be. All she wanted now was to sleep and feel better. She crawled under the chenille bedspread and pulled the cover up around her face. She lay like that, trying to will herself to sleep, but it was too bright in the room. She should have closed the curtains, but she couldn't be bothered to get out of bed again. She pulled the cover over her face, but felt suffocated. After a bit of fidgeting she managed to contrive a sort of eye mask with the blanket that left her nose and mouth uncovered. It was still too bright though. She took off her jumper and then folded it over the top half of her face. Much better and it smelled better too. God knows what Gerry would think if he came in and saw her sleeping like this. But who cared? Just as she fell asleep she thought she heard the door open but she was too far gone.

Mid Afternoon
Dreich with Sudden Showers

He was lying next to her when she woke up. He slept silently, turned away from her towards the door. She no longer had the cover pulled around her face but was now nice and toasty with Gerry close. He'd taken off his jumper and just had his T shirt on. She lifted the blankets to see what else was happening and was glad to see he still had his boxers on. Her legs felt restricted and itchy in her jeans so she climbed out of bed to remove them. As she kicked her jeans off her ankles, Gerry stirred and she stopped still, frozen, keen to get back into bed and curl into him without him waking. After a second or two she carefully lifted the sheet again and slid into the bed.

She hesitated before wrapping herself around Gerry's back but, in the spirit of just doing things, she went ahead. With the two of them squeezed into the bed, she didn't have much choice anyway. Her face fitted nicely into his left shoulder and she breathed slowly trying to match his breaths. His T shirt smelled slightly of the wood fire and she could faintly make out Gerry's own smell which was warm and pleasant. She sighed, feeling properly relaxed for the first time in a week, weeks even. It was so much easier when you could just have what you needed and nobody was trying to make you say or do more than that.

They lay like that for some time until Laurie became gradually aware that Gerry was awake. He said nothing, but she could feel the change in the air. She felt electrified and caught; her finger tips tingled and itched.

She wasn't sure whether she should feel relieved or annoyed when she heard a gentle tap at the bedroom door. The boy said nothing, just tapped quietly again. She knew he'd probably give up if they stayed silent, but it didn't seem fair to pretend they were asleep. That was the sort of thing parents would do.

"Is everything okay Jamie?" asked Gerry without moving.

"I was just thinking it might be a good idea to go for a walk."

Laurie groaned. But before she could protest that it was too cold, Gerry was yanking the blankets off the two of them. He sat up and looked at Laurie.

"We'll be down in a minute. Grab a warm coat from the boot room."

He leaned down and kissed her. After a moment Laurie pulled him down on top of her, suddenly desperate. He pressed his weight against her and she felt the air go from her, making her charged and breathless.

Then he leapt up, grabbed his jumper and headed for the door.

"You coming?"

"What?" She sat up in the bed, furious. "What are you playing at?"

He smiled at her. "There's time enough Laurie."

She turned from him, blushing furiously. She'd be fucked if she was going to look at his stupid, smug face now.

"You sure you don't want to come with us?"

She ignored him. He closed the door.

She lay in the bed thinking about how she was going to get home on her own from here. She cursed the day she'd met Gerry and wondered aloud how she could have been so stupid. Her anger ebbed away as she heard the heavy front door slam and she realised that she was in the house alone. The dark green walls of the bedroom pressed in on her as she started to think that a house as old as this in such an isolated spot had surely had many deaths within its walls. Maybe even in this bed. She sat up and looked at the bed. There was no headboard so it was hard to tell how old it was without raising the bed skirts and having a look underneath. She took a deep breath and tried to steady herself. She knew rationally that being fearful of ghosts was ridiculous and childish, but she couldn't help it.

Once she'd started down the track of thinking about spirits it was hard to get away from it. When she was a little girl she'd had frequent nightmares and had developed routines surrounding bedtime and middle of the night toilet visits. Her parents had been thoroughly dismissive of any talk about ghosts and had told her repeatedly that there were plenty of real things to be scared about without making things up, but it made no difference. She was still afraid to look in the mirror late at night just in case somebody scary was looking over her shoulder.

For weeks after her mother's death, she'd been convinced that her mother was sitting in the chair by the window watching her in her bed. It didn't matter how much she reassured herself during daylight hours that there was no reason why her mother would wish her harm, when it was the middle of the night she was petrified. She couldn't move, her hands clamped themselves shut and she strained through the dark to try and make out her mother's face. She reasoned that if her face was happy or even calm, she could live with her mother showing up and sitting quietly on a nightly basis. But she couldn't make out anything other than a shadowy shape hunched in the chair. She couldn't even be remotely sure that it was her mother rather than some other dead person. But she read somewhere that it was quite common for the recently bereaved to think they saw the deceased. But who was to say that it wasn't relatively common because the dead really did come back to check on their loved ones? Why should rational scientist-types have first dibs on explanations? What was that saying about heaven and earth and not knowing everything?

Still, thinking about things sensibly would be good in the night or in strange old houses in the country. She dressed quickly and walked as fast as she could out of the room and down the stairs. She wasn't going to run – partly because she could just see herself falling down the stairs and breaking her neck and also, more importantly, she wasn't going to give any ghost the satisfaction of seeing her running scared.

Slowly and with a great show of calm she turned the handle of the front door and stepped outside. She saw Gerry and the boy making their way up a slope that led to the tallest hill that stood behind the cottage. No doubt it had some unpronounceable Gaelic name but even if she knew what it was called, she'd still be inclined to think of it as The Tallest Hill. It was much more straightforwardly descriptive than Fairy Dell or Place of Mist or whatever its Gaelic name translated to. Regardless of what it was called, it was pretty high. She knew it wasn't a mountain, but if she got to the top of it, it would be the closest she'd ever willingly get to a mountain.

The notion of climbing things because they were there was ridiculous to her. Ridiculous and manly. She doubted any woman would ever say that. Any *normal* woman anyway. A woman might say it if she was trying to impress some mountaineer, but she still thought it unlikely. It would sound silly coming from a woman anyway. You did things because they were there if those things were washing or making the dinner or picking up a found ten pound note. Not climb a dangerous, near vertical bit of rock that was likely snowy or shrouded in mist and required a significant amount of planning to tackle. Planning, equipment and money to tackle. Definitely not something a woman would waste her energy on.

Because it was there! Ridiculous. She was already out of breath and questioning her sanity and she was only about a fifth of the way up a tiddly little hill!

Jamie looked back at how far he and Gerry had come and when he saw her struggling up behind them she watched an expression that said *for-fuck's-sake* cross his face and then he turned his back on her and kept going, not bothering to alert Gerry to her attempt to catch up. She couldn't even muster the puff to yell; she just got her head down and pushed on. It didn't seem at all far and yet it was taking her an age to get anywhere near them. She decided to try distraction as a means of moving her on. She thought about what she could make to eat later, but that made her realise how hungry she was. Then she tried to enjoy the nature around her as she knew lots of other people would gladly do in this situation but there wasn't much to look at unless she stopped and looked back at where she'd come from and she wasn't at enough of an elevation for the view to be any different to what she'd seen out of the cottage window.

She looked down at her feet and tried to focus on the small things. But the small things consisted of grass, rocks – some small, some bigger- and occasionally, what appeared to be shit. Whether it was from sheep or cows, she couldn't tell. She was no naturalist, clearly. Although, if she thought about it, it probably was sheep shit, because it didn't look like your typical cow pats as it was too small and sort of knobbly. For fuck's sake, she thought to herself, this is what she was reduced to: a nice enough looking young woman in the prime of her life with a degree (admittedly an Ordinary arts degree wasn't going to light up the universe, but still, it was something), her health (she needed to do something about her lung capacity judging by how tricky this was for her) and her whole life ahead of her. And she was doing *what* a couple of days before Christmas? Hanging out with other Bright Young Things in a throbbing Metropolis somewhere planning exciting events? No. She was sweating up a hill (not even a fucking mountain!) in a sort-of chase for a man who was vague about himself and a teenager who was vaguer still if not actually a downright liar about his circumstances, in order not to be alone in a probably haunted, definitely damp and bloody freezing so-called cottage in the middle of nowhere! The last part of this thought rang very clearly in her mind, filling her with a hot, white light that stopped her dead in her tracks.

She clenched her fists and screamed once, very loudly, very theatrically. At once she was both exhilarated and mortified. She didn't need to look at Gerry and Jamie to know they'd stopped and spun round to look at her. Probably there were sheep straining all over the hillside to see what had happened. She closed her eyes, took a deep cleansing breath through her nose and let it out slowly through her mouth. She half expected to open her eyes to see Gerry running down the hill towards her, but when she opened her eyes Gerry and Jamie were still in the same place. In fact, Jamie immediately carried on upwards whilst Gerry looked back, one hand on his hip and what might very well have been a look of amusement on his face.

Bastard, she thought, he isn't even shocked! I'm a joke to him. She looked down to the house and, remarkably, it was further than she'd thought. She couldn't face being the big, moody baby again so she set off towards Gerry who at least, seemed to be waiting for her.

It took a few minutes to march up to him. Almost everything was easier to do when you had some anger pushing you on. Sometimes she pictured a big wheel in her head like the one on the TV show Wheel of Fortune, except the wheel in her head was called Wheel of Fury and it would spin and spin (making her feel angrier still) until it came to a halt on any one of a hundred things that made her furious. There were some topics (bosses, her ongoing lack of ready cash, other people's general stupidity) that always had a place on the wheel and there were also weekly – sometimes daily – hot topics.

At her old work there would usually be something happening to drive her mad. Like her boss deciding he was going to make tits of all of them in an effort to increase sales. It was all a bit too much for Laurie. The first time they'd done one of the so-called "sales games" she'd tried hard and had even, horrifyingly, done a very enthusiastic air punch when she'd made enough. That was actually the worst thing, when she realised that not only had she done what she'd been told in a respectable time, but that she'd on some very basic level loved it. That was the first time she'd seriously considered killing herself in a toilet stall during her lunch break.

She shuddered. She was so out of there.

"I thought you weren't coming," said Gerry when she reached him.

"For fuck's sake Gerry, can't I change my mind?"

He smiled annoyingly. "Of course you can." He gave her a hug. "I'm glad you did."

There wasn't much she could say to that so she knuckled down to the pace that Jamie had set.

"Onwards and upwards," she said to Gerry.

It wasn't exactly that it was hard work getting up the hill. It wasn't like actually climbing something: looking for toe holds; testing how much your arms could take. It was just the ongoing pushing upwards that did you in. That, and that it was hard to tell how far you'd come and how far you had left to go. She kept looking back for the first twenty or so minutes but there was little change to gee her on. She gave up looking backwards and just let her mind drift. She wished she had a stereo with her or a biscuit or a book about her someplace. That way she could promise herself something to keep going. But she had nothing, no treat or incentive to keep her motivated. All she had was the sure knowledge that she couldn't go back down until she'd reached the top. There was just no way she was prepared to lose face to that extent.

She saw Gerry shooting her looks now and then to check if she was okay. He was probably worried that they were going to need mountain rescue. Imagine that, needing mountain rescue to be taken down from a hill! How mortifying! She kept on powered by bloody mindedness as per usual. She didn't like Gerry looking at her in that concerned way. It reminded her of the look on people's faces after her mum was diagnosed and then again when she'd actually died.

It was people being nice to you that did you in. It was like they were trying to make you cry. If you cried, they knew they were okay. They knew no one they knew had died or was dying. They knew they themselves weren't dying. It made some people feel special to proffer kindness to the bereaved. They were the types that liked to tell you some sort of pearl of wisdom that had served them well. Served them well under what circumstances? She'd like to know. Served them well under the circumstances of having to basically parent your parents when one of them was dying? As Jamie had said earlier, un-fucking-likely!

The truth was that no one really knew what it was like unless it had happened to them. Some people made a good guess, but the phrase "I know how you feel" should be torn from the English language. It meant so little and caused a million repeated nips of pain for those who had to listen to it.

God, where was all this bitterness coming from?

She stopped and looked around.

It was all very pretty in a photograph kind of way. She knew that people all over the world would love to see what she was seeing now, but it left her cold. Give her a city any day. She preferred the moving landscape of people and cars and signs and adverts and stray bits of rubbish and animals. All this hill and grass and empty nature made her feel too big and human. She liked the picture to keep changing. All this static beauty made her feel emptied out and switched off. She liked to think about people as they passed: what they were wearing; who they were talking to; where they had come from; where they were going to. She preferred to be a part of a flickering card trick of one thing after another after another.

"It's beautiful, isn't it?" asked Gerry, standing on a rock one leg bent at the knee. He had one elbow on the knee and was surveying the land as if he was filming a documentary.

She nodded. You couldn't actually disagree with the observation. But there were all different types of beauty, and Gerry was welcome to his type. She just hated the idea that if you didn't like the peace and quiet of nature that you were somehow less worthy, more shallow – someone not capable of stillness. As if stillness was so great. Who ever accomplished anything sitting around? What an annoying notion. These fake-buddhist books that you could buy all over the place had a lot to answer for. Feng Shui! Meditation! Yoga! These things were all fine where they belonged, but did they belong in Scotland? She thought not.

"Are you okay Laurie?"

He was staring at her. Intently, but kindly and not in an annoying way. He was nice, Gerry. She should cut him some slack.

He came back down towards her. She felt like lying down and making him take over, make some decisions, be the grown up. He'd manage fine. But the ground looked very uncomfortable and, in fact, it would be hard to find a relatively flat bit to get comfy on. Gerry was standing on a lumpy bit of grass that gave him half a foot of extra height to look down at her from. She wondered if it was a flattering angle to be looked at. It wasn't flattering for Gerry to be looked up at from. But nobody looked good from underneath. Not even models. She'd seen that on one of those reality modelling shows about which angles were good and which ones you must never let a photographer snap you from.

Gerry climbed down from the bump and stood next to her.

"What are you thinking about?"

"Isn't the woman meant to ask that?"

He waited patiently for her to answer.

She shook her head. "You don't want to know."

"I do. I wouldn't have asked otherwise."

He looked at her so calmly that she couldn't help herself.

"Lots of things: models, nature, stupid questions, stillness, death, flattering angles."

"Death?"

She looked down.

"Are you thinking about your mum?"

238

She closed her eyes, but it was too late. She felt the wetness gather behind her eyelids. She opened her eyes slightly to let the tears out but it was as if that only encouraged them. She gave up and just let herself cry and Gerry grabbed her and held her. He said nothing, just held her up. He must have realised that she was close to letting herself drop. She knew that if she did drop, there was no way she'd be walking back down again by herself.

Gradually the tears stopped. She was almost sad she couldn't just keep going and going. She loved that feeling of empty, numbed exhaustion that came after a long and wringing cry. But this seemed to be a quick tip of a cry. Cleansing, but not quite rejuvenating.

She sighed and Gerry gave her a squeeze and set her back on her feet.

"Come on, we'd better catch up with Jamie." She frowned. "Where is he?"

There was no sign of the boy.

"Shit," said Gerry before darting off up the hill and around behind a crop of pine trees.

"Fuck," said Laurie, suddenly feeling very ill-equipped.

Later Still
Drab and Drizzly

"Gerry! Gerry, wait!" She struggled after him as he powered up the hill. He paused long enough for her to almost catch up with him, no doubt fearing that if he didn't, she'd disappear too and then he'd have two fuck-wits to search for.

"He can't have gone far, surely," she said, feeling panic knock about in her chest.

He looked back at her briefly, but all she could see on his face was worry. She realised he was muttering to himself.

"What? What are you saying Gerry?"

"I'm saying: how hard can it be?"

He sounded furious.

"What do you mean? How hard can what be?"

"I always manage to lose sight of the obvious thing." He was talking to himself, not her.

He had the look about him again that he'd had in the hospital. Only now she was responsible for him. She hadn't been able to walk out of the hospital and never look back. Now if she went off (if she was even able to go off, which she doubted) anything could happen. If they did, it would be at least partly her fault. What was she thinking though? Things had already gone to shit. It was

240

all much too late. She should have told Gerry earlier. "Gerry, Gerry," she clutched at his sleeve. "There's something I need to tell you."

He shook her off. "Not now Laurie."

"No, no, you don't understand." She pulled at him again, harder.

He stopped and turned to her. "What?" He looked even more unhinged now, if that was possible.

"Jamie told me that someone died in the accident he was in."

"*What* accident?"

"The accident that brought him to the hospital, obviously."

He shook his head, clearly confused.

"Why did you think he was at the hospital?"

"I don't know, I thought he was just there to meet Ed or something."

"At that time in the morning? It's hardly business hours, is it?"

"Well? What happened?"

Gerry stopped and put a hand up to the side of his head. "I don't know, he wouldn't tell me anything much."

Laurie stopped walking. "Anyway, why didn't you ask some bloody questions, eh?" He stared at her. "If you had we might not be in this mess."

His shoulders dropped. "I know, I know. It's all my fault. I just can seem to get it together." His voice was whiny and irritating.

"You're right." She nearly jabbed him in the chest. "If you hadn't been so hell-bent on being the big," she paused, "saviour of the piece, this would never have happened."

241

"Saviour?" He stopped and blinked at her. "What's that supposed to mean?"

"You know what I mean."

She backed away slightly. The expression on his face was close to being frightening. But she went on, she couldn't help herself.

"Obviously things went wrong in the army." She said. "Obviously you fucked up when you were younger." She looked away, knowing she was going too far. "But you can't spend the rest of your life trying to atone for that stuff. It doesn't work like that."

Now he was on the verge of crying again. But she had to be tough.

"Oh, for fuck's sake, we aren't going to get anything sorted if you're just going to get all self-pitying." She strode past him. "Come on," she said over her shoulder.

Why was she always the one who had to keep it together? At what point was she allowed to be a mess and just really let go? She had her moments, but that's all they were – moments. She had a feeling that if she ever did have some sort of mental breakdown and ended up on a secure ward, within hours she'd be patting the nurses and saying, "there, there," to the doctors.

There was nothing for it but to press on.

There were various little knots of trees as the hill ascended. Jamie could be in any one of them, watching them and laughing. Or maybe he'd gone off in a fit of pique and was now regretting his actions, but too embarrassed to show himself. Or maybe he wanted to come back to them but was injured or unconscious.

"Okay Gerry, focus." She stopped and looked back

at Gerry. "What would you have done in the army?"

"I would have sent some privates on to scout the area out and I would have used the detailed maps I would have been issued with."

"Your tone is not helpful."

He scanned and rescanned the hill.

"What are we going to do now?"

He didn't seem to be listening. "Jesus, it's getting dark. What was I thinking even setting off at this time "Fuck. We aren't even going in a straight ascent. Fuck. I'm not even following basic training."

She needed him to calm down and get focussed. "Look. It's the stress, isn't it?"

"What?"

"I said it's the stress." She made her voice calm and steady.

"That's what it's for, Laurie."

"What what's for?" What was he on about?

"The training."

She looked at him blankly.

"It's so you don't have to fucking think under great stress. It's all about automatic responses, muscle memory. I mean, this is nothing."

"Okay, okay." They couldn't afford for him to lose it at this point. "But what are we going to do now?"

He took a deep, steadying breath. "Call to him." He cupped his hands around his mouth and yelled the boy's name a few times. There was no response. "Not panic."

"Should we split up? Should I head back?" She looked up and down the hill "Should I stay here?"

What was the best thing to do? It was getting dark very quickly.

"No. We stay together." Gerry walked on again, calling Jamie's name into the dusk.

At first Laurie was too shy to call as well, fearing her voice would sound pathetic, but she soon gave it a go. As expected, her shouting was rubbish – sounding like Penelope Pitstop or some second rate horror actress. She couldn't even yell convincingly.

She scanned and rescanned the horizon. She willed him to show himself. Even if he was a bit injured it would be okay. Not too injured. Nothing spinal or in the head area. But a sprain, even a broken leg or dislocated arm. She could see that being okay.

"Come on, come on," she muttered to herself, stomping up the hillside. What had they done? Who the hell takes some kid from a hospital and runs off with them? Regardless of what sob story you got from them, regardless of how you might feel about the situation – there were proper channels for this sort of thing: police officers, doctors, social workers. They couldn't all be useless, could they? There must be lots of effective, kind, organised professional people making sure that children weren't abandoned or murdered by callous or hapless parents.

Who were she and Gerry to think that they knew better? And now what had happened? They'd gone and bloody lost this child. Instead of being the heroes of the hour – plucking a child from abuse, riding off on a white charger to a warm and loving foster family – they would be the villains.

Gerry was tramping up the hill in a zig-zag shape. She

hurried after him as best she could. It would be typical if she got herself lost.

Then she saw a flick of something. It was hard to tell in the thickening twilight. It was probably a rabbit or a sheep or something. She strained hard to make out the movement at the edge of a stand of trees.

"Look, is that something up there?" she asked, pulling at Gerry's sleeve.

"No."

"No, it is." She pointed up repeatedly, uselessly. "Look!" Gerry couldn't make anything out. "Look!" She pulled at his sleeve again.

"I am. There isn't anything." He shook her off.

"Look harder!"

The boy came into focus as he moved towards them. His face became visible as he stumbled over the loose rocks and Laurie recognised the fear and gathering shame. He sat down heavily.

A little "oh!" escaped from Laurie. They both rushed towards him but he stood up again holding a hand out to show he was okay.

There was no point in telling him off. Probably the last little while had been punishment enough. She knew she would have imagined all sorts if she'd been alone on the verge of darkness on a hill in winter. All sorts of things.

"Jamie!" yelled Gerry.

"Don't," she stayed Gerry with a little nip on his arm. "Don't say anything. Don't frighten him."

Jamie jumped down from a little rocky outcrop above where she and Gerry had stopped. He stood silently, waiting for his talking to.

She put an arm around the boy's shoulders and he suffered the touch for a long minute. She could feel his heart banging and wondered if he could feel hers.

Then he stepped away and started to walk back down the hill. There was no need to say anything.

Gerry stared after the boy, his face knotted in thought. Perhaps now he was realising they had to get in the car and take him home. Get shot of him immediately. Then he set off after Jamie who was making quick work of the rest of the hill.

Again, Laurie followed.

Evening
Clouds Gathering

They managed to maintain their silence until they were inside the cottage. Then Gerry started up.

"What were you thinking?" he asked, his voice much too loud in the little hallway and his height making him seem to loom over the others.

Jamie wasn't going to be cowed. He squared up to Gerry, his hands fisted. "What were *you* thinking?"

Gerry's shoulders dropped down a little. He shook his head. "Just to go for a walk." He opened the door to the living room as he spoke.

"Not then," the boy said.

"What?"

Gerry and the boy stared at each other. Neither seemed able to back down.

Laurie touched Gerry on the arm; he obviously couldn't think straight. "At the hospital, Gerry."

"You said you were in trouble." Gerry said. "I wanted to help you."

Jamie snorted. "You wanted to help me?"

Laurie glanced between the two of them. Gerry looked exhausted and Jamie's face had an unpleasant sneer.

"Come on in here," Laurie said, ushering them into the

living room. "There's still a bit of a fire left." She nudged Gerry. "Come on, let's get warmed up."

Neither Gerry nor Jamie moved. Gerry stared into the fire and the boy stared at Gerry. The boy obviously had more to say but she couldn't be bothered trying to get it out of him.

Why did teenagers have to make everything about themselves all the time?

"Look. We're all knackered." She put her hand on the boy's elbow and he stared down at her hand, forcing her to drop it. She persevered. "Things will look better in the morning."

The boy smirked.

"Really Laurie? Things'll really look better in the morning?" His tone couldn't have been any more sarcastic. He sounded like a teenage caricature on a comedy show.

"Sometimes Jamie," she said, trying hard to sound reasonable and patient, "people say things because they happen to be true."

"Whatever." That tone! It was so slappable.

It was hard trying to like him, he wasn't exactly easy company. She was fast coming to the realisation that the problems he said he was having at home were probably because he was such a little shit. Still. She was in this situation now and falling out with him wasn't going to help anyone. Perhaps if she tried to imagine he was a difficult customer at work; that might help. She had received some training on difficult customers, but it was so vague as to be pretty much useless and what she used to do was hang up on them and then pretend she was still speaking to them very politely so that her supervisor wouldn't know.

Anyway, Jamie was as sharp as anything. He'd know she was patronising him straight away and it would only cause more trouble. She rubbed her eyes trying to think of the best thing to do. Gerry was standing, shoulders slumped, in front of the fire. The boy looked at him with undisguised irritation, then bent to the fire and started poking about and blowing on to the little flames he eked out.

"Good stuff Jamie." She knew she sounded like a Brown Owl, but she couldn't help it. "Why don't I get some food together then we can have a chat. OK?" Gerry didn't look at her but just kept looking at the fireplace. To be fair, Jamie turned and nodded very seriously. She had to try and remember that he was only fifteen, just a kid. This had to be a very weird situation for him, being in the company of two complete strangers in a strange place, especially at this time of the year.

"Okay." She stood with her hand on the door. "Will you be okay?"

Gerry nodded, looking at her for a moment. The boy nodded too and slumped back in the chair, eyes closed.

"Are you sure?"

The boy's face creased into a tough guy sneer, but he still didn't open his eyes. "Obviously."

She walked out of the room before she did something rash.

In the kitchen Gerry had unpacked the few items of food they'd managed to scavenge from his flat. There were two tins each of beans and chopped tomatoes. There was also a packet of instant potatoes and a bag of porridge.

"Ace," she muttered to herself. She rooted around in the

cupboards for more stuff, eventually finding some tins of soup. There were two vegetable soups and one minestrone. She opened them up and dumped them into a stock pot and put the stove on. While that heated up she leaned her elbows on the window sill and looked out of the window. It was pretty much black outside now and she couldn't make out much except for the edge of Gerry's granny's car which was parked at the side of the house and the shape of the outbuilding and the ominous looking outline of the woods. She strained to make out individual trees, but it was useless. There was just the darkness of the sky and the darker still mass of the trees. She had an instinctive fear of the woods at any time of day – never mind at night. The problem with woods was you had no idea what was going on in there. The first few trees might seem safe enough, but who knew what was lurking within?

"What are you looking at?" Jamie was standing next to her. She'd been so intent on thinking about what was going on outside that she'd paid no attention to what was going on in here. She felt wrong footed, as if she'd been caught doing something wrong.

"The woods." She nodded towards them.

He squinted out at them. "I can't see anything."

"No. Neither could I."

They stood staring out into the unseeable trees. After a moment, she said, "What do you think's going on in there?"

She watched their thin reflections in the window and saw him turning towards her. He was smiling – this was a variation on the last person on earth thing.

"Bears, stags, prehistoric beasts."

She nodded. "Yeah. And hobos, lost children, aliens."

He laughed. "Bigfoot."

"Yeah. Bigfoot."

He smiled shyly at her. She frowned. "Why did you go off like that?"

He shrugged. "I just got further ahead of you two and I wanted to just," he sighed, "sit down on my own for a bit."

"It's dangerous going off like that when it's getting dark."

"I know."

"We were worried, Jamie." She was trying to keep her voice concerned and not annoyed.

He shrugged again. "I was fine though."

"You didn't look very fine."

His face clouded. "What would you know? You don't even know me. Neither of you do."

She decided to be patient. "Would you like to talk about why you were at the hospital?"

He looked down at his hands which were leaning on the counter top next to Laurie.

"Come on Jamie. A problem shared and all that." She shouldn't push him. That tactic never worked well on TV. She should let him open up slowly, confident that he would be listened to. He'd feel better if he talked about the accident. She had to keep in mind that his friend had died.

She nudged him gently with her elbow. He glanced up at her and then down at his hands again. He moved his hand a little closer towards Laurie's, almost touching her.

Laurie could feel her breath slowing as she considered what to do now. He didn't move his hand and he didn't look at her.

She took a step towards the stove and stirred the soup which wasn't even bubbling.

"This will take forever," she said, lifting the pot to see if the ring was even on. It was, but barely. She started to turn back to the window, but Jamie blocked her way. He stood so there was no way she could move past him without touching him.

"Excuse me Jamie," she said with great politeness.

He didn't move. He was about the same height as Ed, but broader. If you were to superimpose Ed's head on to Jamie's body, you wouldn't think of it as a child's body – in fact, Ed would look much better for Jamie's body. It would make him seem more manly.

There was no room for her to step backwards because of the stove.

"Jamie," she said, still calmly.

"What?" he said, leaning towards her as if to kiss her.

She gave him a firm little push as if her were a puppy. He stepped back, his hands held palm first in front of himself.

"God, I thought you were into it!" He was acting as if she had offended him.

"What! No you didn't, you couldn't possibly have." She didn't want to cause any trouble, but this was getting away from her.

"Why not?" he asked, the peevish tone of his voice much more like a child's now.

"Because, obviously, I'm much older than you."

"You're nearer to my age than you are to his." He smiled as if he'd gained something.

"But that still doesn't mean anything." She shuddered. "God, you're fifteen. It wouldn't even be legal."

"So you mean if I was older, it would be possible."

"God, no! Don't put words in my mouth."

Now she was flustered and he was a cocky young man again.

She took a deep breath. "Jamie, I can only imagine that this is because of the," she paused, "unusual circumstances." She had to get things back onto an appropriate track quickly. She could see he had given up but was too embarrassed to make things right. It must be shit being a boy and being led around all the time by sex.

"Anyway." She made an effort to sound completely normal. She'd have to try her family's tactic of pretending unpleasant scenes had never happened. "Back to what we were talking about."

He smiled. Thank God, she thought, he wasn't holding a grudge.

"What? You mean hobos and aliens?"

He was going to be really attractive when he was older, you could see it in him. But she'd have to be careful not to be touchy feely with him again.

"Ha ha," she said, showing him everything was A-Okay.

"I think the soup's ready," he pointed behind her, his arm extended so that he touched her upper arm with the side of his forearm. He held his arm there and she stood and narrowed her eyes at him. He nodded at the stove. "Watch it doesn't burn."

He withdrew his arm and, smiling at her broadly, he walked out of the kitchen.

"Little shit," she muttered to herself.

"I heard that," he called to her from outside the door.

For fuck's sake. Who was the adult here?

She found a tray, put three bowls onto it and ladled in the soup concoction. It would have to do. She ran the tap for a while until the water was completely clear then filled three glasses. She found spoons and chucked them on to the tray and picked it up, being careful not to spill anything. She'd overfilled both the bowls and the glasses and navigating through two heavy doors and across the uneven wooden floors was going to be challenging. Clearly no one would be making an appearance to help her.

As she neared the living room there was no clue as to what the atmosphere was like between Gerry and Jamie. At least arguing gave you something to work with: a role to fill, a side to take. But silence was difficult.

She bumped the door open with her hip. The two of them were raking through a big old cardboard box. They seemed companionable enough and she felt a weary relief.

"Here we go boys." She put the tray down carefully on the coffee table. "And not a drop spilled," she said, running her finger through a spot of soup on the tray and then sticking her finger in her mouth. Neither of them looked up. "Come on! Get it whilst it's hot." It was no great feast or anything, but still, manners.

She tapped Gerry's back with her toe and he looked up to her blankly. She smiled at him. "Come on: soup."

He blinked. "Yeah, of course." He rolled back on to the balls of his feet and stood up. He put his arms around

254

Laurie and hugged her hard. She was glad of it and stood with him for a long moment.

"Will I just help myself?" asked Jamie and Laurie stepped out of Gerry's arms.

"Yeah and here, drink this. You need to keep your fluids up."

He smiled. "Yes nurse!"

She picked up a bowl and handed it to Gerry who was standing waiting.

"There you are, now sit down."

He sat down where she nodded and she put his water on the floor beside his chair.

"Okay," she said, taking her own soup and sitting down.

It was okay, if not delicious. But it was hot and she was hungrier than she'd realised. For a while the only sound was the soup being spooned up and swallowed.

"There are some chocolate biscuits for afterwards," Laurie said, remembering she'd put some in the bag with the flask.

"Oh goody – a treat," said Jamie.

Laurie looked at him, but his eyes were on Gerry who was just looking down into his near empty bowl.

"Do you want some more Gerry? There's a wee drop left." She wasn't finished her own yet. He shook his head.

"What's wrong with him?" asked Jamie.

"Leave him," said Laurie with more force than was required.

"What's it to you?"

"Just leave him alone."

"Or what, I'll have you to deal with?"

"We're trying to help you, but you aren't being all that forthcoming, or, in fact, nice."

"What? Do you want all the gory details?' Jamie asked. "Do you want me to tell you everything? Do you want me to cry?"

"There's no need to be like that Jamie." She put her soup bowl back on the tray. "What happened?"

"When?" He sounded bored.

She persevered. "At the hospital."

"Well," he paused. "At the hospital I met this weird old guy who was crying and this young," he looked at her, "bird, who thought she knew fucking everything."

She narrowed her eyes at him.

"And then I went off with them because I was bored of my shitty mum and my shitty school and my shitty life."

He glared at her. She glared at him. Gerry said nothing.

"We were only trying to help Jamie," she said, trying not to lose her temper.

He shrugged. "I don't know why." He spoke quietly, his head drooping forward.

"Because we were worried about you."

"It was Gerry that was really worried, eh?" he said. "If it had been up to you, you would have left me with Ed."

"That doesn't mean I wasn't worried by what you said."

"Not worried enough to do anything though." His voice was flat.

"Well that's the difference between me and Gerry," she said. "He's a man of action."

They both looked at Gerry who was staring at the box the two of them had been going through when she came in.

"That's right, isn't it Gerry? You're a man of action, aren't you?" What was she doing? Gerry wasn't in a care home.

He nodded but kept looking at the box.

The boy's face had lost its insolence and he had a similar expression to the one she was surely wearing. This was all so difficult. She couldn't keep up with Jamie's twisting moods. What on earth was she supposed to do? She wasn't equipped to deal with teenagers. And Gerry was turning out to be of no real help.

She couldn't even drive them back if Gerry lost it. She wondered if Jamie could drive. She sat and watched the boy who was also staring at the cardboard box. Perhaps she should try distraction.

"What's in the box?"

"It's Christmas decorations. He got them down for you."

"Oh good," she said and dropped on to her knees beside the box.

It was an old Dewar's whisky box. She saw a pen knife lying next to it.

There were several brittle, yellow layers of tape that had been cut neatly open. The top of the box had balls of crumpled up newspaper acting as a protective layer and some of these had been tossed on to the floor – no doubt by Jamie. She paused before reaching a hand into the box.

Amongst twists of newspaper she felt various softly spiky flat objects. It was like that Halloween game where you felt around in a dark box and there were things that felt like eyeballs or intestines. Except here what she was feeling was like nothing so much as hardened stars and pieces of bone.

She pulled one out and looked at it. It was a snowflake, or a rough approximation of one at least. It was made out of a flattened star of porcelain that had been painted a pearly ivory. Little daubs of glitter had been touched on here and there. It was clearly old and a bit chipped in places, but Laurie felt a strong desire to keep it in her pocket to touch at times of stress. She held it in her hand and turned it over a few times, stroking its points.

She laid it on the table and then reached into the box and took each of the ornaments in the box out in turn. They were all snowflakes. Each of them was the same dusky white, but they had slightly different shapes. There were twelve in total.

"There should be another one in there," said Gerry who was sitting watching her.

"Really? I couldn't feel anything else." She reached back into the box and ran her hand through the newspaper.

"It's probably near the bottom." He kneeled down beside her and reached into the box. His hand glanced against hers in the box and she turned and looked at him. She leaned her head forward and touched his forehead with hers. They blinked at each other and she would have kissed him if Jamie hadn't been sitting on the chair in the corner watching them.

"Found it," said Gerry, stroking her hand in the box with his thumb.

He pulled what looked like a saucer out of the box and gave it to Laurie. It was wrapped in tissue paper.

"She's thorough your mum, isn't she?" She smiled at

Gerry. It had to be a woman who'd taken such care with these small items.

"She had to be – they're fragile." He sat back on his heels. "Go on, unwrap it."

She carefully peeled back the paper to reveal the porcelain star inside. It was obviously for the top of the tree, but it was like no tree-topper she had ever seen. It was about the size of her hand and the six points of the star were rounded and short. The back of the piece had a cone shape of porcelain fitted to it to attach it to the tree. What was remarkable about it was the way it had been decorated. It was the same white as the snowflakes, but it had a tiny painting taking up most of the front. She recognised the picture straight away. It was the mountain from the dining room. There was more snow cover on it, but it was the same mountain.

"I know this, don't I?" she asked Gerry. "Is it that painting? Well, that mountain?" She pointed over her shoulder to the kitchen.

He nodded again. "She's very thorough."

She frowned, not following.

"My mother," he smiled.

"Do you mean your mother made it?" She pointed at the snowflakes laid out behind her on the table. "These?"

He nodded with a shy look of pride.

She was impressed. She hadn't pictured the doctor's wife as so artistic.

"You seem surprised," he said.

"I am, I suppose." She held the mountain star closer to her face and scrutinised the picture. For such a small item, it was very detailed. Up near the top of the mountain she thought she could make out a stag. "These are beautiful." She put down the mountain star and picked up a snowflake and tilted it to run the light over its sparkly surface. "Did she make all of them?"

He nodded. "She wanted to be an artist."

Laurie frowned. "She's obviously talented enough. Did she end up working as an artist?"

"No," he smiled.

"Why not?"

He shrugged. "Different times." He reached over and picked up the star. "She had my dad to look after and then me, of course."

"Look after?" Laurie tutted. "Why? Was your dad disabled in some way?" Immediately she really hoped he wasn't.

Gerry sighed. "Things were different then, weren't they?"

"I suppose." She turned the snowflake over in her hand so that the glitter caught the light. "It's a shame though. These are great."

"They are. I remember when she made them." He examined the mountain star. "Well, when she started to make them." He held it up to the light. "She did one every year from when I was five until I went into the army."

"What's the story with the star?"

"I'm not sure really." He put it down.

"Haven't you ever asked her?" She had a cheek lecturing him on how to communicate with your family, but he didn't know that.

"She worked on that off and on for years. She changed it a little bit every year." He motioned towards the dining room. "It was the same with that painting. She did a bit here and there. I don't know if she's finished it yet."

He walked out into the hall and came back a moment later, carrying the painting. Jamie and Laurie watched him take it over to the fireplace and lean it against the wall on the mantelpiece. He stood back and looked at it.

"It's kind of spooky," said Laurie.

"I used to think that, but now I'm not so sure," said Gerry, hands in pockets, leaning back slightly to study the painting.

Laurie got up and stood next to him. "I like it. I really like it." She reached forward and gently ran her fingers over the crest of the mountain. There was no stag near the summit on this painting, but there was a smudge of white in amongst the trees near the top that could have been a person. The more Laurie looked at it, the more she felt sure that it was a person – Gerry's mum. She thought of staying this but kept quiet. If he hadn't noticed it, then he didn't deserve to be told about it.

"Is your parents' house full of her paintings?" she asked.

"Oh no. She didn't do anything else. She didn't have the time."

"That's all she did?" Laurie was shocked. "God, what a waste!"

"Maybe she's gone back to it now she's older. I don't know."

"How come?" asked Jamie. Laurie had almost forgotten he was there.

"How come what?"

"How come you don't know what your own mum's doing?" The boy sounded quite angry.

"Who do you think you're talking to?" asked Laurie, turning to face him.

"It's okay Laurie." Gerry patted Laurie on the elbow. He turned to Jamie. "I never really got on with my parents and then when I left it was under a sort of cloud." He shrugged. "And now I don't see them much."

"Do they even know you're back?" The boy sounded outraged.

"Back?"

"From the army? Back in town." The boy stared at Gerry.

Gerry shrugged. "I phoned them when I came home. Like I said before, I wasn't well." He crouched down by the coffee table and picked up a snowflake. "I left the army . . ." He turned the snowflake in his hands.

"What? Under a cloud?"

Gerry half-laughed, but the boy wasn't joking.

"Sort of." Gerry looked at the snowflake.

"What was that all about?"

Gerry kept looking at the snowflake. The boy leaned forwards in his seat.

"What was it *about*?"

"It was a long time ago."

"What? Back when it was different times?" The boy laughed briefly. "It can't have been that fucking long ago."

Laurie was taken aback by the anger in the boy's voice.

"Eh?" he shouted at Gerry, standing up quickly and kicking him in the thigh.

"Fuck's sake!" shouted Laurie, leaping forward and standing between the boy and Gerry. "What the fuck is wrong with you?"

The boy sat down heavily, put his head in his hands and started to cry.

"It's okay," said Gerry. He reached up for Laurie's hand and pulled himself up "You're angry, Jamie. I understand." The boy went on crying, his hands in front of his face. Laurie stared stupidly at the boy, not sure whether to comfort him or tell him off. Everything kept changing too quickly.

Gerry sat down on the armchair and Laurie perched on the arm.

They stayed like that for a few minutes. The boy's crying petered out and he sat silently looking at the fireplace.

Eventually Laurie spoke. "I think it's time we all went to bed." She got to her feet and touched the boy's shoulder. "Come on," she said, guiding him to his feet. "We're all over tired." She led him to the door of the living room.

He didn't look at Gerry at all.

She led him out into the hall and stood at the bottom of the stairs with him.

"Try and get a proper sleep and we'll speak in the morning."

He nodded and put a foot on the first stair. She looked at him, at the nape of his neck and his down-turned shoulders. He needed a rest. They all did.

He looked back over his shoulder at Laurie. His face was blank with exhaustion. "It's just . . ."

"It's okay," she said, pleased that he was finally listening to her and doing as she said. Maybe now he'd had a little outburst they could get things moving. "Go on now." She patted his shoulder blade very gently and gave him a little nudge. He trudged up the stairs and she watched him reach the top and go into his room. She stood for a second and watched the closed door to make sure that he was staying put and then she went back into the living room.

She closed the door and sat down next to Gerry on the floor. He put his arm around her.

"Are you okay?" she asked him, moving as close as she could. "What was all that about? Boys eh?" She was amazed that Gerry was taking it all so calmly. She didn't know how well she'd react to being attacked by someone she barely knew.

"Ach," he rubbed briefly at his leg. "The army's full of angry boys. Sometimes they need to take it out on someone."

She took a deep breath. "Do you want to talk?"

"About what?"

"About this? Or what's happening between us? Or, I dunno, about what the fuck we're going to do tomorrow?"

"I don't really want to talk just now." He kept stroking her arm.

"It isn't good not to talk about things though."

He said nothing, just kept up a steady rhythm, stroking her arm.

"Seriously Gerry." She pulled her arm away gently. "What's going on?"

He sighed. "I'm just thinking some stuff through."

"What sort of stuff?"

"Well . . ." She knew he was forcing himself to speak. "About Jamie . . . And about some of the young soldiers I knew back in the day who didn't come out of things as well."

"Oh." What could she say to that? Nothing in her life compared. Of course her mum dying was hard, but at least it was fairly civilised. She had an idea of what to do and how to behave. But for people to be blown up or shot? How could anyone prepare for that?

"I just look at Jamie and I think about these boys who should have been mucking about with their mates," he shrugged, "and now – " He spread his hands out. "That's it: they're finished." He shook his head but he didn't seem tearful. "They had no time to make their mark. No time at all."

"You must have seen horrible things." She tried to pull back so she could look at him, but he pressed her to his side.

"I did. We all did." He touched her thigh with his other hand. "But there's no point in talking about it. It won't change anything." He flicked his hand up to her inside leg and touched her through her jeans.

"Yes, but your nightmares Gerry. You said they weren't going away."

He was rubbing her and still holding her into his side. She couldn't move.

"I'm awake just now." His breath caught. "Let's deal with one thing at a time."

She didn't have the energy to persist.

The Middle of the Night
Sudden Storminess

She'd never been so frightened in her life. She'd been woken from a deep, dreamless sleep, expecting some sort of catastrophe to be happening, but it was just Gerry. It was like he was on fire, the sounds he was making. There were no recognisable words coming from him, just that mixture of smothered screams and a harsh, scratching shout repeated over again and again. At first she tried to wake him. She shook him gently, but to no avail. She was frightened to turn the light on, because she didn't want to see what sort of face went with that sort of sound. After a minute she curled herself around him hoping that he'd sense her comfort through the dream and it would help him to navigate back. She wondered if he knew he was dreaming, but was unable to wake himself. She lay with her head on his chest and listened to his frantic heart. Eventually he stopped. He didn't wind down. The shouts just stopped. His heart gradually slowed.

"It's okay Gerry, I'm here."

She didn't know if he was awake, but she repeated herself.

There was a scratching sound at the door.

"Laurie? Is everything okay?"

"It's okay Jamie. Just go back to bed."

She could feel him hesitating outside the door.

"Honestly, it's okay. We'll see you in the morning."

Jamie's bedroom door closed.

Gerry sat up, gently pushing her off him. He turned and put his feet on the floor.

"Gerry, can I turn the light on?"

"No, don't just yet." He opened the drawer in the bedside and took something from it. She heard sloshing. His hip flask.

His voice sounded rough. They sat in silence for a few minutes.

"I'm sorry I frightened you."

"It's okay Gerry. Don't worry." She reached for his hand. "What happens in your dream? Is it always the same?"

He took a long drink.

"Here." He handed the flask to her.

She knocked back a glug and stifled a cough. How people could drink whisky for pleasure was beyond her.

He sighed. "It's not always exactly the same thing. But mostly it's Afghanistan." His voice was flat. "It's the summer usually, but sometimes it's the winter."

"What happens?"

He took the flask back and drank again. Then he sighed. "Various things."

She waited. She didn't want to browbeat him for details.

"I saw this little boy get . . ." He took a deep breath then exhaled slowly. "I just saw him reach out for this box. He reached for it and that was it. Gone." He drank again. "He must have been about nine or ten. He probably put the explosives there." He tapped her in the side with the flask.

She pretended to take another drink and handed it back to him.

"It wasn't like it was my fault or anything. I mean, I know that, but in most of the dreams I see him. Not dying. Just standing and watching whatever else is happening." She felt him shaking his head. "His face is so clear to me. It can't really be his face. But I know he's that boy," he said. "I just know it and then I'm calling out to him to be careful and then I wake up." He turned to her.

"You weren't calling anything out tonight. You were just screaming."

He drank again.

"You know, he wasn't even the only person I saw that happening to. I saw it a few times. I don't understand why that's sticking with me or that it isn't even his death that I see."

Laurie leaned over and wrapped her arms around him. "I don't suppose the details matter do they?"

She felt him shrug.

"I want to make you feel better Gerry." She cringed in the darkness. It was such a pathetic, nonsense thing to say. But she meant it.

Gerry considered for a minute. "I want to feel better."

That seemed obvious to her, but Gerry went on.

She could feel him wind up. "You can't unsee what you saw. I want to be better, get better – but it's too late." He brought his hands up to his face and rubbed his eyes.

They lay in silence for a few minutes.

She began hesitantly, "I think if you're able to say you want to get better that you probably can. You know? It's your brain processing things, isn't it?"

He said nothing, but she felt okay to go on.

"I used to dream about snow all the time when my mum was ill. And it wasn't even the wintertime when she was at her worst. But I felt really lonely at first in the dream and then it would snow and I'd feel really tired and I'd lie down in the snow and then I'd wake up."

"What did it mean?" He pulled her close.

"Fucked if I know."

She could feel him smiling. "Was it a nightmare?"

She considered. "Not in the way yours is. I didn't scream or anything. But it made me wake up with a sort of," she searched for the words, "feeling of dread."

"Dread?"

"Yeah." She was embarrassed to use the word. It sounded so overblown and old-fashioned. But dread was definitely the feeling she'd woken with.

The rest of the time over those months she'd felt mostly harassed. She was the one who took her mother for chemo appointments, to the chemist's, out for lunch once a week so she wouldn't feel separate from society. Her brother was too busy with his own job (forgetting of course that Laurie worked too). Her father closed in on himself even more than usual. He played more golf. He went into work more as well. She knew that he'd been offered plenty of time off to take her mother to her appointments, but why bother when Laurie would do it? Ed had tentatively suggested that maybe she should say she couldn't make the next appointment; that she'd used up all her holiday time – which she had, long before, she was taking sickies mostly – but Laurie flew into a rage. He had only suggested what she'd been thinking, but she couldn't be seen to shirk her duties. It was very important that everyone saw how stoic she was. Not that anyone ever commented on it or thanked her or anything.

Mostly, she'd just felt she had too much to do and not enough time to do it. She didn't think too much about how she'd feel when her mother died. And she'd known from the beginning, on some level, that her mother would die. Despite what well-meaning people kept saying to her about new discoveries and medical miracles. Her mum was a goner; it was obvious. As soon as she'd had her diagnosis, even before it, back when there was a lump that could have been a cyst or something benign or treatable, her mother's head had gone down and it had never come up again.

During those months Laurie had occasionally seen something on TV that had made her cry. Sometimes she'd force herself to cry, deliberately imagining the funeral, picturing herself from outside herself as if she was watching a film. But generally, she just pressed on and did what needed to be done. It was only when she had the dream about the snow that she seemed to have a more appropriate feeling.

Gerry put his hand on her chin and pulled her towards him for a kiss. He tasted of whisky. She thought back to the two of them on the floor in the living room earlier. It was better than she'd imagined. She liked the weight of him on top of her. It made her feel grounded and pinned. It was nice being with someone older, someone who knew what they were doing. It was all very well being gentle and kind, but sometimes you wanted to feel like the weaker sex. Sometimes you wanted to feel like you weren't making every single decision. Get her, she was starting to sound like a bodice ripper.

He didn't seem interested in sex now though. But that was to be expected after his nightmare. Maybe she should make the first move. But it was too late now – she'd started thinking about it all. Somehow if it happened unexpectedly, quickly, she was able to do it.

But when she had to think about it her arms and legs were slow to respond and her mind went blank. She couldn't think how she should move. All her brain would give her was scraps of porno images and that completely put her off. Partly because she started to see what she was doing through a pornographic lense where everything looked fake and forced, including the sounds she made, and also because she had a sort of montage of the dead-eyed facial expressions the women made in those films. On the one hand she thought, you know, make money however you want, but, on the other hand, she couldn't get over the idea that all these women were victims in some way, that they were trapped in a well paying, seemingly glamorous nightmare where all anyone saw were their horrific fake tits and shaved fannies. It was like an ongoing assault where they didn't realise they were being raped. It sickened her.

"It was nice earlier, wasn't it?" Gerry's voice was husky and tentative.

"Yes it was." She hugged into him, relieved. "You're not bad for a washed up mentalist."

"Ha ha." He squeezed her a little too tightly. "Now let's get some sleep. There's a lot to be sorted out tomorrow."

She didn't press him for details.

271

Early Doors
Overcast

Gerry wasn't there when she woke and she curled over into his side of the bed to take up his warmth, but it was cold. He'd been up for a while then. After the night before, Laurie felt as if things with Gerry could definitely go somewhere. She didn't know where, but at least she had a glimmer of direction.

She got dressed as quickly as possible in the freezing cold room but was still exposed enough to feel as if she was made of glass. As she reached the bottom of the stairs she could hear the two of them outside. She went into the kitchen first and made a quick cup of coffee, for the heat as much as the caffeine. She wondered what sort of mood Jamie would be in today and also if the two of them had decided to go home. She hoped they had. She'd like a change of clothes, if nothing else. Her jeans felt damp.

She wished she was able to eavesdrop a little to gain purchase on the mood of the day but the door was too thick to hear anything other than that the two of them were talking. She could tell they must be sitting on the bench under the living room window. She pictured them holding their coffee, looking out on to the hills and the morning sky. It was a shame to disturb them really and she couldn't help but feel that with her there, things would probably not flow quite as smoothly. Still, it couldn't be helped. She was here and that was that. She opened the door, quite prepared to whimper pathetically as soon as the cold hit her, but it was as crisp as new money. Bracing – but clean and sharp.

"Morning gentlemen," she announced.

They looked up at her and Gerry moved to give her his seat.

"No, no. I'll sit over there." She pointed to a low wall that ran round the side of the house. She sat on the wall which was cold and sharp, but she wasn't going to be asking for a seat on the bench. It was impossible to get comfy but she acted like her bum wasn't damp or rapidly becoming numb and took a long drink from her coffee which was now lukewarm.

"So. What's the story then?" She tried to sound easy going, but she could hear a touch of panic in her own voice. Jamie glanced at Gerry.

Gerry smiled and looked to Jamie. "Well?" His face was so kind and calm. He was like a different person to the Gerry of the night before.

She could see how Gerry could be an inspiration to all those young soldiers. You would think he had all the answers, if you didn't know him outwith his competent, daytime self. She liked this side of him, but she liked him more knowing he wasn't as grown up as he seemed. She liked the fact that other people would see him as this big, clever, calm guy. Yes, he was a bit lacking in ambition and he was doing something inherently pointless for a job, but you felt he knew what he was all about; he was a proper man. Probably particularly so to a kid like Jamie who maybe, probably, didn't have a father around, or at all.

Laurie smiled kindly at Jamie. "I think your family will be worried."

"My family?" said Jamie, his head down. There was no charge to his words, more an accepting hopelessness.

Gerry nodded although Jamie wasn't looking at him.

"What was that in the night?" The boy glanced up at Gerry, then at the ground, embarrassed.

"What do you mean?" Gerry frowned, not following.

Of course Gerry's dream would have frightened the boy – alarming noises in a strange house in the middle of nowhere. Not mentioning the fact that until that day he'd never met Gerry before.

Laurie watched the light dawn in Gerry's eyes.

"Oh," he said. He pressed his forefinger into the bridge of his nose. Laurie waited for him to say something, but Gerry just sat staring at nothing.

"Jamie," Laurie said. "There are things you don't know about."

Jamie all but snarled at Laurie.

"This has got nothing to do with you."

Laurie was taken aback by the venom in his voice. "Alright Jamie, settle down."

"This has got *nothing* to do with you." He jabbed a finger at her.

"Okay, okay." Gerry held a calming hand out to Jamie. "Laurie is just trying to help." He put his hand on the boy's shoulder. "I think you should apologise."

The boy sighed heavily through his nose. Then he glanced at Laurie and muttered an apology.

"Thank you," said Laurie. She found it hard to keep the smug tone from her voice.

They sat quietly for a minute, each staring in different directions. Laurie thought the discussion was over, at least for now, but Gerry cleared his throat.

"When I was in the army -" He paused and seemed to be ordering his thoughts. Laurie wondered if he'd ever told anyone apart from her and the doctors what was going on with him. What was he going to tell Jamie now? A Disneyfied version of events where he had done something unpleasant but necessary? Or would he break down into tears again and give Jamie a rambling, distressed version? Neither option was very good.

He looked fairly calm, but she was prepared to step in if she needed to. Honesty was great and all that, but there was no point in needlessly upsetting yourself, especially for an essential stranger.

"Well. I saw some . . . that included some," he cleared his throat, "difficult events that I found very . . ." He sighed but didn't go on.

Jamie looked suddenly concerned. It was very difficult to get a handle on this kid. He was so changeable.

She didn't want to step on Gerry's toes, but it seemed important that the boy had a bit of an understanding. "Traumatic. I think that's what Gerry's trying to say." She looked at Gerry and he was looking away off to the hills, his eyes wet. She noticed that the hand holding his coffee cup was fairly steady. That had to be promising. Maybe the whole notion of a problem shared was true to an extent.

Jamie waited. Now there was no trace of aggression at all.

She shook her head. "Any more than that's up to Gerry, I think."

"There's time for that, isn't there?" Gerry asked the boy.

Not if I can help it, thought Laurie, picturing a bath and her pyjamas. The thought of spending Christmas up here was horrifying. She had no idea if Ed would have chucked her stuff out by now or not. But she reasoned that if that happened she'd be able to go to her dad's house and stay there for a bit. She could just tell him the flat had been sold or her flatmates had lost their jobs or something. As hellish as going to her dad's would be, at least it would be warm and there was a telly to watch all the terrible Christmas programmes on.

"Okay," She looked at the two of them. "So what's the plan then? We can't stay up here forever."

"Don't sound so cheerful about it," said Jamie, back to annoying teen again.

She tried to appear practical. "But we can't stay here. We don't have enough food for one thing."

"We could hunt. There'll be rabbits up there." He indicated the trees behind the house.

"Hunt?" laughed Gerry. "Very survivalist."

The boy was hurt. "I could do it. I've done it before."

"You've hunted before? Where?" asked Gerry.

The boy shrugged. "In the country, with my Grandad."

Laurie thought back to a documentary she'd seen on serial killers. They always seemed to start off killing small animals. Oh God, had she been right not to trust Jamie?

"With your Grandad?" Gerry asked, almost inaudibly.

"Yeah. A little bit." He was clearly lying. He probably just wanted to look manly to Gerry.

"Anyway," said Laurie. She needed to get them back on track and back to the City. "What would we hunt with? There probably isn't anything to hunt with here." If they left soon they'd be back for lunchtime. She knew she should probably be worried about what was going to happen with Ed and her flat and her job and everything. But all she could think about was getting washed and warm and clean and eating something nice like a baked potato – definitely not a rabbit.

"Actually, there is some stuff," said Gerry. "There was anyway, years ago."

"Look," she said, sick of trying to be subtle. "I want to go home. I've had enough of this. It was a stupid idea in the beginning and I don't know why I ever came here." She looked at Gerry. "We need to get Jamie home before we get into trouble." She looked at Jamie. "Jamie, we need to help you get in touch with a social worker or something and get your home situation sorted out and we," she flicked her index finger between herself and Gerry, "have got some stuff to sort out. Don't we Gerry?"

Gerry looked at her with a peculiar little smile on his face. Maybe he thought it was funny that she was referring to herself and Gerry as "we". Maybe he thought that their going home would be a natural time to draw a line under things between them. Maybe he had no intention of ever taking her home and she'd have to try and hitch out of here. She waited, but neither of them said anything.

"Well? What's happening?" She stood up, on the verge

of shouting. They both looked at her as if they were going to laugh.

She felt herself begin to cry. "I cannot be bothered roughing it, when I don't fucking need to! And besides which, it's Christmas Day tomorrow!"

Gerry stood up and reached a hand out to her. "Laurie, look . . ."

"No Gerry! I'm not listening to any more of your shit. This was all a stupid idea. We shouldn't be out here. I want to go home!" Her voice rose to a mortifyingly squeaky level. "I'm fucking freezing!" She backed away from Gerry.

Jamie laughed. "Boo hoo! Poor princess Laurie can't hack a bit of cold."

"What do you know about anything?" She pointed at Jamie. "You're only a kid! And you," she pointed at Gerry, "you're no better! It's like being with two stupid little kids, playing at being men! It's fucking ridiculous! You both need to grow the fuck up!" She'd gone too far, but it was too late. She couldn't bear to look at Gerry.

She threw her half-empty coffee mug over the wall and then climbed over after it and started trudging up the slope towards the trees at the top. Neither of them tried to stop her and why would they? What a drama queen! How embarrassing, she'd behaved like a bloody teenager. That's what came from hanging around with an adolescent and a mentalist.

"Laurie, come back! Laurie!"

"Fuck off Gerry!" She shouted back over her shoulder. She refused to turn round and look at him.

But after only a few minutes, she couldn't stop herself

from glancing back at them. They were both on the bench and they seemed to be chatting companionably. Bastards, she thought miserably, wishing she'd brought some food with her. God knows how long it would take for her to be able to go back down and face them again.

Late Morning
Threat of Rain

She woke to the sound of a car making its way up the main road. All she'd done was sit down for a rest – she must have drifted off. What time was it? She stood up. It was so quiet here she could make out the driver changing the gears as the car climbed the steep gradient. She wondered idly if she'd be able to run down in time to get a lift back to somewhere she could catch a train or a bus back to civilisation. But then she remembered that she had pretty much no money with her. She supposed she could hitch or if the worst came to the worst she could phone her dad or her brother. It would be hard to explain but she'd rather put up with a grilling than stay here another night.

The car came to a stop at the bottom of the cottage's track and then turned slowly in. Oh God! Who the fuck was it? The police? She scrambled to her feet and clambered back down the hill to the cottage.

"Gerry! Gerry!" she called out uselessly. Would the police have a wee car like that? Surely not! More likely it was a social worker come to get Jamie. Would there be time for them to hide in the woods? She clambered over the wall into the garden, noticing absently that her mug from earlier was no longer there.

"Gerry! Gerry!" She flung the door open, nearly hitting Gerry in the face with it.

He grabbed her. "What is it Laurie? Are you hurt? Are you okay?" His face paled.

Laurie felt a brief flare of satisfaction.

"There's somebody coming Gerry, quick! Do something!"

"What? A car?" He was completely unruffled and made no move to run.

"Gerry? Come on!" The childish panic in her voice embarrassed her but she couldn't help it. She tugged at his sleeve.

He smiled at her and nodded. "It's okay Laurie. It's all okay." That must be the army training, she thought fleetingly even as she began to realise he wasn't going anywhere. She pushed him out of the way and stood at the foot of the stairs trying to see into both the bottom rooms as she called out wildly.

"Jamie! Jamie! We have to go! Quick, grab your coat! Quick! Where are you?"

He appeared and came smoothly walking down the stairs towards her.

"It's okay Laurie." He smiled at her calmly. What the fuck was going on? Had they been kidnapped by aliens? Who were these two unflappable automatons? Maybe he didn't realise what was going on, maybe he thought she was playing a prank. "I'm not joking Jamie, we have to go. There's a car coming!" He stood on the last step and smiled down at her. She plucked at his cuff. "Come on!"

He shook his head. "It's alright Laurie."

"But Jamie, they'll take you back."

"It's okay." He shook his head, smiling as if he pitied her.

She felt like wiping that smile off his face. She turned to appeal to Gerry, knowing already that it was useless. She could hear the wheels turning on the gravel. Gerry turned to look over his shoulder out of the front door.

"Oh," he said, his shoulders slumping slightly.

"Oh?" shouted Laurie, "Oh? We're fucked and all you can do is say oh!"

Gerry glanced back at her quickly, a flick of irritation crossing his face and then over her head to Jamie. "Did you call him?"

Laurie turned back to Jamie who nodded confidently. She looked out at the driveway but Gerry was obscuring her view.

"You didn't need to phone him as well."

"Jesus Christ," she muttered, elbowing Gerry out of the way. "Call who? What's going on here?"

Climbing out of the Ford Fiesta was Ed's mum. Laurie stood dumbly as Sandy brushed herself down and glanced around at the scrawny garden and the paint-peeled cottage.

"Laurie," she said nodding politely.

Ed had told her whatever he knew, she could tell by the look of grim satisfaction on her face. There was nothing worse than that told-you-so expression. She'd never seen it before on Sandy. It brought her features into stronger focus, perhaps due to her mouth being drawn into an almost straight line.

If she was here then so must Ed, she thought, looking into the body of the car where of course, joy of joys, Ed

282

was reaching into the back seat for something. He looked up at Laurie then reached for the door and climbed out. She stood and watched him as he came around the car and held out a packet of biscuits.

"Hob Nobs? Are you joking?"

"Put the kettle on Laurie and let's get this all sorted out," said Gerry.

Laurie looked at Ed's mum and shook her head.

"No."

"Laurie, don't be difficult," said Gerry, squeezing her arm. "Let's be adults here."

"Don't be difficult!" She was completely wrong-footed here. "Let's be adults?" She stood between Gerry and Ed, not sure who she wanted to punch more. "Can somebody please just explain what's going on here?" She made an effort to bring her voice under control.

"I phoned Ed," said Jamie.

"But why?" asked Laurie. "And how? There's no phone?"

Jamie pulled a tiny mobile out of his pocket and waved it at Laurie.

"Oh. Of course." What an idiot she was. "What's going on here?" She felt herself going red. "I thought you couldn't go back because of the police and your parents and everything?"

"The police?" said Gerry.

"Yeah, well, you know." She nodded towards Ed and made a *keep quiet* face at Gerry.

"I never said anything about the police," Ed said.

"You said there'd been an accident." She took a step towards Jamie. "That someone had died," Laurie said.

The boy shrugged.

"Look," said Ed, stepping forward. "We need to sort things out here." He looked at Jamie and then back at Laurie. "What's going on? I've got a duty of care here and until . . ."

"What gives you the authority?" interrupted Laurie.

"Because I'm in loco parentis," he said patiently.

"No you aren't – you aren't even a qualified play worker or whatever it is you're doing at college." She couldn't seem to stop herself sounding like a fishwife.

Ed went on, "and I'll be in that position until we can locate his parents or caregivers."

"Parents? Caregivers?" Laurie tutted. "Gee whiz, you've really got it together now, haven't you?"

"Well, actually," said Gerry.

But before he could finish speaking the sound of another car came crunching up the drive way. They all turned in the car's direction.

"Now what?" asked Laurie.

They all stood and stared at the Volvo Estate. There was an older woman behind the steering wheel and a younger woman sat glaring out at them from the passenger seat.

"Oh fuck," said Jamie.

"Fuck indeed," said Gerry.

Laurie's eyes flicked between Gerry and the boy and back to Gerry again.

Of course.

There'd been some half formed thought bobbing about at the edge of her brain, but she hadn't paid it any attention.

Jesus Christ.

How bloody melodramatic. She was such an unbelievable fuckwit.

The younger woman ran her hands over her hair and leaned back in the seat with her eyes closed. She appeared to be counting. Gerry moved over to the driver's door and nodded. The older woman stared up at him. Gerry opened the door for her and she stepped out and then clutched him to her, starting to cry.

Everyone shuffled and shifted, unable to stop staring at Gerry and the woman. Then the passenger car door slammed and the younger woman stood and coughed once. Gerry and older woman stepped apart.

The older woman looked at the younger woman and then back at Gerry.

"Jenny." Gerry couldn't take his eyes from the younger woman's face.

Jenny laughed harshly. She was so like Jamie, it was startling – the same dark eyes and sharp chin; the same high forehead and thin lips. But it was the laugh that brought the similarity into sharp focus. "Well this is a lovely little get together."

Gerry nodded with a look of sad resignation.

The older woman frowned at Jamie, who looked down at his feet, shame-faced.

"What were you thinking? You had us worried half to death." She shook her head, but her face was full of concern. "There are easier ways, you know."

He muttered sorry, still not looking up.

Jenny tutted. "Get your stuff together. We'll talk on the way home."

Jamie's head whipped up to look at Gerry who was staring at this Jenny character.

"But Mum!" Now he sounded like a child.

"But nothing. I said we'd talk in the car. Get going!" She pointed up the stairs. Jamie still didn't move. "Now!" Jenny didn't shout, but her tone was firm and she was clearly no push over.

Gerry couldn't seem to tear his eyes away from Jenny. Jenny was very deliberately not looking at Gerry.

Finally Jamie made a little huffy sound and thumped up the stairs. They stood and listened as Jamie slammed his door shut, opened it again and slammed it shut harder.

"Fucking hell," thought Laurie, but she must have said it aloud, because they all turned and looked at her.

"You must be Laurie," said the older woman. "I'm Margaret, Gerry's mother."

She reached out a hand to shake. Her hand was warm and smooth and she gave Laurie's hand a reassuring squeeze.

"Please excuse my son's lack of manners." She turned to the assembled company. "I expect it's the circumstances." She smiled at Ed and his mother. "Are you the man from the Community Centre?"

Ed nodded. "Yes. Ed MacDonald."

"I'm so sorry about all the trouble my grandson has caused you. We will, of course, make sure there are no further problems."

"Hello," said Ed's mum. "I'm Edward's mother, Sandy."

"Lovely. How nice to meet you." The two older women shook hands. This was too weird and polite for Laurie.

"Are these for us?" Gerry's mother asked Ed, pointing at the Hob Nobs. "Come on then, let's have some tea. I brought milk."

Tea? Laurie felt she needed something a lot stronger than tea. Where was Gerry's hip flask when she actually needed it?

Margaret walked into the house and they had no choice but to follow her in.

Laurie turned to look back at Gerry and Jenny. Gerry stepped forward and, without glancing at Laurie, gently shut the front door.

Late Morning
Clearing Slowly

Margaret led the way into the living room but stopped short when she saw Laurie's attempt at decorations with the old artificial Christmas tree and the ornaments. She reached out and ran her fingers over the mountain star. She smiled.

"I hope you don't mind," said Laurie. "Gerry said it would be okay."

Gerry's mother turned and looked at Laurie, studying her face. "I don't mind at all." She tapped a finger on the top few snowflakes. "I'm surprised Gerry remembered about them."

"They're very pretty," said Laurie, sounding to herself like a suck up, but she meant it.

"They are, aren't they?" said Ed's mum, stepping forward and looking intently at the star. "I've never seen anything like them."

"Nonsense," said Margaret. "They're just silly decorations." She blushed and shrugged. "Now let's get organised," she said, changing her tone to that of professional hostess. "Why don't you sit down," she indicated the sofa. "Laurie, could you come and help me?"

Ordinarily, being bossed around like this would have gotten Laurie's back up, but there was something about

Margaret that she liked. She followed Gerry's mother out of the room, glancing back briefly at Ed and his mum who were standing looking at the scrappy Christmas tree as if they were at an art gallery.

Once they entered the kitchen, Laurie was at a loss as to what to do to help. Margaret quickly assembled the cups and saucers, filled the kettle and laid the biscuits out. Clearly she had done a lot of entertaining. Laurie imagined there were a lot of Ladies Circle and PTA meetings that she'd organised in her time. She looked like Laurie's idea of a doctor's wife. Her hair was a nice clean silvery grey, cut into a neat little bob that swung pleasingly about her oval face. She didn't look much like Gerry except for around the eyes which were similarly twinkly. She did appear to be quite tightly-wound, but that was probably down to worry.

"This is a strange situation, isn't it?" she said suddenly to Laurie. "Not the best of circumstances to meet your boyfriend's mother. Or his child, for that matter."

Laurie wasn't sure where to begin. She looked out of the window at the trees she'd been sleeping under all but ten minutes before. She wished she'd had the good sense never to have talked to Gerry in the first place. She should have just broken up with Ed and been single for a while, advertised for flat mates, saved up and gone to Australia like any other directionless twenty-something would have done. What was she thinking of getting together with a weird near forty-year-old with family issues?

She sighed.

"I don't think you could describe Gerry as my boy-friend, really." She unscrewed and re-screwed the lid of the sugar canister. "And he didn't say anything about being Jamie's father," she said out of the window. Her face burned with the shame of being such a fool.

"Gerry didn't say what?" Margaret frowned at her.

"Gerry didn't say that Jamie was his child." She was such an idiot. It was so obvious now that was what was going on. "He didn't say anything to me or Jamie."

"Jamie?"

"Well, Jamie didn't know." She sighed. "It must have been a shock for him."

Margaret looked briefly at Laurie and then turned back to the tea tray.

"He knew that Gerry was his father." She didn't look at Laurie. "Unfortunately, it seems he contrived this whole ridiculous situation. And he isn't called Jamie," she turned to Laurie, wincing as she spoke, "he's called Paul."

Laurie felt as if she'd been slapped. She considered just grabbing her stuff and going.

"So basically, everyone knew but me?" Her eyes teared up. She had been so dim-witted, she could hardly believe it.

Margaret raised a hand to touch Laurie's arm in comfort, but the look on Laurie's face stopped her short.

"I'm sorry." She stood for a moment, thinking. "From the brief conversation I had with Gerry on the phone, I don't think he actually knew until this morning." She took a step closer to Laurie. "He took Paul's phone and found our number on it. I think he was planning on phoning Paul's mother, but then he realised . . ."

"I see," said Laurie, leaning against the counter. "Why didn't he tell me?" She sounded pathetic. She didn't know why, but she wanted very badly not to give Margaret the impression that she was as much of a monumental tit as she was appearing.

This time Margaret did place her hand gently on Laurie's arm. "I didn't speak to him for long and you know what Gerry's like – not, shall we say, tremendously communicative." She smiled at Laurie in an attempt at we're-in-this-together humour.

Laurie didn't smile. "So . . ." She rubbed at her temples, "Let's see if I've got this straight." She had a headache coming on. "Jamie, sorry, Paul, knew all about Gerry and this whole," she waved her arm around herself, "mess was down to him? And Gerry realised this morning that Jamie, sorry, Paul," she sighed, "was his never-seen son. Then Gerry phoned you and told you to come here. Jamie, Paul, meanwhile phoned Ed?" She tried to laugh bitterly, but just sounded pathetic. God, all that "Paul's dead" rubbish. This was like a stupid afternoon play.

"For fuck's sake!" Laurie said, sitting down heavily at the table. "You couldn't make this up. I was just trying to help Gerry and Jamie! I don't need this hassle!" She started to cry. She didn't care any more about making a show in front of this woman.

Margaret hovered over her. "I'm so sorry Laurie. Gerry said things got . . ." she took a deep breath, "away from him."

Laurie shook her head and looked up at Margaret. "Things got away from Gerry quite a while ago."

"I know," said Margaret. "But he won't let us help him." Now the older woman's eyes filled up. God, they

291

were great criers, you had to hand that to Gerry's nearest and dearest.

But she felt sorry for Margaret. It couldn't be easy having only one child and that child making themselves unavailable. She seemed nice enough – not at all as posh or cold as Laurie had imagined.

Well, quite posh, but not cold. Laurie wiped her eyes with the heel of her hand.

"I'm sorry Laurie. Really I am." Margaret shook her head. "All I've ever wanted is for Gerry to be happy." She kept shaking her head. "I don't know where I went wrong, I really don't."

Now Laurie patted Margaret on the arm. She was wearing some sort of silky blouse under a knitted tank top thing. The blouse felt soft and almost damp. It was the colour of a late night sky and it seemed to pull Laurie closer to it. She stroked the fabric while Margaret wept quietly without a loss of decorum. If you walked past the kitchen and glanced in you would think Margaret was just standing waiting for the kettle to pop. She stood straight as tears rolled quietly down her face. Her mascara didn't even run and yet it was obvious to Laurie that she wasn't faking her upset. She really was broken-hearted at Gerry's lack of contact.

How could Gerry not want to see his mother? She was far nicer on first appearances than her own mother had been and Laurie would give almost anything to have even that vague, unsupportive presence in her life still. It used to happen to Laurie when she was a teenager that she'd fall in love with a boy's family and would hate to eventually give up hanging out with someone else's more successful family life. She wondered if she might be able to go and see Gerry's mum after all this was over. Maybe she could offer herself up as a surrogate daughter. She could talk to Margaret about art or anything.

She'd already proven what a good daughter she was when it counted.

But then the thought occurred to her that Margaret was at least five years older than her own mother would have been and that she couldn't face going through all that death and pain again. She didn't want to see anyone else hooked up and fading unless she absolutely had to. She pulled her hand away from the silky arm with a final pat.

"You haven't gone wrong with Gerry," she said to Margaret. In light of all this, Laurie certainly didn't want the burden of Gerry. She needed to think clearly. She'd be far better off on her own. The thing was to stop Margaret crying so they could get the show on the road and she could extricate herself from all this drama. "He needs help."

The woman smiled sadly. "He won't take any. His father arranged for him to see a colleague." She turned away and poured the water from the kettle into the tea pot. Laurie was glad to note that she didn't warm the tea pot first – or any other tea superstition. "A really first rate psychiatric specialist. But he wouldn't go. He was, of course," she gave a forced little laugh, "far too polite to say no outright." She put the lid on the teapot with a firm clunk. "But he didn't arrive for his appointment and he didn't get in touch again until this morning." She reached into her handbag and took out a biscuit tin. "We thought it best to wait for him to get in touch this time." She opened the tin and shook out a pile of Kit-Kats on to a plate then she picked up the tea tray and pivoted on her heel. She nodded at the kitchen door.

Laurie held the door for her then followed her back through to the living room. Ed and his mother were still sitting as they had been. Both of them had their hands tucked neatly between their knees. Ed's mother had a polite smile on her face. Ed looked down at the carpet. His mother moved to stand.

"Oh no," said Margaret nodding for Ed's mum to stay seated. "You stay there. Now," She put the tray down and hovered over it, "what would you like in your tea?"

"Oh, just milk thank you," said Ed's mum, smiling away as if this was just a nice little social visit and nothing out of the ordinary had happened. Laurie looked at Ed to see if she could try and work out what he was thinking. He looked up at her and nodded curtly. This was all very strange and unsettling. Now that the boy's mother was here then why were Ed and his mother – and herself for that matter – still here? They should drink up and hit the road. But she really didn't want to be stuck in the car with them for a couple of hours. Especially as Ed's mother had just passed her driver's test. She was wary enough in real life, never mind what she'd be like behind the wheel. She could just imagine – face close to the wheel, shoulders as far up as they'd go, driving at 40 on the motorway. God knows what she'd be like on these windy country roads.

But did she want to go home with Gerry? She still couldn't believe it. She'd had a strange feeling about the boy from the beginning, but she couldn't honestly say why that was. And her priding herself on working out who the murderer was on crime shows! When had Gerry worked it out? Surely not straight away? It must have been this morning. There had been a kind of smugness about the two of them when she'd come out into the garden. But then, surely Gerry would be decent enough to tell her and not just surprise her like this? But she hadn't given them a chance. She remembered chucking her coffee cup over the wall and blushed afresh.

Laurie blew the surface of the tea she seemed to be holding. "Oh," she said. "Thanks."

Margaret smiled politely at her.

"So," Laurie said to Ed. "What now?"

He shrugged helplessly. "What do you mean?"

She frowned. She'd almost forgotten how annoyingly obtuse he could be. "What about Jamie?"

"Jamie? Do you mean Paul?" Ed looked confused.

"Yes, Paul." She could feel herself looking at Ed as if he was the idiot. "He was calling himself 'Jamie'."

"Why?"

She looked at Margaret. "Well, I presume so that he wouldn't give the game away to Gerry."

Margaret looked away with a tightening of her lips.

"What game? What are you on about?" said Ed with more irritation than he normally showed.

"Gerry didn't know that Jamie, Paul, was his son."

"What are you talking about?" asked Ed impatiently.

Laurie raised her eyebrows at Margaret. He was her son and she knew this story better. Let her explain it.

Margaret sighed. "When Paul was born, Gerry was away in the army. He and Jenny," she sighed again, "went their separate ways, when Jenny found out she was expecting."

"So?" asked Ed.

"Don't be rude Ed," said Laurie, surprised by his tone.

Ed glared at her. It was a look she'd never seen from him before and instantly it shamed her. "Rude? Don't be rude?" He thumped his cup down on the table. "You have no idea how polite I'm being. No idea!"

He stood up and walked out muttering to his mother, "I'll be waiting in the car."

Ed's mother turned to Laurie and narrowed her eyes, "I don't see why you'd be surprised." She jabbed her chin at Laurie. "You've broken his heart, you know."

"You don't know what you're talking about," said Laurie quietly.

"One day you might be a mother and then you'll get an idea of what it's like seeing someone treat your child so," she screwed her face up in concentration, "casually." She jabbed a finger at Laurie. "He's worth more than this."

"But . . ."

Ed's mother cut Laurie off with a chop of her hand.

"But nothing." She was much more impressive in her anger. "I know he's not the right person for you." She leaned forward, still holding her cup. Laurie waited for her to slop tea all over herself. "That's been obvious from the start." She was clutching the cup so tightly, Laurie wouldn't have been surprised if it shattered. "But have you ever considered that you aren't the right person for him?"

Laurie looked down at her tea cup.

"You haven't, have you?"

Laurie shook her head. It was like being back at school.

"You don't think much about other people do you?" Ed's mother didn't wait for an answer. "You're a pretty girl Laurie and when you've stopped being so," she exhaled heavily, "*selfish* I'm sure you'll be good for somebody, but you need to start thinking about other people, instead of yourself all the time."

Laurie sat quietly, waiting for her to let it go.

"I know you don't have a mother now to guide you . . ." the woman's voice softened.

Laurie's head snapped up. "Nobody's ever guided me."

Ed's mother raised an eyebrow as if to say, well look what's happened. Laurie could feel herself start to cry. It was the type of crying that left you ragged and dirty looking. Perhaps she could hold it off by not speaking. She looked down at her hands.

"You have to sort your life out, Laurie." Laurie heard the tea cup finally being placed on the table. "You can do what you like with your life, go anywhere."

Laurie heard Ed's mother stand up. "Just try and treat people with some respect."

Laurie counted slowly to ten.

"Thanks for the tea." Laurie felt her hovering damply next to her. "I wish I had the possibilities that you have." Her hand fluttered over Laurie's shoulder and then she was off.

Laurie sat still, trying to stave off the tears that lurked behind her eyes. What Ed's mother had said was like a script from some TV movie. She knew she could do whatever she liked with her life and she knew she was lucky, but really, what was the point of it? She'd still be herself wherever she went; she'd still have no clue about what she really wanted.

At least if you sat at home bemoaning the fact that your life didn't turn out the way you wanted it to, you still had the fiction that things might have been different, if only . . .

Laurie and Margaret sat in silence for a few minutes. Laurie couldn't bring herself to look up from her lap, let alone form any words.

Margaret cleared her throat quietly. "If you don't mind me asking Laurie, how old are you?"

Laurie took a deep breath.

"I'm nearly twenty-five."

Maybe she should have given herself a few extra years so she was closer in age to Gerry. She couldn't be bothered with another disappointed mother.

"When I was twenty-five I was trying to get pregnant. It took two years and it was the only thing I thought about all that time."

She refilled her and Laurie's cups and picked up a biscuit.

"We came up here every opportunity we could."

She took a small bite of the biscuit, chewed quickly and swallowed.

"I dreamt all the time about climbing a mountain. A snow-capped mountain that was filled with birds and animals that were watching from all the trees and bushes." She filled her tea up again. "They all had human eyes. They weren't at all frightening – just watchful, like new babies." She smiled to herself.

Laurie waited for her to go on but Margaret sat back in her seat and sipped her tea.

Laurie couldn't work out what was expected of her. It was an unusual situation. Here she was: a fair bit younger than Gerry, shown to have treated her boyfriend shabbily, sitting mutely next to her fling's mother who was reminiscing about some freaky dream from years ago.

Paul entered the room silently. The sneaky little idiot had probably been ear-wigging the whole time. He perched on the arm of his grandmother's chair and she reached up and rubbed his shoulder blade. He turned and smiled at her. They were obviously close.

Laurie waved her finger between the two of them.

"Did Gerry not know about all this?"

Margaret looked at her. "It wasn't a secret. But he wasn't in touch much and things were very one-sided. He'd send us a Christmas card and phone now and then." She sighed. "Often I didn't even know where he'd been posted."

"That must have been hard," Laurie said.

Margaret nodded. "But at least we saw Paul and Jenny."

Paul smiled at his grandmother and then looked at Laurie. He blinked at her. If you didn't know the situation, you'd think he was a lovely young boy, so nice with his grandma.

"So what are your plans now Laurie?" he asked innocently.

Laurie looked at him calmly. "I don't know, Paul."

She was still the adult here. He'd better not get the notion that somehow the two of them were equals. "Your father and I will need to have a chat."

"Your father and I," he mimicked her.

"Paul, stop it," said Margaret.

"I tried to help you and you lied to me." Laurie stood up. "Don't forget that."

"You wanted shot of me, more like," Paul said, standing up and facing Laurie. "You just wanted him to yourself."

"Come on, that's enough," said Margaret, catching Paul's hand. "It's not Laurie's fault."

"Don't worry," said Laurie "I'll leave you lot to sort out your own situation."

Margaret's eyes flicked left to right, scanning Laurie's face. She made no move to say anything and Laurie left the room.

She passed the still-open front door, forcing herself not to look out at Gerry and Jenny. As she went upstairs she thought about what to say to Gerry but she couldn't think where to even start.

The bedroom was as she'd left it a few hours before. She pulled the sheet up and tucked it in, making as neat a job of it as she was able. Then she smoothed the quilt out and plumped the pillows.

She glanced around to make sure she hadn't left anything. But, of course, she hadn't brought anything to leave. She sat down at the window and looked out at the hills. From here she could just see the top of Gerry's mother's car. She stood up and looked down at the car. Gerry and Jenny were inside it, talking. She could only see the top parts of their faces from this angle. All she could tell was that they weren't shouting and they weren't kissing.

Despite her earlier nap, she was numbingly tired. She felt she might be coming down with something. She rubbed uselessly at her eyes which felt as if they'd been wiped down with sandpaper. How long was she going to have to wait here? She heard a car door open and close and then the front door creaked open. She lay down on the bed.

"Paul? Let's get going." That must be Jenny.

"Hang on Mum," Paul shouted back, "there's something I need to get first."

Laurie heard him swinging around the banister and then banging up the stairs. She'd be glad to see the back of him. He was old enough to know what he was doing, wasn't he? She was when she was fifteen.

There was a soft tap at the door. What now? She groaned inwardly, trying to make no noise so he'd just go away. Hadn't she been involved enough in another family's drama?

"Laurie?"

Why was he whispering?

"What do you want?" she asked roughly.

"Can I come in?"

He was still whispering.

"Do what you like. It's your family's house isn't it?"

He opened the door a bit and looked around it warily.

"I'm decent," she said.

He stared at her.

"Just come in, will you." She pointed at the chair. "Sit there." She didn't want a repeat of any funny business.

He came in and closed the door. He stood with one hand behind him. She waited. He looked over her head.

"Well?" she said. "What is it?"

He took a breath. "I'm sorry about everything."

She raised an eyebrow. "Are you?"

"I am. I was a dick downstairs. Everything's just a bit weird." He shook his head.

"I've always known about Gerry." He hesitated. "But I never wanted to know him, you know?"

She supposed there were plenty of kids who didn't have contact with their dads. It was probably uncommon to have both parents together these days.

"Like, my mum never had any time for him after everything."

She nodded. You could hardly blame the woman.

"And, she didn't say much about it, but I knew he wasn't really talking to my gran."

"I know," she said. It was hard to think of Gerry the way she knew him. He'd been such a shit with his family.

"So, last week I went to the hospital and waited around a couple of times to see him. And I found out that he works late at night." He scratched at his top lip where the faintest hint of a moustache was in evidence. "So when my mum was asleep the other night I went down there and I saw him in the cafe."

"Oh. The cafe." Laurie nodded remembering that messy, stupid night. It seemed ages ago.

"Yeah. I was sitting over by the door and he was really upset."

"I know." She stood up and walked over to the window to perch on the windowsill.

"I'd already phoned Ed for a lift home when you came along. And then you two were talking and I thought, you know, like how come everyone else gets to know my dad and I don't?"

She sighed. "I hardly know him at all really. I only met him last week."

"You still know him better than I do." There was a brief flare of anger in his eyes.

"All that stuff about being abused and your friend dying and everything," she said. "Why did you do that?"

He shrugged. "I don't know." He picked at the bed spread. "Haven't you ever just done something without thinking it through?"

"Yes. And look how amazingly well that's worked out." She tried to smile, but her heart just wasn't in it.

"Sometimes I just wish everyone would go away." He came over and stood next to her and looked out of the window. They both watched Jenny leaning against the car with her arms crossed.

"What? Like a last-one-on-earth type of thing?"

He nodded.

"It would be lonely," she said. "That would have its appeal for a bit, but you'd get sick of it. And scared."

He breathed out heavily through his nose. "What was that all about last night? Was he having a nightmare?"

She nodded.

"What about?"

"Och, you know – army stuff."

They both kept looking out of the window. Jenny scratched her head then smoothed her hair down.

"She's pretty."

"Don't worry, she doesn't want to get back together with Gerry." He nodded down at his mum. "She's got a boyfriend."

Laurie shrugged. "It isn't any of my business."

"Isn't it?"

She elbowed Paul gently. "Come on, you'd better get going."

"Okay." He pushed himself up from the window sill. "See you later."

She shrugged. "Anything's possible."

He walked out of the room trailing a waving hand behind him. He'll probably be alright when he grows up, she thought, trying to be kind.

She stayed at the window and watched him getting into the car. Jenny glanced up at the bedroom window and Laurie nodded to her, unsure of whether she could actually see her. She looked around the room and then got to her feet. If she set off now she should be able to find somewhere with a phone. She waited until she heard the car driving away down the stony drive and then walked to the door and opened it quietly. The last thing she wanted was to get into it with Gerry or his mother. She crept down the stairs completely silently then stood in the hallway and looked around. She would be glad to get away from all this complication and intrigue and domestic drama. She hardly knew Gerry enough to miss him and she was sure a few days staying with her dad would soon invigorate her enough to get organised again.

"Laurie." He stood in the doorway of the dining room.

Her heart sank. So much for a quick getaway. She couldn't even think what to say to him.

"Are you okay?" His face was all concern.

"Okay?" She laughed quietly. She'd prefer to not encourage Gerry's mother to come out and get involved. "Peachy Gerry, bloody peachy."

"I'm sorry Laurie. I didn't forsee any of this happening." He shook his head. "We were going to tell you this morning and then . . ."

Laurie didn't trust herself to say anything.

"Still," Gerry smiled. "At least you've met my family now."

"It's not a joke Gerry." All of a sudden her mouth was so dry. "You knew, didn't you?"

"Not at first, no."

"But you worked it out before this morning, didn't you?"

He shook his head. "Not really, at first all I was thinking about was, you know, help this kid. I knew it was my chance to do something right for a change. I was just feeling so shitty and everything." He ran his hand through his hair. "But then some things started to ring a bell of sorts."

"What things?" She was angry, but she was still curious about what had tipped him off and yet she'd had no clue.

"He seemed to know his way around here and then I suppose I saw Jenny in him, but I didn't really realise what I was seeing." He gripped her shoulder and she felt herself give in to it. "But then I recognised myself in him and I knew who he was."

So typical. He sees himself in the boy and that's all it takes for him to get interested after all these years.

"And, what? It didn't occur to you to let me know who he was?" She leaned up close to his face and jabbed her finger at him. She wasn't going to relent now.

"Gerry?" It was his mother. "Is everything okay?"

Gerry looked at Laurie and then over to the door of the living room.

"Well?" Laurie said to him.

"Look, let me do this," he nodded at the door, "then we'll go for a walk and sort everything out."

Could she even be bothered to sort it out? What was the point anyway? She didn't need a therapist to tell her that a relationship needed to be honest.

He squeezed her shoulder. "Please?"

"Okay. But I'm not hanging around for hours." She'd go as soon as the door closed behind him.

"Thanks Laurie." He looked at her with such naked gratitude that she felt ashamed.

He leaned down and gave her a shy peck on the lips. She would have to steel herself. She gave him a little push.

"Go on," she said. "You two need to talk." She tried to smile. She hoped it was convincing.

He took a deep breath and then opened the door to the living room, glancing back at her. She gave him the thumbs up and he entered the breach, with his head dipped slightly as if he was going out into rain.

She stood listening to Gerry and his mum talking quietly in the living room. She was amazed by how quietly they were speaking to each other. What a show of self-restraint. Mind you, it was probably this buttoned-up aspect to the family's nature that had stopped Gerry from doing the right thing from the start. She got the impression that appearances and community feeling would be very important to a family doctor. There would have been shame in Gerry's walking away, but would there be more shame than getting his teenage girlfriend pregnant in the first place? She doubted that the teenage version of Gerry would have thought of that. It was all act now, think later when you were young.

She looked at herself in the mirror by the door. She was a state. Her hair needed washed and her eyebrows looked as if they were on the verge of developing personalities. She wondered when the bloom of youth – if she still had it, even – would be wearing off.

Bits of Gerry and his mother's conversation drifted out to her. They could be discussing dinner or the day at work if you didn't know better. They were so calm and polite. It made her think of the Royal Family.

"I've no idea."

Gerry sounded tired.

"But you must have some sort of an idea." Gerry's mother's voice rose a tiny bit and betrayed very, very slightly now that she was forcing politeness somewhat.

"I really don't," said Gerry. It sounded as if he was getting ready to finish the conversation and come out to the hall.

She realised quite suddenly that she had absolutely no interest whatsoever in getting involved with Gerry and his family any further. She should say something to Gerry, but he of all people should understand the desire for a clean break. Besides which, she didn't owe him anything, did she? Really, what on earth was she doing here? What was she doing generally?

She decided to go out of the back door to make sure that they didn't see or hear her. As she passed the remains of the tea tray, she picked up a Kit-Kat and stuck it in her pocket. That might come in handy if she had to wait a while for a lift.

She legged it as fast as she could down the drive. If someone was to see her now they'd call the police – she looked a person on the run from some demented picker-up of hitch hikers. She imagined herself explaining it to some grizzled old policeman.

"He seemed so nice." Tears would flow. "He said he was taking me to a phone."

"That's how they get you in the car miss." The policeman would pat her on the shoulder in a fatherly way. "It's a classic ploy."

She'd sniffle in a feminine way into a hankie provided by the policeman.

"You were lucky this time miss." He'd shake his head. "There were others," – here he'd pause, raising an eyebrow – "who weren't as lucky."

She slowed down once she made it to the main road. Of course, it started to snow. What were the chances of her freezing to death out here? She stuck her tongue out and caught a few snowflakes. She should have pinched one of those decorations to remember this whole sorry escapade. This reminded her of the photo in her coat pocket. She took it out and stopped walking to look at it properly.

Gerry looked so much younger and more together in the picture. But she liked him the way he was now. She liked the fact that he looked as if he'd been around. All he needed really was a bit of focus and some sleep and less drink. She ran her fingers over the picture, remembering the night before on the living room floor and then later, the way he'd held on to her with his heart beating so fast and his skin clammy and shivery like a sick child.

She looked back up the hill to the cottage and then

308

down the road which they'd driven up the morning before. She took a few steps forward and stopped again, looking around at the hills and the darkening sky.

She sighed. There was no point in making life any harder than it needed to be. Maybe this would all prove to be illuminating in some way on the methods of the world and the people contained therein. Things could be worse, she could be sitting on her own on a bench in a park surrounded by weirdos in the bushes. Or she could be wandering around aimlessly in a shopping centre, wasting the day with nowhere to go and no one to be with. Besides which, it was really cold and it was Christmas Day tomorrow and she didn't want to die in a ditch on her own with no one she knew very well looking for her.

She turned around and started to walk back up the hill towards the cottage. She pulled the Kit-Kat out of her pocket.

Fuck it, she thought, ripping the wrapper off, live each day like a tiger.